I0628647

Hunted

A Rory Mack Steele Novel, Volume 3

Eugene Lloyd MacRae

Published by CreateSpace, 2013.

This is a work of fiction. Similarities to real people, places, or events are entirely coincidental.

HUNTED

First edition. February 8, 2013.

Copyright © 2013 Eugene Lloyd MacRae.

ISBN: 10-099173923X

Written by Eugene Lloyd MacRae.

Chapter 1

BEING HUNTED WASN'T SOMETHING HE ASPIRED TO. It wasn't something he desired. It just happened.

HAZY LIGHTS FLASHED in front of Rory Mack Steele's eyes. Wind whipped hard against his body and then disappeared. Vague shadows moved at the edge of his vision. He felt a soft, feminine body behind him and the light floral scent of a delicate perfume floated around his head. He felt the soft body move away and then it settled against him again. Something white appeared in front of his eyes. He fought hard to focus. It was the crotch of white silk panties. Why was he seeing that? The thighs were tanned and shapely. Then a silvery cloth covered the panties over to his disappointment. He struggled to remember where he was. And why was he lying on his side? There were voices and flashing lights around him. The floor beneath him vibrated with a low, powerful roar. And then it all faded slowly as a wispy darkness covered his eyes.

Chapter 2

RORY WOKE UP AGAIN, this time in a heavier fog. Light slowly filtered through his eyelashes. Lifting his head slightly, he realized he was lying face down on a green canvas army cot. That didn't make any sense. His army days were long behind him and he'd sworn to himself that he would *never* sleep on another army cot once he got out. Laying his head back down, Rory tried to make sense of where he was. He vaguely remembered a party but this didn't feel like a normal hangover at all. This was something different.

Rory smacked his lips a few times. There was something familiar about the slightly sweet taste on his lips but his brain was so fuzzy he couldn't quite place it. It reminded him of a gas used by his dentist a long time ago. Nitrous oxide...was that it? But that was a sedative. He shook his head softly a few times trying to clear the cobwebs from his head. He couldn't remember when or why he was given a sedative.

Slowly turning his head to the left, Rory realized the cot was up against a wall made of large, redwood logs. He could smell the strong, lingering scent. Redwood logs? That didn't make any sense either. *Where am I?*

His hands and arms felt weak as he slowly turned his body and all he could do was flop weakly onto his back. The room went for a spin and he closed his eyes, holding tightly onto the edges of the army cot. It took a few moments but the spinning finally slowed and then stopped. He slowly opened his eyes again. A pine cone shaped glass chandelier hung in the center of the ceiling and the light hurt his eyes. He closed them tightly. After a few moments, he slowly opened them again, trying to adjust to the light. The ceiling came into clear focus. It was made from highly lacquered tongue-and-groove redwood planks. Turning enough to get his left elbow under him, he propped himself up on his side, trying to get a better view of his surroundings.

He was in a redwood log room about twelve feet by twelve feet in size. But for an expensive looking room, there wasn't a single piece of furniture anywhere. There were no pictures on the walls, no lamps, no radio, no television, not even the type of knick-knacks you would in a log cabin. And there wasn't a single window in the room either. That didn't make any sense.

Rory's right hand rested on the side of his pant leg and he felt silk. He looked down at his body and realized he was wearing a tuxedo. Why? His mind vaguely flashed back to a black tie event he was attending rather than a party. *When was that? Last night? Was it longer?* Rory lay back again, staring up at the ceiling. He tried to think, tried to make sense of it all. He found himself drifting off...

A door banged open loudly somewhere below the foot of the cot. "C'mon sport," said a nasal voice, "everybody else is down in the holding area, time to get this show on the road."

Chapter 3

RORY WAS SLOW TO REACT PHYSICALLY, but his brain automatically placed the accent as Midwest. *That's good. At least my brain is working. But what does he mean by the holding area? That doesn't sound good.* Rory saw two men he didn't know tower over him and he tried to move his sluggish body.

Two pairs of rough, strong hands yanked him to his feet.

Nausea hit him and the world went for a spin again.

The men dragged his body towards the open door. They smelled of sawdust and rough wood.

Rory dragged his feet deliberately, not particularly wanting to go wherever they were taking him. He felt like throwing up from the movement.

The two men turned sideways to get him through the open doorway.

Rory's head lolled to the right and he struggled to glance up at the man who had spoken. Finally focusing in, Rory estimated the man to be in his late 20s, possibly early 30s. He noted his face was dotted with pockmarked scars, probably from severe acne in his teens.

"C'mon buddy, use your feet, it'll make your head clear up faster," growled the man on the other side.

This one sounded a little bit older, maybe in his early 40s.

They turned Rory left and dragged him down a long hallway,

Rory slowly turned his head to the left to look up at the other man. This one had whiskey on his breath. *Smells like Jack Daniels. And that accent...Brooklyn? Is that where I am?*

"Walk buddy, you're going to need to get walking so you can run," the younger man urged.

The older man gave a harsh laugh.

Why would they need me to run? That doesn't sound good.

"C'mon buddy," the younger man urged again.

Rory closed his eyes as he tried to remember where he was. *Do I know these men?* Nothing came to him. Whoever was responsible for him being here had definitely drugged him or gassed him. And whatever they had done to him must have caused him to lose his short-term memory. Rohypnol, the date rape drug came to mind. Rory pushed that thought from his mind quickly. There was no sense letting his imagination run wild. He had to deal with cold, hard facts. The problem was he didn't have any.

"Use your feet," the older man growled.

Rory *could* feel his feet starting to work again as they dragged him around a couple of corners.

But he still refused to cooperate.

He didn't know these men.

And something in the back of his mind said not to trust them.

He had to find some advantage.

As they dragged him down the hallway, Rory noted the walls were made from redwood logs, just like back in the room. And like the room, there were no pictures or decorations of any kind.

There was nothing that might help him to identify where he was. There was nothing to help him know who these men were.

They dragged him passed a number of doors on both sides of a long hallway. Turning him to the right, the two men dragged his body around another corner where he was dragged past more doors.

Rory realized he wasn't in a cabin. He had the feeling those doors they were passing led to bedrooms much like the one he had been in. This place was more like a large, upscale lodge and it gave Rory the impression that whoever built this place had a boatload of money. And for the first time, Rory realized the two men dragging him were dressed in green and brown camouflage clothing. Camouflaged hunters in a fancy redwood lodge. *What would hunters in a fancy lodge want with me?*

Rory's head was finally clearing and his body was working much better. He was considering making a move against the two men when they suddenly dragged him around another corner and approached a large pair of wooden, swinging double doors.

The two men pushed the doors open with their shoulders, slamming them back against the wall and hauled his body through into a room.

Rory was turned roughly to his left and dragged towards a large group of men who were also dressed in tuxedos similar to his. He didn't recognize anyone in the group.

"Welcome to the party," barked the older man.

Rory was shoved hard towards the group of men. His legs gave way and he stumbled forward.

A couple of the men in the group put their arms out and caught him.

As Rory regained his balance, he slowly turned and watched "acne-face" and "whiskey-breath" move back to stand guard on either side of the double doors. I won't forget you two, he thought to himself.

They sneered back at him, jutting their chins out in defiance. They obviously knew what he was thinking and were ready for anything.

"Ah! Finally, everyone is here," said a course, loud voice from above.

Rory looked up and saw a man about fifty feet away looking down over the room from a fancy, wrought iron, second-story railing.

He now realized the room he was in was huge, much like a large high school gymnasium. The ceiling was crisscrossed by large, gleaming redwood logs that acted as beams for the roof. The room was lit by a number of elegant crystal chandeliers hanging high among the beams.

As Rory's attention returned to the man above him, he realized he wasn't alone up there.

Rory slowly turned as he looked up.

The entire room was completely surrounded and overlooked by the wrought iron railing that ran around the entire second floor. And there were men, dressed in green and brown camouflage clothing, evenly spaced along the second-floor railing. They were all looking down on Rory and the other men. The two men had called this the holding area. This did not look good.

"So," the man from above said slowly, "finally we get everyone here. Let's get everything started."

Rory quickly sized up the speaker.

He was about 6' 4" tall, in his early 50s, with salt-and-pepper hair. The man had a ruddy complexion, like he had spent a lot of time outdoors; a barrel chest, thick arms and he wore the same green and brown camouflage clothing like the others. He was speaking into a thin microphone that extended from his right ear similar to those worn by singers in concerts. By his demeanor, Rory had the impression he was the Bossman. So what did Bossman want from all these men in evening attire? What did Bossman want with him?

"Ladies," the Bossman said as he gestured down and to his left, "we are going to get things started by letting all the wives go over and get together with their husbands."

For the first time, Rory realized there was also a large group of very scared women over on the right side of the room. They seemed to range in age from their early 20s to late 50s. But one thing stood out, they were all very attractive. And every one of them was dressed in evening wear or ball gowns and dressed to the nines. *What in the world is going on here?*

"Just the wives. I repeat...*just the wives*," Bossman emphasized to the women as he held up a finger. "Do it now, ladies."

Immediately a number of the women began to move across the floor over to the group of men.

Rory watched as wives, with a combination of fear and relief in their eyes, joined their mates around him. They immediately began hugging and kissing and shedding tears. The reunion was touching but Rory had a feeling it was not going to last very long.

"Now, *gentlemen*," the Bossman continued from above, "those of you who are *single*, you can now move over to my left to join the ladies. Let's go, gentlemen," he commanded as he clapped his hands together, "single men over to the single ladies. Do it now."

Rory took a deep breath as he watched the continuing re-union of husbands and wives around him. It was very touching. Then he began the walk over to the single ladies side of the room.

Suddenly, a pair of warm, luscious lips pressed against his and caught him completely by surprise!

Chapter 4

RORY WAS VERY AWARE OF A FIRM, shapely body pressing against his chest. Well-toned arms wrapped around him in a tight bear hug. "Lady," mumbled a perplexed Rory through compressed lips, "I think–"

"Quiet!" hushed a dark-haired beauty as she kept her lips half pressed against his. But her eyes were not closed in a romantic kiss. They were darting back and forth, looking at the people beside her.

"I think that must've been some kind party if I ended up being married," Rory said out of the corner of his mouth. He could taste black-cherry lipstick and he smelled the light hint of a vanilla perfume.

"Shhhh," whispered the woman as she broke off the kiss. She glanced up at the men looking down on them. She looked directly up at the Bossman. She grabbed Rory's hand and led him further behind the crowd of husbands and wives. She was moving them away from the Bossman's gaze.

The woman wore a black, silk dress that floated just below her knees, clear hose and black, high-heeled shoes. She was tall, almost the same as his 6'-2" in her high-heels. Rory definitely didn't know her and he couldn't remember ever seeing her before.

"Uh, this marriage didn't happen to get consummated last night did it?" Rory asked. He glanced down at her long, shapely legs as she walked, "Because that would be absolutely–"

The woman quickly turned and pushed her lips back up against his to quiet him. The woman's brown eyes stayed open as she looked up into Rory's silver-blue ones. "Just play along or they'll kill us!" she warned under her breath.

Rory's body went rigid with the warning. The confusion and wonder at what was happening turned to a very heightened sense of danger. He kept his lips pressed against her lips as his eyes quickly looked around. "What's going on?" he asked in a low voice.

"I overheard them talking before they took me out here," the woman whispered. She looked up into Rory silver-blue eyes this time as her lips brushed against his, "I heard them say–"

"Okay," the Bossman said from above, "I want to thank everyone for their excellent cooperation. This is going to make things so much easier, you'll see."

The woman broke off the kiss and looked up at Bossman. There was definite fear in her eyes. Whatever she had overheard, Rory was certain it was serious. *Deadly serious.*

Bossman had a smile on his face as he rubbed his large hands together. "So nice to get all you husbands and wives back together again," he said as she looked down at Rory's group, "this is going to work out nicely." Then Bossman turned and looked down to his left, "Now, as for you singles, I want to apologize for putting you all through this ordeal. We usually know exactly who our guests will be. But sometimes mistakes are made or our information isn't entirely correct. You can understand how that happens."

"Are you going to let us go?" a young woman asked from the singles group in a very panicky, but hopeful voice. She was wringing her hands over and over as she looked up.

The Bossman smiled sardonically at the young woman. Then he looked around at the men on the upper level, "Gentlemen," he said as he held out his arms, "the young lady has asked an interesting question. What's your answer?"

Suddenly, every man looking down over the railing of the second floor had a powerful bow in his hand. Arrows rained down on the screams and shouts of all the single men and women. Before they could move, every one of them was pierced by one or more cruel hunting arrows as the answer ended their lives. Blood stains spread over their tuxedos and evening dresses.

Screams and cries continued on one side of the room among the husbands and wives as deadly silence descended on the other.

Rory was stunned as his new found companion buried her face against his shoulder. He wrapped his arms around her, playing his part as he searched the room with his eyes, looking for answers, looking for a way out.

Bossman's eyes were hard, watching over the room below as cries of anguish and disbelief continued to ring out. After a few moments, he called for quiet. When there was no real response he bellowed, "I...want...quiet!"

The husbands and wives worked hard to comply, afraid of the reprisals that might come their way if they didn't obey. After a few tense moments, sniffling and small cries were the only sounds left as quiet descended on the holding room.

"Now," continued the man from above as he suddenly switched on a smile, "as for the rest of you, we are going to play a little *game*." He emphasized that last word and let the thought sink in.

Rory noted the Bossman's smile didn't reach his eyes. And the coarseness in his voice seemed to intensify. There was pure evil intent behind that voice and smile and Rory's body was ready for a fight, whatever came next.

His companion must have sensed his readiness to fight because she whispered in his ear, "Not yet."

"Each couple," continued Bossman as he raised a finger like he was teaching a class, "will be taken outside and given fifteen minutes to run. You will be given time to either find a hiding place or make a run for freedom before we set out after you. Do you understand?"

"What are you planning to do?" demanded a tall man who took a step forward. He was obviously someone accustomed to being in charge. His wife was clasping his right hand with her two hands, trying to restrain him.

"Well, *Sir*," Bossman said forcefully as he looked directly down at the man. "In this *game*, we plan on hunting you down to put an arrow in your heart. Just like we did with *them*." He pointed down to the pierced bodies of the single men and women. Blood was beginning to pool on the brown, ironstone slate floor beneath the dead bodies.

Fear immediately ran through all the captives. There were cries of fear and outrage as they realized what it meant for all of them. The wives turned to their husbands for solace and protection.

"Of course, we don't plan on killing your wife right away," the Bossman said in a louder voice as he gestured towards the man's spouse. "We plan on enjoying the pleasures of her body *before* we kill her!" he added with an evil grin.

That comment caused the husbands and wives to clutch each other tighter.

Rory noted every man standing around the railing above them was enjoying the fear being created in the room below. This was all part of the deadly *game* they were playing.

"That's why we love hunting *only* husbands and wives," continued the Bossman. "The single guys, they usually run and leave the lady behind to save their own skin. Oh, there are a few heroes from time to time. But by and large, it's every man...and woman...for themselves. But husbands usually will fight and do everything they can to save the woman they love. That makes it so much more fun for us. And more exciting when we get to ravage the wife before the husband's dying eyes."

Rory scanned the upper balcony as cries of anguish sounded all around him again. How many were there? Rory quickly estimated their total to be about five dozen men. Possibly 60 in total when you added in acne-face and whiskey-breath over by the doors! They were the hunters. And all the captives below, including Rory, were the prey!

"So," continued the Bossman as he rubbed his hands together in anticipation, "who would like to go first? Any volunteers? Anyone wants to get this thing started *with a bang*," he asked with a cackle.

Chapter 5

RORY LOOKED AROUND at the husbands and wives in the holding room. Fear and terror filled their eyes as they held each other tightly. Rory didn't blame them. He couldn't see any way out for anyone, including himself. Rory was surprised when he felt his right hand jerked hard and he was pulled by his new found companion away from the back of the crowd. She pulled him around to the front of the husbands and wives again and towards a spot below Bossman's position above.

"We'll go," she stated loudly as she looked up at Bossman.

Rory looked at her and wondered if he was hearing correctly. *What kind of mad plan is this? Is she serious?*

Bossman looked down from the balcony, "My, my," he said, "don't I just love an assertive woman." Bossman leaned against the railing and breathed coarsely into the microphone as he appraised her body. "And a very beautiful and sexy one at that," he added. Then he turned his attention towards Rory.

Rory saw Bossman's expression turn hard as he looked down at him.

Bossman extended his hand and smiled sarcastically, "And, of course, we salute the brave man who expects to protect her." Then he lifted his head and nodded to someone across from him on the second floor. Within moments, acne-face and whiskey-breath appeared beside Rory and his new companion.

"This is gonna be fun, buddy," whiskey-breath said to Rory. "Your woman looks real fine and I can't wait to catch up with her," he added as he ogled Rory's 'wife'.

Rory realized both acne-face and whiskey-breath were now carrying bows like all the other men.

And very quickly, four more men with bows in their hands joined them.

Rory tried to check out the number of men still above them. Did these four come down a staircase from above? Rory desperately wanted to know how many men he was up against. Was it 60 or 64? More?

"Let's go," whiskey-breath said as he gestured to another set of double doors off to the right, on the other side of the holding room.

Rory noted they would walk past the double doors they had dragged him through earlier. He began calculating the odds and wondered if he could duck through them and get away. Could he pull the woman with him?

HE AND HIS NEW COMPANION began walking towards the double doors, led by acne-face and whiskey-breath. Rory saw both acne-face and whiskey-breath now had backpacks with a quiver full of arrows. He didn't see any other weapons beyond the bow each man carried.

The woman with him turned her head away as they walked past the pierced bodies and the spreading pool of blood on the ironstone slate floor.

Rory glanced back and realized the other four men now escorted them from a safe position a number of paces to the rear. All of them had their bows in hand; arrows notched and ready to fly. There was no way out. There was no way he could duck out the side double door and live. Then another thought struck him; was this simply going to be an execution in the next 15 to 20 minutes?

Rory and his new companion were led through the double doors and out onto a large open veranda outside. The air was crisp and fresh. The veranda swept across the full side of the redwood lodge and appeared to wrap itself right around the building. Rory noted a number of chairs and tables set in various places up and down the veranda. Everything was made from rich redwood materials, just like inside.

Dead ahead, about two hundred yards away, was another redwood log building about the same length as the redwood lodge. As Rory looked across the entire length of that building he noticed there were no windows. That seemed odd. The roof was covered entirely with black ironstone slate. There were several black pipe chimneys and exhaust fans on the roof. He wondered what the building was for. Could they use it to hide if they escaped?

Rory and his new companion were led across the veranda and down a wide set of stairs.

As Rory looked towards the back of the unusual building, he could now see the edges of a couple of other large buildings. The first was about two hundred yards behind the back of the building and the next was a couple of hundred yards beyond that one. Of particular interest to Rory was the fact that the two buildings were shaped like hangars for airplanes. He had enough skill to fly a small plane. Was this a possible escape route to freedom?

They were led twenty feet along a path to a well-worn cross-path and acne-face and whiskey-breath turned left to follow it.

Looking left, Rory could now see the building they had been in was a two-story, redwood-log structure. It reminded him of a big hunting lodge. Looking past the two hunters leading the way, Rory noticed another hangar-like structure a couple of hundred yards ahead, in line with the building on the right.

His new companion was on his right as they walked and she moved right against him.

"Why exactly did we volunteer for this?" Rory asked her under his breath.

"I didn't want to stay one more minute in there with those guys," she answered in a low voice. "What if they had figured out we're not married?" She looked furtively back over her shoulder, "I figured we'd be better off out here and not dead on the floor with the others."

"I see," Rory's said succinctly.

"I may have been wrong," she said as she bit her lip.

Rory appraised his new companion. She was definitely beautiful with black, shoulder length hair, white teeth and a lightly tanned, clear complexion. She had small diamond studs in her ears but no other jewelry. Rory wondered if she realized neither one of them wore a wedding ring. He folded his left hand under to hide his ring finger. Then he used his right hand to clasp her left, to hide her own ring finger.

She gave him a weak smile.

He gave her a small nod of assurance. A feeling he wasn't sure he felt himself.

As they reached the end of the path between the two buildings, Rory glanced to his right. In the distance, he could distinctly see a large, open area. *Is that a helicopter landing zone?* Beyond that open area, he noted the tops of trees, which meant there was a drop-off or hill on that side. Beyond the trees, he could see rugged, snow-capped mountain peaks.

Acne-face and whiskey-breath turned to the left again, following another well-worn path.

Rory and his beautiful companion continued following them, like two lambs being led to a slaughter. But Rory was determined not to go easily. He worked to stay calm and coolly appraise every piece of information he could take in. He noted the early morning sun was now dead ahead. *That means we're now walking east.* A few moments later they were walking across the front of the lodge on their left. *That means the lodge is facing south.* Rory noted the wide veranda did wrap completely around the redwood lodge. Despite the situation they were in, Rory couldn't help but be impressed with the whole structure. The front of the two-story lodge was amazing. A large peaked roof of western red-cedar shingles jutted out from the main roof and towered over the main entrance. Two-story, gleaming glass windows, reflecting the morning's blue sky and white clouds, flanked either side of two large entry doors. The massive entry doors were also made of gleaming glass. The irony struck Rory. He thought about all the single men and women he had seen die in front of his eyes only a few moments ago. There was all that beauty on the outside of the lodge, yet so much evil on the inside.

Acne-face and whiskey-breath continued to lead the way, not even looking back once.

Glancing right, Rory took note of two more large, hangar-like structures behind the first one he had seen. The curved, galvanized steel roof of each building was painted in camouflage greens and browns. Several hundred yards past those structures, he noted the tops of trees again. *Another hill or drop-off. And beyond that more mountain peaks.*

"Keep your eyes to the front, mister," snapped one of the men in the rear, "this ain't no walk in the park." The other men behind him snickered at the remark.

Rory peeked over his right shoulder. He estimated the distance to the front and back group of men. Realizing he had no chance to reach either group, he decided to be patient. *But how long do we have? And where are we headed?*

"I said eyes front," snapped the man again.

Rory complied but kept his eyes moving side to side. They were now passing a large, U-shaped log structure on the left. There were several double-doors all around the inside of the U-shape. Rory had the solid impression this building was a garage of some type. *Maybe there's a vehicle inside that we could use to escape.* Several smaller log sheds dotted the ground behind the garage-like structure. He looked discretely to his right. *More log sheds.*

Looking dead ahead, Rory noted the tops of trees again. Which meant they were coming to the edge of another hill or drop-off. *We're in some kind of huge compound, planned around the central lodge and on a plateau in the middle of some wilderness. This doesn't look good. Do they kill us and drop us over the edge?* He looked at the woman. *No, first they said they would do things to her.* Rory clenched his fists with the thought. *I've got to find a way out.*

Once past the garage-like structure, the six men marched Rory and his companion three hundred yards over scrub grass to the edge of a hill. That confirmed Rory's theory that they were on a plateau of high ground, on three sides at least.

From the edge of the hill, Rory could see lush, green forest in all directions ahead of them. He now knew what was about to happen. Rory thought back to the Bossman talking about the *game* where they would hunt the husband and wife. They would be sent over this hill and told to run for their life. They would be given a chance to escape. But as Rory looked at the terrain below them, he realized the chance to escape was only an illusion. The trees were spaced too far apart to do them any good. There were bushes and other nooks and crannies to hide in. But it was apparent it wouldn't take long before someone found you. And even more sobering was the fact that the hill fell away slowly for quite a distance. Rory estimated it would take several hours of running downhill through this open, treed terrain before they could reach trees and brush dense enough to hide in.

This was an open killing field. And it went down a long, long way. This *game* was set up to offer zero chances of escape for the hunted. And a perfect chance to kill and rape for the hunters.

Chapter 6

"**OFF YOU GO**," whiskey-breath said, "you have fifteen minutes before we come and get you." He held up his bow in emphasis. Then he looked down at the woman's legs and rubbed his rough beard, "Lady, this is gonna be a real pleasure."

One of the other men, young and dirty blond with a bushy beard leered at the woman,"Yea. Ain't she got great legs. Me and Dylan already took a peek under that dress and I can't wait–"

Rory's companion drew her right arm back and made a fist, "You're lucky I didn't poke your eyes out with my heels when you did that, you pig–"

"We're the ones who're gonna to do the poking, lady," tossed a burly man with a red goatee. He leered at her, "If you know what I mean."

Rory caught her arm in mid-swing with the crook of his arm. "They're just trying to get us riled," he said to her in a low voice. "They're trying to bait us into doing something stupid."

"Don't worry lady, your husband will protect you," the blond-bearded man said with a husky laugh.

"Yeah," red goatee said, "until I put an arrow in his heart." The men all laughed and continued to feast their eyes on the woman's body.

The woman glared back at them, unwilling to yield.

"Let's go," Rory whispered to his companion. The woman finally relented and Rory and his companion set off down the hill. She alternated between looking at where they were going and glaring back at the men, anger burning in her eyes. But after a few moments, anxiety replaced anger in her eyes and she asked, "What...what are we going to do now?"

Rory just glanced back at the men without saying a word and continued walking down the hill, leading her between two tall aspen trees. His eyes swept the terrain nearby and below, trying to formulate a plan.

The woman glanced back and then looked at Rory again. Her voice was shallow and revealed mounting fear, "Shouldn't we be running?"

Rory still didn't say a thing as he stole a quick glance of his own back over his shoulder at the men. He noted each man carried a small canteen at their waist. Each man also carried a hunting knife in a sheath attached to their belt. Bows, arrows and hunting knives appeared to be their only weapons of choice. But it was still more than anything Rory and his new companion had to fight back with.

whiskey-breath put his hands to his mouth and yelled out, "Don't worry mister, we won't peek as you run and hide. That makes the hunt a whole lot fairer and a whole lot more fun that way." Then he added, "For us."

Rory watched the men laugh. Then they turned around and began to walk back out of sight. But as they walked back over the crest of the hill, they were spreading out. The hunters were obviously making a long line across the crest of the hill to ensure Rory and the woman couldn't double back and try to hide in a building. Rory and his companion would have no choice but to move down the hillside, where they would be completely exposed once the men started their hunt. This whole thing was a set up with a complete advantage for the hunters. Rory doubted they could get very far before being caught.

Rory fought the urge not to run like the woman suggested. That would be certain death.

Once the men finally disappeared over the crest of the hill, Rory reached out and stopped his companion.

That caused the woman to look back in fear, wondering if the hunt had started. When she didn't see the men, she asked again, "S-shouldn't we be running?"

"Just wait a moment," Rory whispered.

The woman's hands shook with fear, the panic in her eyes beginning to rise. "This is crazy," she whispered in a shaky voice.

Rory took his companion's elbow, "This way," He guided her to the left, past a large Lodgepole Pine, as he watched the crest of the hill.

The woman looked confused. Instead of continuing *down* the hill, he was moving them back up the hillside at an angle. "B-but...shouldn't we be going down that way to get away," the woman asked in alarm as she pointed down the hillside. When Rory didn't answer, she began to panic and tried to pull away, "This doesn't make any sense."

"Shhhh," Rory cautioned as he kept his voice low, "you have to keep your voice down. We can't let them know what we're doing."

"But I don't know *what* we're doing!" the woman said in a higher, panicked whisper. "We're losing time! We should be going down that way, not back up the hill."

"Shhh," Rory cautioned her again. "Fifteen minutes isn't enough time to get very far. I see a lot of Aspen and Lodgepole Pine. That pops up after a forest fire. They've done a controlled burn and cleared a lot of the forest down this hillside."

"But we can hide. Right? We can hide."

"There *are* a lot of trees but there's so much open space, it won't do us any good. Take a look. It goes down a long, long way before we could really hide. They've created a perfect hunting ground with all the advantages on their side."

The woman looked up the hill to where the hunters had been, "Oh great. And here we are making it easier for them by climbing back up. This is totally nuts. *You're* totally nuts!"

"Maybe. Maybe not," Rory said as they reached a clump of trees just below the edge of the hill. He bent down and pushed some branches back, revealing an older, rusted piece of metal. He grabbed the front edge of the metal and began to pull. "Help me with this," he said to his companion.

The woman looked at it and then bent over and grabbed onto the rusted metal. She began to pull with Rory, "What is this?" she asked in a low voice.

"It's the hood off a car. It's upside down. That's probably why you don't recognize it. I noticed it as we came over the hill," Rory explained. With a strong tug, they pulled the rusted metal out of the brush and started dragging it back down the hill. " I'd say it was off an old 1950s Cadillac," he added. "One of these guys is probably a collector."

"What kind of an idiot am I with?" she said in a louder voice. She stopped helping him pull, stood up and threw her hands up into the air in exasperation, "We need to run!"

Rory continued dragging the up-side-down car hood down the hill to the edge of a slight drop-off. Once he got it there he balanced it with the front nose just over the edge.

The woman stood just up the hill with her hands on her hips, "Are you crazy? You expect to collect old car parts at a time like this!" she asked incredulously.

"No. I expect to use it as a sled," he answered. Rory carefully held it in place as he sat down on the front portion of the upside-down car hood.

The woman walked down and stood beside the upside-down car hood with her arms now crossed. She had a look of pure skepticism on her face as she looked at the piece of rusted metal Rory was sitting on.

"Unless you expect to run down the hill in those shoes," Rory said.

The woman looked down at her black, three and a half-inch high heel pumps. Then she looked back at the upside-down hood, giving it some thought. "Do you think it'll work?" she finally asked.

Rory shrugged. "The odds are we'll hit a tree and die before we get too far. But what are the alternatives?"

The woman looked back up the hill. She tapped her right foot on the dirt as she thought about his plan for a moment. Then she took in a deep breath and let it out. "Okay, so what do I do?"

Rory jerked a thumb over his back, "Climb on board, sit down and hang on."

The woman raised her eyebrows, "In this dress?"

"I'm sure those men will appreciate your modesty," Rory said. "But I think that will disappear the moment they get their hands on you."

"The man has a point," grumbled his new companion. She carefully gathered her black silk dress in the front and gingerly put a foot on the rusted metal. The upside-down hood moved a bit as the woman took a couple of halting steps to stand just behind Rory.

Rory could feel her getting into a sitting position. After a moment, Rory was pleasantly surprised as a pair of long, shapely legs in clear pantyhose wrapped around his waist and locked on at the ankles.

"Keep your comments to yourself," the woman warned as she laid her head on Rory's back. She wrapped her arms tightly around his chest.

The front of the hood was curved slightly upwards and Rory gripped the edge, holding it like a steering wheel. He began to rock back and forth, trying to get the hood to slide over the edge of the small drop-off. He rocked gently at first, praying the drop would give them enough momentum once it slid over. Rory continued to increase the rocking motion until the hood slowly and finally slid over the edge.

The hood seemed to hang for a moment and then it took off down the hill over the grass and dirt

The speed was manageable as Rory leaned a few times to steer the hood away from several large trees in their path. He was surprised he was actually able to steer it that well.

Then the hood slid over a steeper hillside edge and they were suddenly rocketing over the dirt and grass, small stones scraping and scratching at the metal underneath them. Trees and bushes shot by in a blur. A large pine tree suddenly loomed dead ahead.

Rory shouted, "Lean left!" He could barely be heard above the rumble of their make-shift sled and he yelled louder.

The woman heard him this time. She leaned with him and they slanted to the left, just barely missing a collision with the pine tree. Then they rocketed across an exposed tree root and were launched skyward.

The hood landed with a jolt, twisted to the left and they were now sliding downhill sideways.

Steering was nearly impossible now as the make-shift sled picked up speed at an incredible rate.

The woman screamed in Rory's ear as he tried desperately to straighten the sled and regain control. He over-compensated and they careened to the right and slid sideways towards a stand of birch trees. Rory spotted a small opening and fought to straighten out the sled. He barely managed to get the narrower profile of the hood through the stand of trees. But his relief was short-lived.

They hit a mound of earth and were suddenly airborne again. They seemed to hang for a moment and then gravity took over.

They dropped swiftly.

The woman screamed.

The hood hit the ground with a metal clang and bounced twice as it tried to throw them off.

Rory fought desperately to keep a tight grip on his steering wheel as the make-shift sled sped downhill at a clip that even scared Rory.

The ground leveled off for a bit and then they were suddenly airborne again.

Rory's heart sank as he realized they were now flying over the tops of the trees!

The sled began to plummet back to the earth and Rory braced himself.

A monstrous evergreen tree had fallen over and lay at an angle with the top towards them. The sled landed with a dull thud on the upper branches. It slid down the evergreen boughs like a ramp. Pine needles were ripped away and filled the air as the sled scraped and clawed its way down the side of the tree. The hood hit the mound of earth the roots had torn up when the tree had fallen and Rory and the woman were launched with a tremendous jolt into the air again. The ground came up to hit them hard. They bounced several times and then they shot like a bolt down a steeper section of hillside.

Trees and bushes flashed by as Rory struggled with all his strength to keep them from tipping over. The trees were a lot closer together now.

Rory was barely able to steer between them.

The sled was hissing as it picked up speed. It shot down the grassy hillside, large evergreen trees slapping at them on both sides.

They suddenly pierced into denser bush and the woman screamed.

The make-shift sled hissed and bounced off tree roots. Their sled slanted to the right and tried to throw them off.

Rory held on tightly.

The woman behind him squeezed so hard around his chest he had a hard time breathing.

The sled straightened out as it hit something with a metal clunk. They were airborne for a moment. Then they landed with a bang and the sled continued hissing downhill.

Suddenly the ground under them leveled out. The make-shift sled cut straight through a thick stand of Pine boughs and shot into the open, suddenly hissing through the tall grass of a large clearing.

Rory was helpless as they sped towards a clump of rocks, bushes and trees two-thirds of the way across the clearing.

Rory yelled, "Hold on!" a moment before they smashed into the obstruction.

The front of the hood dug into the bush and the back of it tipped up like a wild bronco, nearly throwing them off. They hung in the air for a moment, looking down. Then the back of the hood slammed back down onto the earth, coming to a final rest.

Chapter 7

IT WAS A FEW MOMENTS before the woman behind him spoke. "You sure know how to take a girl for a ride," she said as she tried to calm her shaking body.

"Wait until we go out in the whole car," Rory commented as he willed his heartbeat to slow down, "that'll be a lot more fun, I promise."

"I think I'll pass for now," she said as she unlocked her ankles and struggled to rise. She got to her feet and pushed her black silk dress back down.

Rory pushed himself to his feet. His legs were shaky. He wasn't sure if it was the shakes after an adrenaline rush or–

The woman stepped back and started to turn when her legs gave out.

Rory reached out and grabbed her arms, keeping her upright. He could feel her whole body shaking. "Are you all right?"

The woman nodded her head and licked her lips, "Y-yeah. It's just...getting away from them. I just realized how close...and all those people dying...."

Rory could see the mixture of fear and anguish in her eyes.

"That...that could've been me," she said in the tight voice, "that could've been *us* lying up there..."

"But it's not, thanks to you," Rory said quietly.

The woman started to say something and then she closed her eyes tightly.

Rory wondered if she was going to start feeling survivor guilt. She was definitely going through a roller coaster of emotions.

The woman opened her eyes after a few moments and nodded, "I'm okay. I'll be okay."

Rory held her for a few more moments to make sure she wouldn't collapse and then he slowly released his grip. He took a deep breath, taking a few minutes to gather himself as well. Despite getting away, this still wasn't over. Far from it.

The woman crossed her arms over her chest as if she was trying to hold herself together.

Rory knew they had to get to cover but first things first. He bent over and struggled to pull the hood toward a denser set of bushes. "Can you help me hide this?"

"Why?" she asked, her body still visibly shaking.

"I don't want them to figure out how we got down the hill so fast. I want them to keep looking for us as long as possible up there," Rory explained. "Right now we have a time advantage. If they use binoculars and spot the sled, we could lose that advantage." Rory stopped lugging the hood and looked up at the woman. "I don't know, I'm just winging it here," he said as he shrugged his shoulders.

"That's what I said to my friend last night. I'll just go to the event without a date and wing it. And look where that got me," she replied as she walked to the hood and bent over.

Rory had to smile at that. The small joke told him she wouldn't totally collapse on him.

The woman grabbed the far side of the hood and set her feet.

"So, it *was* a party that I vaguely remember," Rory said as they dragged the upside down hood through the grass and towards his projected hiding spot.

"Well, a cancer benefit actually," corrected the woman, "it was a fundraiser put on by Trent and Emily Corrigan. Their daughter had survived cancer number of years ago. You don't remember anything?"

"Not really," Rory admitted. "They must have drugged us. And whatever they used caused a problem with my short-term memory."

Together they pushed the hood into the center of the bushes.

"It was a modified gas," the woman said as she stood up and brushed dirt from her hands.

Rory let branches spring back to cover any sign of the upside-down car hood, "How do you know that?" he asked as he turned to the woman.

The woman crossed her arms again, as if trying to hold back tears, "I woke up and overheard several of the men talking. The gas must have worn off quicker for me. But it was like I was paralyzed and that scared me. I could hear them talking, but my body wouldn't respond when I tried to move. And they took advantage of the situation. That's what that pig up there was talking about," she said with anger. "I was lying face down and I could feel someone in the room lift the back of my dress up."

"I'm sorry," Rory said. He could see the humiliation in her eyes.

"If I could have kicked their eyes out with my high heels," she said in anger, "I would have. But I couldn't move. All I could do was listen to their filthy talk as they flipped me over on my back and lifted my dress up again in the front. That's when I heard them talking about killing anyone who wasn't married. I was so scared until I spotted you."

"I'm not sure how they expect to get away with this," Rory said as he shook his head. He felt his anger rise. "People will be looking for us by now–"

"Maybe not," interrupted the woman as she blinked away a few tears.

Rory looked at her. He could see her experiencing a rush of emotions again. And this time, her face was showing a sense of defeat as well. He couldn't imagine someone not looking for them. But something about the way she said it told him it might be a reality. "Why not?" he asked her.

The woman wiped a tear away and then tightened her arms across her chest.

Rory took a step forward and placed a hand gently on her shoulder, "Why won't somebody be looking for us?"

The woman took a deep breath before she continued, "They only took a small number of people overall from the black-tie event. The rest were left behind deliberately. The men who were looking up my dress talked about setting a high-intensity fire after they took us. It may be a long time before anyone starts looking for us."

Her revelation stunned him. Rory took a step back and looked back up the hill towards the lodge and the compound, contemplating their situation in the light of this new information.

"If that's true," Rory said in a low voice, "then they covered their tracks and our kidnapping pretty well. If they used a high-powered accelerant, someone will eventually figure it out. But when they do, the police and fire investigators will probably focus on an arsonist. They won't have any reason to look for missing people at that point in the investigation. And with a couple of hundred bodies to go through, it may be a long time before DNA tests show bodies are missing from the remains they find."

After a few moments of silence the woman held out her hand, "I'm Missy Amos, by the way."

"Rory Mack Steele." Rory shook her hand, "Family and friends call me Rory. Only my granny called me Rory-Mack since she's the one responsible for the name. I wish we could have met under better circumstances, Ms. Amos."

"You can call me Missy," she said.

Rory nodded. Then he cocked his head as he looked at her, "Hey, how did you know I wasn't married, to pick me out that fast up there?"

Missy folded her arms across her chest again and blushed, "I just happened to ask some friends at the event about you last night...."

Rory gave that some thought and then grinned broadly, "Really–"

"Oh, get over yourself, Casanova," she mildly protested, "what do we do now?"

Rory gave her question some thought. "First, let's get back over to that side of the clearing," he said, "they should be looking for us up there right now. If they somehow spot us down here in the open, we'll lose the edge we've gained by getting down here so fast."

"Can they see us all the way down here?" Missy asked she looked back up the hill anxiously.

"If they use binoculars they could," Rory told her, "but I imagine it will be some time before they resort to that. They'll expect us to be somewhere close by when they come back over the hill."

Missy nodded her head in understanding.

They moved quickly through the grass and back to the tree line they had come speeding through on the make-shift sled.

Rory looked north and south along the tree line, "Let's go this way," Rory said as he gestured to the south, "If we can climb that high spot of ground, we can take a look around."

Missy Amos followed Rory as they moved south and into a denser stand of trees. They wove a path back and forth between high pines as the ground slowly rose under their feet. Rory turned them to the east and they headed for the top of the rise. Rory's Tanino Crisch dress shoes and Missy's high-heel Gucci pumps made the trek up the hill slow.

"Do you have any idea where we are?" Missy asked after a bit of time.

"I'm not really sure yet," Rory answered as e glanced around. "I'm not a real botanist but I think I recognize some of the plants and trees around us. Once we get up on that ridge, I'll have a better idea."

After a bit more time they began to approach the higher crest and some open ground, Rory did his best to make sure they had trees between them and the viewpoint from the lodge. Rory helped Missy over some loser rocks as they approached the highest spot. But once they reached it, what Rory and Missy saw from the top of the crest made their situation a whole lot worse.

Chapter 8

AHEAD OF THEM stretched miles of dense, green forest leading to snow-peaked mountains that looked impassable. And when they looked to their left and right, they saw an equal stretch of dense forest, also leading to more rugged snow-capped mountains.

"Where are we?" whispered a stunned Missy.

"When you see Rocky Mountain Juniper and Rocky Mountain Maple," Rory said, "you can only come to one conclusion."

Missy's eyebrows shot up in surprise, "We're in the Rocky Mountains?"

Rory nodded, "That's what it looks like. We're somewhere in the Rockies. The problem is the mountain range extends all the way from Canada down to New Mexico. There's no telling how far we are away from any city or town."

"H-how do we get out of here?" Missy asked in a shocked, shaky voice as she looked at the wilderness around them.

"I don't think we can," Rory said in a quiet voice after a moment

"Why not?"

"From what I saw when they marched us to the hill up there, it looks like we're in a valley surrounded by high mountains. I didn't see to the north, but if it's the same, then we have no way out, except over those high mountains. And since we have no climbing gear or clothing to keep us warm at altitude, it's not going to happen. They've trapped us in a perfect hunting ground," he added ominously. Coupled with her information about the high-intensity fire, Rory realized every avenue of escape or the possibility of rescue was dissipating for them.

"So what are we going to do?" Missy asked him quietly.

Rory thought for a few minutes. Then he took a deep breath and let it out, "The first thing we're going to have to do is find water. Without it, we won't last more than a few days, no matter what."

"Are we just going to stay down here for days? What about the people back up there?" Missy asked him. Her eyes flared with anger. "Are we just going to hide down here and leave them on their own–?"

A faint scream echoed down through the trees.

Rory turned and looked up at the plateau.

"They've sent another couple over the hill," Missy said in dismay. She turned and took a few steps back down the hill.

Rory watched her heading back, "Where are you going?"

"We need to do something!" she said as turned to look back at him, "they've sent another couple over the hill." She stood defiantly and pointed in the direction of the lodge," I'm willing to fight those bastards."

"I believe you," Rory said softly. "But it could take us hours to get back up there. And when we do, we have no weapons. How do you plan to fight them?"

Missy's face took on a look of anguish as the words hit her hard. She turned to look back in the direction of the lodge.

Rory understood her feelings.

Another faint scream echoed down through the trees.

Missy started down the hill again.

Rory's own hands were balled into fists, ready to fight as well but he knew they would only be throwing their own lives away right now.

Missy stopped, staring back up at the plateau.

Rory's fingernails cut into the palms of his hands as he watched his companion. He completely understood her anguish. She was going through another whole set of emotions.

Missy turned away from the plateau and crossed her arms hard, obviously frustrated at her inability to do something.

Rory willed himself to relax his fists. He had to stay pragmatic for both of them right now. He stepped down to Missy and held her shoulders as he looked into her eyes, "You did an incredible job of helping us to escape. We can't just throw that away. This hurts me as much as it hurts you. But we're no good to anyone dead. Every couple they send over the hill means six more hunters in addition to the six looking for us. And no matter how hard we fought, once we got back up there, we wouldn't last very long against a dozen armed men at the very least. In fact, they've set this whole thing up to make sure we wouldn't."

Missy nodded reluctantly but the pain was still evident on her face.

"Right now," continued Rory, "they have no idea where we are. That gives us an edge. But eventually, those hunters will probably come down this far looking for us."

Missy's eyes took on a look of fear as she realized the actual eventuality of confronting those hunters again.

"We'll have to be ready," Rory said. "I don't know how, but we will fight back." Rory's voice took on some heat of his own, "Maybe we can make our own bows and some arrows and give them a little taste of their own medicine, put one on their heart."

"Just find me a pointy stick," an angry Missy growled, "and I'll shove it where the sun don't shine." Missy gave the finger to the hunters back up the hill.

Rory smiled at her grit and determination, "I'll make sure you're not behind me when we go back up the hill."

Missy stuck her tongue out at him.

"So," Rory said, "first things first. We need to survive. And then we find a way to fight back. Deal?"

Missy took a deep breath and let it out before she nodded.

"Good. Now let's keep moving south," Rory said.

"Why that direction?" she asked as she started to walk with him.

Rory pointed ahead of them, "See that higher ridge of trees? Everything looks a little greener up there so we should be able to find a stream. We need to find water, remember?"

Missy nodded.

"Can you walk in those shoes?" Rory asked as he looked down at her high-heeled dress pumps.

Missy shrugged, "I'll be okay. I do better in these than I do in flats. Good thing I didn't wear my 6-inch spikes."

"Six inches?"

"Us girls will do anything to attract men." She waved Rory on, "Let's go."

MISSY SHOES WERE A bit of a deterrent for fast movement but not as much as Rory had expected. Still, he was careful not to move too fast in case she ended up twisting an ankle. Rory's expensive slip-on dress shoes were getting scuffed and that irritated Rory. He had grown up poor and simply hated it when anything he had spent hard earned money on was ruined. As far as he was concerned, this was just putting another nail in the Bossman's coffin!

"What's that?"

Rory turned.

Missy had turned and was pointing back up towards the lodge. A plume of thick, black smoke billowed into the sky somewhere up on the plateau.

Rory looked at it for a moment and then shook his head. "I don't know." But inside, he knew it couldn't be good. He felt his fists tighten into hard balls of anger again, "Come on, let's keep going."

Missy nodded and the two new companions trudged on in grim silence as the sun rose in the sky.

The trek was slow because they had to take a zigzag path as they climbed the ridge. Rory knew if they didn't keep trees between them and the lodge, they could be easily spotted from higher ground. But the zigzagging was also adding extra distance that was sapping their strength because of the unexpected heat from the sun combined with their exertion. That wasn't good. Rory had to remove his tie, slipping it into his pocket and undid the top button on his dress shirt. Within an hour of slow, steady hiking they were finally nearing the ridge of trees they had been aiming for. As the ground rose under their feet, their pace began to slow.

"Keep an eye out for any tramped down areas," Rory instructed her, "we're looking for anything that looks like a trail made by deer or other small animals. A trail like that could lead us to water."

"Okay," Missy nodded in understanding, "I haven't noticed anything like that at all so far." Her voice was raspy and tired.

"Even flocks of birds could lead the way," Rory added as he looked up into the blue sky.

"I noticed a bunch of finches flying in that direction," Missy said, pointing a little to their left and higher up along the ridge of trees, "at least I think they were finches."

"As long as you don't spot buzzards flying over our heads, we'll be okay. Let's go up there and see."

After ten minutes of slow hiking further up and through the pines, they came to a wide, shallow stream that tumbled lazily over flat rocks.

"Looks like you earned your first wilderness badge, Missy," Rory said as he moved down the bank of the stream.

"Thanks, but I'll take a drink instead. I'm a little parched right now." Missy wiped glistening sweat from her brow as she approached the stream just behind Rory.

Rory bent down and moved his fingers back and forth through the water as Missy came up on his right, "That will have to wait a bit, I'm afraid. This water is too slow moving. Actually, most of it is dead still. It would have to be filtered before we could drink this. We can't afford to get sick."

Missy thought for a minute and then reached down and began to take her high heel shoes off, "I can be a campfire girl if need be," she stated with full confidence.

Rory turned a bit as he squatted and watched her movements with a puzzled look.

Missy grabbed the hem of her black silk dress and lifted it straight up, flashing long shapely legs and lacy, black underwear beneath the clear pantyhose. She put the hem under her chin to hold the dress up, put her thumbs into the waistband of her pantyhose and pushed them down and off her legs. Her dress dropped back down to cover her and she held the clear pantyhose out to Rory, "Here. I saw this on a television show. You can use this to filter the water."

Rory simply nodded as he looked up at her. "Or we could simply go upstream, to find faster-moving water that will be clean." He jerked a thumb back over his shoulder, "I think I hear a waterfall in the distance back up there in the trees so it's not too far."

Missy looked perplexed for a moment and then placed her hands on her hips as she held her pantyhose in her right hand. She gave Rory an angry look. "And why exactly did you allow me to take these off," she said, thrusting the pantyhose at his face.

Rory gave her a sheepish grin, "It seemed like a good idea at the time."

Missy gave him a growl of frustration.

"You should put them back on," Rory said as he stood up, "they'll keep you warm later when nightfall hits."

"Oh, you'd like that, wouldn't you, *mister*?" Missy snarled as she struggled to put her shoes back on. "Tricking me into getting a cheap thrill."

Rory shook his head, "I didn't–"

Missy turned in a huff, heading over to a clump of trees, "I'll put them back on," she shot back over her shoulder to him, "in *private*, thank you very much."

"Just watch out for the bears," Rory called as he watched her scramble over some rocks in her high heels.

Missy wheeled right around and headed back for him, "I'll put these on later, *alone*!" she stated emphatically as she shoved the pantyhose into a small side pocket of her black dress.

Chapter 9

MISSY AND RORY slowly hiked further upstream, weaving in and out of the sunlight as they moved through a forest of tall, fragrant pine trees. Finally, they saw a high, fast-moving waterfall just up ahead.

"Isn't it pretty?" Missy said. She started for it but Rory reached out and stopped her advance for a minute.

"Did you see someone?" she whispered in fear.

Rory shook his head no, "Just being cautious is all."

The waterfall was about 100 feet high and plunged over the black rock into a small glistening lake. Rory noted a larger, faster-moving stream flowing away from them on the other side of the small lake. The stream they had followed up here probably received most of its water during periods of flash floods. Rory scanned the scene around them and listened intently for a few minutes.

Missy stood absolutely still, listening intently herself and scanning the terrain around them.

Everything looked safe and secure.

Rory put his hand in the small of Missy's back and slowly moved with her into the small clearing around the waterfall.

Birds were singing and everything seemed idyllic but Rory wanted to remain cautious.

"Can we drink now?" Missy whispered.

Rory nodded, "Try to drink closer to the falls, where the water is moving fast over those flat rocks. It's the cleanest. We can't afford to get sick."

Missy took her time in her high heels as she stepped across some wet, flat rocks. She squatted down and began to drink from the clear, cool water.

The sounds of the waterfall and the stream were soothing, but Rory stayed on full alert and kept watch.

Missy picked her way carefully back to the shoreline, passing a hand over her lips, "That's better."

"Can you keep an eye out while I take a quick drink?" Rory asked her.

Missy nodded her head.

"The falls are noisy, so let me know if you hear the smallest sound of anyone nearby. Okay?"

Missy looked around apprehensively, "Do you think one of them is nearby?"

"Don't worry, I just don't want to get caught off guard. Better safe than sorry," Rory said, not wanting to panic her. He stepped over the flat rocks to quench his own thirst. He kept his head up as he scooped up water in his hands and drank. At one point, he stopped drinking for a moment to pick up several small, round rocks from the shallow water and slipped them into the side pocket of his tuxedo. Then he drank some more of the cool, refreshing water. Once he was finished, Rory felt a little safer. No one had taken advantage of them being in the open.

Moving back across the flat rocks to Missy, he then led her off to the side of the small clearing to some larger rocks, "Why don't we just sit down and rest for now."

Missy sat on a rock, smoothing her black, silk dress down over her knees and sitting in a prim and proper manner in the middle of the wilderness.

Rory shook his head a little and smiled. She was quite the woman. "We passed some blackberries and raspberries as we hiked up here," Rory told her, "I also saw some stands of white-oak trees loaded with acorns. It's not that far back down the stream. Between that and the water, we should be able to keep our strength up."

"Where did you learn all these woodsy things," Missy asked as she wiped her brow and relaxed a little after all the tension.

Rory looked off into the distance. "Survival training," he answered. "I served in The Black Watch for a number of years."

Missy looked puzzled, "Black Watch? What's that?"

"It's originally an old Highland Scottish regiment. I served in the Black Watch or Royal Highland Regiment in the Canadian Army," Rory added as he seemed to be peering into the distant past.

"Ah, that's what that accent of yours is, Canadian. I wondered. So what's a Canadian doing in an American city attending a black-tie event for cancer?" Missy queried. "Are you a Canadian tycoon, Mr. Steele?"

Rory shook his head, "No. My family operates Highlander Investigative Services in Toronto and New York. Nothing fancy or high profile," he added. "We do background checks, gather evidence for divorces, find people who have been left money in wills, boring stuff like that mainly. I even helped a woman find an old flame one time."

"Oh," Missy said, eager to hear the story, "that must've been really romantic!"

"Not really," Rory admitted, "we eventually had to help her get a restraining order against the guy."

"Ouch," Missy said, "I thought you're going to tell me a 'feel good' story."

"Sorry to be a killjoy," Rory said. "Anyway, we've been fortunate enough to handle a large number of cases all through the USA and Canada. I work out of the Toronto office, but my father was an American and my mother was a Canadian, so I have dual citizenship. My uncle and my sister Skye work out of the New York office. They also have dual citizenship. It really works well when you have reliable people on both sides of the border who can work a case and travel easily anywhere in North America."

Missy nodded her head, "Well, you and your family must be doing pretty well since these black-tie events are usually attended by only the well-to-do."

Rory shook his head slowly again as he looked off into the distance, "No, my wife passed away from cancer. We helped the Corrigan family with a private matter some years ago. When they put on this foundation event, they sent us an invitation. We thought we would stretch the budget and do our bit for a good cause."

"I'm sorry," Missy said sadly. "Was it recent or...?"

Rory shook his head, "No. It was some time ago. We were both 18 when we were married. We grew up together. I was small and got picked on a lot by the other kids. She was the only one who took a liking to me and we became best friends. I remember this one day...the biggest kid in school said something bad about her and I got into a fight with him. He beat me to a pulp. I was bloody, had a broken nose and broken cheekbone, but I wouldn't quit until he apologized. He would knock me down and I would get up and demand he take back what he said about her. Over and over we did that." Rory paused and shook his head, "It was the only fight I ever won because he got tired of beating on me. But...he said he was sorry as he walked away. A year and a half after we were married, she was gone," he added with finality. "That's when I joined The Black Watch."

The two sat side-by-side in awkward silence.

Chapter 10

THE WARM MOUNTAIN DAY should have been a joy but both now sat feeling awkward, despite the idyllic setting. The fragrant scent of pine carried across the air as birds twittered in the trees around them, and flapped their wings, bathing from the edges of the flat rocks in the small lake.

Rory broke the tension, "So...are you an American tycoon, Missy Amos?"

A smile lingered on Missy's lips at his use of her own teasing question, "No, but my father is. I just spend his money and make appearances at these events to give donations for tax write-offs," she added with a rueful smile.

"What does your father do?"

Missy grimaced as she spoke. "He owns coal mines, Coal mines from here to Timbuktu."

"Do I detect some disapproval?"

"Well," Missy said, "while everyone else is talking about getting out of coal to save the planet, I have to explain to my friends why *we* have to keep digging more of it up."

"So, I take it you don't work in the family business."

"No," she said. "My father sent me to law school so I could help him run the business. Since he never had a son, it was determined I would eventually take over. But it's difficult when you're young and everyone keeps asking you why you're ruining the planet. So I changed my life's planned course. I became a defense lawyer instead of a corporate one." She put her hands on her knees, "Now, enough about me. What do we do next?"

"Changing the subject, are we?" Rory noted with a smile.

"Yes," she said with a quick nod of the head. "Let's just move on." She stood up and smoothed her black, silk dress down.

Rory smiled as he looked up to see where the sun was in the sky. "My survival skills are a little rusty," he said, "but I think we can make ourselves some kind of shelter before nightfall. Let's go back down the trail and collect some berries and acorns for our supper and then we can start."

Missy and Rory hiked back down along the small stream, constantly keeping an eye out for movement in the trees around them. They first arrived at the white oak trees and gathered as many acorns as they could, stuffing them into Rory's jacket pockets. Then they moved a little further downstream and gathered some blackberries and raspberries, eating as many as they could. Then they headed back up towards the falls, ever alert.

ONCE BACK AT THE FALLS, Rory hunted around until he found two rocks that were roughly shaped like knives. Each rock had one side that narrowed to an edge. Rory took a bigger rock and began chiseling down those sharper edges to create two homemade rock knives. Once he was finished, he began scanning the terrain around them.

"What are you looking for? Did you hear something?" Missy asked as she began to get nervous.

"No, it's fine," Rory said, "I'm just looking for a likely campsite."

Missy visibly relaxed, "Okay. But why not just camp down here by the water?"

"Because that's what most people would do," Rory told her, "and that's exactly where they'll be looking first when they come for us. I don't want to go too far away from the water but I don't want to be too close either. It's always good to be cautious. We should be okay for tonight, though. We came rocketing down that hillside pretty fast and got a good head start on them." Rory began to move to the east, to higher ground, away from the waterfalls.

"Are you sure?" Missy asked as she quickly began to follow him.

"Not entirely," Rory admitted.

"Oh, great," Missy muttered.

"Don't worry. I'm sure it's going to take them some time to search for us as they move down that hill. And as long as they don't know *how* we got down the hill, it could take them at least a day of searching before they get down to where we slid to."

"I hope so. I'm starting to get really tired," Missy admitted.

"You've done great." Rory scrambled over a ridge of black rock, turned and held his hand down to Missy, helping her up. A few minutes later, he found what he wanted - two trees about 8 feet apart that would work for what he had in mind. "Okay. This will work for an overnight campsite. But we'll make sure it lasts for a few days, just in case."

Missy looked around her, "Real romantic, dear."

Rory looked up at the sun again, estimating their time left before nightfall. "Okay, we'll have to work quickly while we still have some daylight."

"What do you want me to do?" Missy asked.

"Follow me."

RORY LED MISSY ON A brief trek through the surrounding forest until he found a number of young willow trees. He then instructed Missy on how to cut long, thin strips of bark from the young willows using one of the rock knives. As she worked on her own, Rory salvaged more strips from the inner bark of fallen trees and limbs. Before long, Rory began to weave the long strips of bark they had cut and gathered into a makeshift rope. His hands worked quickly and expertly as Missy delivered more material. Once he was finished, Rory and Missy then carried the coils of newly created bark rope back past their proposed campsite and down to the waterfall below. Rory walked further downstream, scanning the ground around the trees as they walked.

"What are you looking for?" Missy asked.

"This," Rory said finally as he moved to a dead, reasonably straight tree limb that was about six feet long. He used his rock knife to hack away some of the smaller branches. Then he asked Missy to help him move it over to where they had been walking. Missy struggled on her end of the heavy limb but she persevered until Rory said to put it down.

"What are we going to do with this," Missy asked as she stood beside Rory, trying to catch her breath.

Rory began lashing his makeshift rope around both ends of the dead tree limb. "As I said, most people will camp by the water. If those hunters come this way looking for us, they'll probably follow the stream like we did. They should come through here and up to the falls. If they do, this might give them a little surprise and alert us."

"Are you sure?" Missy asked.

Rory shrugged his shoulders, "It's always worth a try."

After securing the rope around the limb, Rory then threaded the makeshift rope up into the trees. He carefully pulled the tree limb up into the air by the rope and had Missy hold it in place. While she did that, he looped one end of the rope around a rock and back six inches above the ground and across the pathway leading up to the waterfalls where he secured it. He looked up at Missy, "Hopefully someone steps into the rope trigger and the dead limb comes swinging down and boom!"

Missy looked at him skeptically.

Rory shrugged his shoulders, "Well, that's the theory."

"Theory?"

Rory stood up and stepped back, looking over their handiwork as he brushed dirt from his hands, "Even if it misses, it should make them think twice and maybe slow their search. Now, let's use those dead leaves on the ground over there to carefully cover over the rope to hide it. We want to hide it right across as much as possible."

Missy worked with Rory to carefully pile dead leaves over the rope to hide it. It didn't take very long and then Rory began to gather some more leaves, "Okay, now we can spread as many dead leaves as we can twenty or thirty yards downstream. Then we can spread more leaves on the other side of the rope along the animal trail leading up to the falls."

"How does this help?" questioned Missy as she began to gather leaves alongside Rory.

"For one thing, it helps to hide the trap we built. And if someone comes up this way and walks on the dead leaves, they should crackle enough for us to hear and alert us."

"Really?" she said again skeptically.

"Well, again, that's the theory," Rory said cheerfully.

"Has any of this worked for you in the past?" Missy asked him.

"Sorry ma'am, that's classified," Rory said.

"That tells me all I need to know." Missy continued to gather and spread leaves along the trail.

ONCE THEY WERE FINISHED, Rory led them back up to a spot just beyond their intended campsite. He searched for a fairly straight dead tree limb that was about 8 to 9 feet long. When he found something adequate, he began working with Missy to strip off the side branches using the rock knife and then they carried it over to the campsite. Each end was placed in a Y-shaped branch on each of the trees that Rory had picked out. Once the top hole of the tent was in place, Rory began leaning dead branches against it on either side to create a tent shape. Next, Rory led Missy over to some large evergreen trees and they used their rock knives to chop away some evergreen boughs. They carried the evergreen boughs over to the campsite where Rory began weaving the boughs expertly through the dead branches. He finished the lean-to walls into a well-camouflaged shelter.

At least this part of Rory's plan impressed Missy.

Rory then asked Missy to gather as many flat rocks as possible and he told her to set them in place inside their shelter to create a fairly flat, raised floor. While she did that, Rory went to work on another roughly woven masterpiece. As darkness was nearing, Rory was finally finished and he approached the shelter as Missy was just finishing her own task.

Missy turned to look at him and then at the item in his hand. Suddenly, it dawned on her, "A mattress."

Rory smiled and slid the makeshift mattress into the shelter. "Placing this on the rocks will help to retain body heat." Then he turned and picked up the other woven item leaning on the wall. "And a blanket," he announced.

"Wow," Missy said as she watched Rory slid it into the shelter, "not bad for a honeymoon abode in the wilderness."

Rory could only grin and shake his head at her willingness to stay cheerful despite the circumstances. "Let's eat. The sun is starting to go down fast."

They sat down and split up the remaining berries. Rory showed Missy how to use a rock to crack the acorns and get access to the nut meat inside. As they ate they engaged in small chit-chat. Rory noted that Missy seemed naturally cheerful and she was absolutely refusing to allow the circumstances they were in to get her down.

As the sun began to set, Rory stood up and stretched. "Okay. You head to bed and try to get some shut-eye. I can take the first watch."

Missy looked up at him and then at the shelter. Then she pointed at the shelter, "Shouldn't we be in there together, to preserve body heat or something like that?"

"One of us needs to keep watch," Rory told her.

"But...are we really going to be able to see anything out here?" she asked as she stood up. "I mean, there are no streetlights or anything," she said as she gestured around them. "I won't mind. As long as you behave yourself," she added with a twinkle in her eye.

Rory looked at her for a moment, then raised an eyebrow, "Something tells me I'm not the one who would have to behave themselves."

Missy gave him a big Cheshire cat grin as she put her hands behind her back.

Rory smiled but shook his head, "We really need to have one watch while the other sleeps, just in case."

Missy gave an exaggerated sigh, "Well, okay. Goodnight. Let me know when it's my turn to take a watch."

As he watched Missy's shapely bottom disappear into the shelter, Rory called out, "And put your pantyhose back on. You'll catch your death of cold."

"Yes, mother," came the muffled reply.

Rory shook his head in amusement as he settled on a flat rock overlooking the waterfall not far below them and pulled a handkerchief from the breast pocket of his tuxedo jacket. He was now glad his grandmother had insisted on teaching him how to fold a real handkerchief into the breast pocket and not use one of those cardboard ones she so detested. Not really classy, she would say.

Rory folded the white handkerchief until it was a diamond shape about the size of his palm. He then used his sharp rock to wear a hole in opposite corners of the handkerchief. Rory then wove himself a couple of slender cords out of the remaining strips of bark. One of the cords was knotted with a loop just large enough to slip over his finger. He then threaded one woven cord through each hole of the handkerchief, knotting them in place. Rory then pulled out three smooth, round rocks from his side pocket. He had found them in the water below the waterfall when they were drinking. He placed one stone in the center of the handkerchief and returned the others to his pocket. Rory now had a rudimentary throwing sling. He folded his new weapon in his pocket and hoped it would be effective in a pinch.

A light breeze sprung up as the sun sank. Light from the moon and the stars twinkled off the waterfall below. Rory surveyed the dense forest around him but his gaze was unable to penetrate the darkness in the low light. His mind drifted off to his conversation with Missy. His teenage bride, Kitty Black, had died from cancer less than six months after their wedding. Rory had found it difficult to forgive himself for not being able to save her. *She was always there for me. And when she needed my help....*

One army shrink said it haunted him. Another said he was looking for ways to atone for a perceived failure. Both shrinks agreed on one thing. It had created a deep drive to help others. Rory wasn't sure about the haunted part, or if it was self-inflicted punishment or penance, but it gave his life purpose. *Except it always seems to lead to situations like this.*

He pushed the troubling thoughts to the back of his mind as a slight chill descended. He lifted the jacket's collar around his neck and crossed his arms to keep warm. This was going to be a long, long night.

Chapter 11

MISSY AMOS WOKE UP desperately trying to scream! Terror filled her heart as she realized there was a hand clamped tightly over her mouth. Another strong hand encircled her waist and began to pull her backward from her bed. Her thoughts went to the nightmares of the men looking up her dress. She began to fight with all her strength, kicking her legs out, clutching desperately at the hand cutting off her breath.

In her ear she heard a harsh whisper, "It's me."

She didn't know who "me" was and she fought with all her might, twisting her body in an attempt to escape. Her shoes struck something hard. She set her feet against it. She pushed with all the strength her legs could muster, trying to free herself and scream at the same time.

"It's Rory," said the harsh whisper again.

She continued to fight until she remembered where she was and who she was with. She stopped fighting.

"They found us," Rory whispered as he continued to pull her out of the back of their makeshift shelter and into the darkness of the trees. He pulled Missy a few feet away from the lean-to before he stopped and listened.

Missy was shaking.

"Move slowly and stay low," he whispered urgently as he took her hand.

Missy nodded woodenly. It was close to dawn and there was just enough light for her to look back and see some movement down by the waterfall. Fear and terror filled her eyes.

Rory moved them very slowly away from their camping spot, the waterfall and the intruders. They couldn't afford to make the slightest sound. Soft sounds of movement came from their left and he slanted slowly to the right, moving away from it. It was agonizingly slow in the semi-darkness and the uneven ground made movement difficult. Rory stopped when he realized Missy was breathing heavily from her panic. He placed a hand on her shoulder and whispered, "Try to keep your breathing down. They might hear—"

That only made it worse and her eyes grew larger, her breathing raspier.

Rory placed a hand gently on her face and turned her head, looking into her eyes, "It's okay. It's okay. Look at me. It's okay."

Missy nodded, her breathing still rapid but slowing.

He waited for her to catch her breath as they crouched together in the semidarkness. "That's it," he whispered. "That's it."

She gulped air and then asked in a raspy whisper, "How...how did they find us so quickly?"

"It's my fault," Rory whispered as he surveyed the semi-darkness around them.

"What do you mean?" Missy asked between choppy breaths.

"Your shoes," Rory said after a moment.

Missy looked down at her shoes and then at Rory, questioning him with her eyes.

"I doubt if many people, especially women, would've gotten down this far wearing high-heeled shoes," Rory explained. "They leave very distinctive prints on the ground. Once they found them, they acted just like a beacon, leading them straight to us." Rory shook his head and chastised himself, "I should have thought of that and found some way to wipe out your footprints as we moved up here."

"I'm sorry," Missy said. She closed her eyes in defeat and swore under her breath.

"That's okay, we're not done yet," Rory said with a firm voice. "Let me know when you're ready. We have to put as much distance as possible between us and the campsite back there."

Missy nodded and indicated she was ready to move on. Rory took her hand again and they began to move further away from the campsite and the waterfall. The going got a little easier underfoot as the sunlight made it easier to see roots, loose rocks, and other impediments. After a few minutes, Rory stopped dead in his tracks.

"What's wrong!" Missy whispered in alarm.

Rory gestured up ahead, "There's a high ridge of rock up ahead."

Missy looked up over his shoulder and saw a clearing not far ahead. And beyond that was the smooth face of a high wall of rock. "Can we climb up?"

Rory clenched his jaw as he shook his head no, "It would be like trying to climb a six-story building. We'd need some kind of climbing gear."

"What now?" she whispered.

Rory gave some thought to their predicament. Looking back in the direction of their campsite and then back to their left, he had the vague feeling that they were being funneled away from the waterfall but towards the stream. *But what choice do we have?*

Missy fidgeted as the seconds of silence passed, "Rory?"

Rory was broken from his thoughts, "We'll have to go this way." He jerked his thumb to their left.

"But won't that put us back near the men again?" she asked in alarm.

"Well, we can't climb that rock face," Rory said. "And even if we could, all they would have to do is look up to see us. A few well-placed arrows...."

"What about going back towards the campsite?" Missy asked.

"If we head back to our campsite, we *know* someone is there," Rory answered. He looked into her eyes, "What other choice do we have?"

Missy looked in each direction and then closed her eyes. She licked her lips. Then she looked at Rory and nodded her head once in agreement. They would have to move closer to the men tracking them.

"Okay," Rory said. He took a deep breath and let it out. "Just stay low and quiet and we'll get past them," he said in assurance. "Ready?"

Missy nodded her head reluctantly and they began slowly moving through the woods again. Missy struggled in her high-heel shoes as they moved over dead logs, around boggy sections of land and squeezed through tight stands of trees. Despite being able to see because of the early morning sunlight, they really weren't getting very far. But they persevered. They had no choice.

Faint sounds came from the trees far behind them.

Rory and Missy paused and then moved on, trying to go a little faster. The trees were wider apart now and Rory had them quickly moving in a crouch from tree to tree to try and stay as hidden as possible. The trail along the small stream was just up ahead. Suddenly Rory raised his hand in the air and stopped dead in his tracks.

Missy froze on the spot. She began to shake as they crouched in silence for several minutes.

Rory turned to her and silently pointed several times at something dead ahead of them.

Missy raised herself a little and peered over his shoulder and through the trees ahead.

One hundred yards away was a man with his back to them. He was dressed in brown and green camouflage clothing, crouched behind a stand of trees just beyond a small clearing. He was watching the trail along the stream that led up to the falls.

"We're not going to be able to get by him," Rory whispered. He went into a squat, watching.

Missy's body shook in fear as she did the same.

Rory made a decision and he glanced back at her, "Stay here."

Missy clutched his arm as she realized what he was going to do, "Let's go back."

Rory looked at her. "We already know they're back there searching for us. These guys are very, very good. They almost caught me by surprise this morning at the campsite. If we go back, they *will* find us eventually. Like we talked about before, either we go forward or...."

Missy looked at him for a long moment and then nodded. She was visibly shaking with fear.

Rory nodded in return and patted her on the knee in assurance. Then he turned and began to slink ahead towards the camouflaged hunter. Moving swiftly and silently from tree to tree, he worked to stay hidden in case the hunter turned around.

Back behind him, Missy watched with mounting fear, her body shaking.

Rory reached the small section of open ground and knelt down. There was no other way to reach the man. *I'll only be exposed for a moment.* The silence was intense as Rory took a deep breath and then moved cat-like towards the hunter–

"Freeze!"

Chapter 12

RORY FROZE IN PLACE AS INSTRUCTED. He slowly turned his head to glance behind him. Another hunter in brown and green camouflage clothing was about ten feet away. He had an arrow set in his bow. The bow was pulled right back and the tip of the arrow was aimed directly at Rory's back. *Maybe if I–*

"Don't even think of movin' mister," the hunter snarled.

The hunter he had been sneaking up on turned around and stood up. He had a large, stupid grin on his face, "I told you we'd find them, Carl. Didn't I?"

Carl nodded in acknowledgment, "Jes like you said, Seth. Although, I don't know how in the hell they got all the way down here. Ya must be some kind o' amateur woodsman, mister." He spat some tobacco juice on the ground.

"Yeah, props to ya. Ain't no one ever done that before," Seth said. He spat some tobacco juice on the ground as well, like some ritual between the two.

Rory tried desperately to figure out some way out of this. His brain raced through all the possibilities.

Seth took off his hunter's cap and rubbed the top of his head, "How *did* you get down here mister? When we couldn't find you the boss shut the game down. That never happened before. We couldn't hunt no others, just concentrate on you. You and your missus caused a lot of commotion when you disappeared. You're gonna be a real feather in our caps, mister."

"Ya, we'll probably get a couple extra to hunt," Carl said enthusiastically.

"That may be," Seth said, "but there's one pair of legs I'm thinking about more right now."

"Ya, mister, where's that hot little wife of yours?" Carl asked in a mocking way. He cautiously moved a little off to the side of Rory, not taking any chances and keeping his loaded arrow trained on him.

"Yeah, where is she?" Seth asked as well. "You didn't just run off and leave that sexy thing all by herself now did you?"

"Na," Carl said. "This one's not the type to run out on his little woman. She'd be round here somewhere. I bet my life on it."

Rory stayed rock-still and silent. He estimated the distance to both men and realized he wouldn't have a chance.

"I gotta say, mister," Seth said with a silly grin on his face, "you don't give up easy. I can see ya scoping us out, wondering if you could take either one of us out."

"Enough foolin' around. I asked a question, mister! Where's ya wife?" Carl repeated in a more commanding tone after a few minutes.

"Yeah. Me 'n Carl been thinking about your wife mister," Seth grinned as he put his hunter's cap on, "we got a real nice peek up her dress earlier. Your wife has got a great pair of legs and we want to see what she has *between them*."

"Ya," Carl said. "Ever since we found her high-heel prints, like sexy little shoes leadin' us to her bedroom, we've been thinking about your wife real hard. If you get my drift...."

The two men laughed as Rory continued to stay silent. They were trying to get a reaction out of him with their talk. He stayed calm, his brain trying to figure out a plan. But no matter how we looked at the situation, he couldn't see any way out.

Seth reached over his back, pulled a hunting arrow from his quiver and set it on his bow. "Funs over, mister," he spat as he aimed the arrow directly at Rory's heart, "Where's...your...wife," he demanded.

Rory tightened his muscles, getting ready to spring. He knew it would be useless but he had to try anyway. He swallowed hard and prepared to feel the arrow enter his heart.

"Whoops!"

All three men looked in the direction of the female voice.

Missy was standing in the trees on the other side of the small clearing. Her eyes were wide open in surprise. She was dressed only in a black, lacy brassiere, black, high-cut lacy panties that left little to the imagination and black, high-heeled shoes that made her shapely legs looked incredibly long.

The two hunters looked at each other in total surprise.

Rory found himself frozen to the spot as well, staring at Missy standing there in her sexy underwear and high-heeled shoes.

Suddenly, Missy turned and began to run away upstream towards the waterfall.

Carl finally broke out in a lecherous grin, "I'll go git the wife. Why don't ya just kill shit-head here and be done with it? Let the others know and then join me for a little fun." With that said Carl quickly unracked his bow, put the arrow back in his quiver and headed off at a jog after Missy.

Seth grinned at Rory as his fellow hunter disappeared upstream. He then unracked his own bow and put the arrow back into the quiver on his back. The camouflaged hunter then bent down and placed the bow on the ground. He came up with a large Bowie knife in his hand, pulled from his boot. "Let's see how you are in hand-to-hand combat, Mister. Oh wait, that's hand to knife combat. Oh wait, that's hand to *Bowie knife* combat." He chuckled at his own lame jokes and then he grew serious and went into a knife fighting crouch.

Rory took a breath and slowly stood up erect. "Thanks," he said to Seth.

Seth stood up straight as well and cocked his head, "Thanks for what?"

"For being stupid," Rory replied. He quickly pulled his right hand from his tuxedo jacket's pocket, twirled his make-shift sling three times over his head and fired before Seth could react. The smooth, round stone buried itself a half inch into Seth's forehead, just over his left eye.

"Actually, it was sling to Bowie knife combat, Seth," he said as the hunter's body tumbled over backward onto the forest floor. "You can thank granny for teaching me Bible stories."

Rory slipped the make-shift sling back into his pocket. Moving forward, he grabbed the fallen Bowie knife and quickly checked Seth's neck for a pulse. Dead. Rory turned and ran hard up-stream after the other hunter.

UP AHEAD, MISSY WAS now running up the animal trail along the stream, headed towards the falls.

Carl was running behind her, grinning as he enjoyed the chase.

Missy's arms were pumping hard as she ran in her high-heeled shoes. The ground was soft with pine needles and the heels sunk in, slowing her down. Carl was starting to close in and she put in a little extra kick to stay ahead.

"C'mon missus, don't make this hard on yourself," Carl yelled at the fleeing Missy. "I'll do that for ya," he cackled.

Missy kept running, struggling to stay ahead of the pursuing hunter.

Carl began to breath heavy and he took the chase a little more serious, running a little harder now after the scantily clad woman.

Missy pumped her arms harder as well, trying to stay ahead and praying she wouldn't twist an ankle running in her high heels.

The hunter kept his eyes on her long, tanned legs and shapely bottom, grinning as he closed in on his prey.

Leaves crackled under their feet as prey and hunter ran along the trail.

Suddenly, Missy took a quick hop in the air, stopped running and turned to face her pursuer.

Carl stopped running about ten feet away from her. He bent over and placed his hands on his knees as he tried to catch his breath. He grinned as he looked up at Missy in her black, lacy underwear. "Damn, you can run, girl. I can see why you're so shapely."

"Please don't hurt me," Missy said in a tiny, pleading voice.

"Oh, don't worry about it honey," Carl said as he wheezed a bit. He looked directly at her crotch, "you'll enjoy every minute of it."

Missy took a step backward and stumbled to the ground with a look of surprise on her face.

Carl grinned lecherously as he straightened up and started to advance on the defenseless, beautiful woman lying on the ground in her sexy underwear.

Missy slowly spread her long, shapely legs wide open.

Carl took the bait. He moved forward faster, hands going to his belt buckle, "That's it, sweetie, get those legs wide apart so old Carl can kneel between them–"

The hunter stopped dead in his tracks as he felt something against his ankle. He looked down and realized what it was. He looked up in time to see a blur hurtling towards him. The hunter instinctively ducked under the blur. But he wasn't quick enough. The six-foot-long tree limb hit him on the top of his head, fracturing his skull and crushing the vertebrae in his neck. His dead body slumped to the ground.

Missy closed her legs and rolled over quickly to her left as the tree limb swung back towards her.

AFTER A FEW MORE MINUTES Rory finally reached Missy. He stopped beside the dead hunter, placed his hands on his knees and tried to catch his breath. He looked down at Missy a few feet away, still lying on her back in her black underwear and shoes. The dead tree limb still swung gently above the ground beside her.

"You keep taking your pantyhose off," he remarked between breaths.

Missy sat up and covered herself with her arms, "If that's all you noticed, then the honeymoon is really over."

Rory gave a small laugh, still trying to catch his breath. Then he shook his head, "You do realize that make-shift cordage rope was never tested. It might have snapped, causing the limb to come down short and kill you instead."

Missy shrugged, "As you said yourself, what was the alternative?"

Rory nodded, "The woman has a point."

She stood up, self-consciously brushing dirt off the bottom of her black panties, "Now, if you don't mind, can we go back and get my dress?"

"Don't bother," Rory said as he took his hands off his knees and straightened up.

"Oh, you'd like that, wouldn't you!" she said with mock indignation as she crossed her arms over her chest.

"Yes, I would." Rory agreed with a nod. "But what I mean is we can use their clothes. He gestured to the dead hunter.

"Really?" Missy looked down at the dead body.

"Unless you'd rather keep running around the wilderness in a dress and high-heel shoes," shrugged Rory, "*or* in your underwear."

"The man has a point," Missy agreed.

"Help me with this one and then we can go back downstream and get the other one. This one is shorter than the other and should be a better fit for you."

"As long as I don't have to wear his underwear," Missy protested.

"I don't blame you."

Chapter 13

MISSY AND RORY SQUATTED DOWN across from each other and worked quickly to strip the greenish, camouflage clothing from the dead body. Once they were finished, Missy stood up tall in her black, lacy underwear and black high-heel shoes.

Rory kept his eyes respectfully down as he handed her the camouflage shirt.

"A little late not to be looking now," Missy said, teasing him.

Rory continued to keep his head down as he extended his arm.

She smiled as she took the shirt from him and put it on, rolling the sleeves up a couple of times. Stepping into the camouflage pants, she slipped them up her bare legs, pulled the belt tight to the last notch and buckled it. The jacket came next. Then Missy sat down, took off her black high-heel shoes and pulled on each of the socks, "Now I wish I had my pantyhose. I turned his socks inside out," she commented, "I don't want any part of him near me any more than I have to."

"I don't blame you," Rory said, "you can retrieve your pantyhose and put them on later if you want."

"Trying to get me out of these pants already?" she said with a twinkle in her eye.

Rory shook his head and smiled as he handed her the water-proof, insulated hunting boots.

As she slipped them on, Rory checked for the fit with his hands, "It's a good thing you don't have dainty feet."

"Hey! That's not a thing you say to a girl," she complained as she started to tie the laces on the right boot.

"Sorry," Rory said. "I didn't mean how it sounded. But they are pretty feet," he added as he tried to make amends.

"Big and pretty still doesn't cut it, big boy," she complained as she tied the laces on the left boot.

Rory held his hands up in mock surrender, "Okay, no more comments about your body parts."

"Oh, so you've made comments about other parts of my body have you?" she said with mock indignation, "Let's have it."

Rory shook his head, "No thanks. We'll be able to travel a lot a faster with those on your feet. How's that?"

"Coward," she said. She stood up and lifted each foot up and down a few times, "they're a lot heavier than my high heels. But at least I won't have to worry about twisting an ankle if I have to run from one of those scumbags again."

"Hopefully, you won't have to do that again," Rory said as he rolled up the pant legs a few times for her.

Missy did the same with the sleeves on the camouflage jacket, rolling them up. The fit was a little big but it would do.

Rory then reached up and shifted the small Bear Grylls canteen on her belt around to the side, "This is where you wear it. Easier to move this way."

Putting her hands on her hips, a twinkle in her eye again, Missy said, "Anything else you'd like to adjust?"

"Nope."

"Your loss, big boy."

"Here." Rory passed the dead hunter's cap up to her.

"Missy grimaced, "No, thanks. I don't need his cooties."

"Even with the camouflage clothing, you still look too much like a woman."

"And that's bad how?" Missy snatched the hat from his hand, "Never mind. Don't answer that." She crushed the cap against her camouflage shirt, trying to wipe the insides. Then she tested the cap for size and adjusted the tab at the back.

Rory began to straighten out her pant legs.

Missy placed the cap on her with a look of disgust and then began to rummage through the pockets of her camouflage jacket. She pulled out a few packaged energy bars. "Breakfast, lunch and dinner," she said.

"I suppose you didn't like what I served you last night?"

"Oh no, dear, that was very romantic of you." She patted another pocket and then slipped her hand inside and pulled something out. "What's this?" Missy asked.

Rory looked up at what Missy was holding in her hand.

"It was in one of the big pockets," Missy explained as she looked at the item in her hand.

Rory stood up and took it from her hand, turning it over, "These are night vision goggles. No wonder they took us by surprise this morning. Once they found our tracks, they probably tracked us all night, knowing we couldn't move without breaking a leg. They're not giving the men and women they send over that hill much of a chance."

"They're cheaters. You can't trust people these days," Missy grumbled as she patted the other pockets in her new outfit.

"That's true," Rory agreed as he contemplated the night vision goggle. His face took on a worried, dark look.

Missy didn't notice it as she bent down, picked up her black, high-heeled shoes and tossed them over into the brush, "Those cost me over fifteen thousand dollars," she griped.

"Really!"

"Well," Missy shrugged, "they're Gucci. But I had to fly to Italy to buy them, so it's only fair to add in all the costs. That's one of those good business things my father taught me. Return on investment and all that stuff."

Rory shook his head as he hefted the goggles and looked off into the distance. He was contemplating what this new fact meant to their survival.

Missy picked up the hunter's bow and examined it closely, "This looks like a pretty expensive item as well."

Rory nodded as he pocketed the night vision goggles. "I don't know a lot about this stuff but I would say someone put a lot of work into that bow."

Missy tried in vain to pull the bowstring back beyond a couple of inches. "Wow," she said with amazement in her voice, "is that ever hard to do. I can hardly budge it."

Rory took the bow, tested it himself, checked its height against his own and nodded, "Actually, this is a pretty powerful Longbow. I never noticed that before."

"Longbow? I remember something about that from history class," Missy mused. "The English used them a long, long time ago, didn't they?"

Rory nodded as he pulled back on the bowstring, testing its strength.

Missy's eyebrows knit together, puzzled, "Why not use one of those modern ones with all the pulleys and stuff? I saw those being used when I was at the Olympic Games."

"Compound bows?" Rory shook his head, "I'm not sure. But these guys seem old school. I noticed the arrows they carried are wooden as well. They're not aluminum or graphite, like everyone else carries these days. I would say this guy probably built his Longbow from scratch as well. The bowstring looks to be made from green silk."

Missy looked closer, "Green silk? Why use that...?"

"I'm not sure. I know some guitar strings are silver-plated, copper-wire mixed with silk cord to give a soft, easy feel on your fingers. They also give you a mellow tone but I imagine being easy on the fingers is the reason. Plus there's that silk is stronger than steel thing. Probably lighter and easier to use this kind of cord."

"Okay. Makes sense, I guess."

Rory nodded as his hands caressed the string, "It looks like an endless loop string as well. He's done an amazing job. I would say these men chasing us pride themselves on their survival skills. They probably track wild game, tell tall stories around the campfire, live off the land and consider themselves throwbacks to a time when men were men, crap like that."

Missy shook her head, "And yet they cheat by using night-vision goggles. They're a pack of a-holes if you ask me."

"I won't disagree. Here, put this on" Rory said as he set the Longbow down and picked up the hunters backpack and quiver of arrows. He showed Missy how to slip it on her back. "This has what's called an Eberlestock Butt Bucket Kit."

"Hey, no lady wants more butt," she griped as she slipped the kit on.

Rory retrieved the Longbow and showed Missy how to slip it over her shoulder and carry it in the kit, freeing her hands. "You might not be strong enough to fire an arrow but take it with you anyway. You never know when or how we can use it," he said as he patted her on the back. He adjusted the sheath holding the hunting knife on her belt around to her right side, "Besides, you wanted some weapons to fight back with, you've got them."

Missy nodded her approval with two thumbs up.

"We'll head back downstream to get the other guys clothes," Rory told her. "I'll take his kit and Longbow for myself so that we're both armed and ready. All set? Let's go."

RORY AND MISSY HEADED downstream toward the other dead body. They took the hike back a little slower, moving from tree to tree to keep hidden in case there were other hunters nearby. Once they reached Seth's dead body they began to strip off his camouflage clothing and gear.

"What the hell happened to him?" Missy exclaimed as she looked down at the smooth stone lodged in his forehead.

"I went Rocky on him," Rory said. He rolled the body over to remove the backpack and bucket kit. They piled the clothes and gear in one spot and then Rory stood up.

Missy stayed kneeling beside the pile of clothing, looking up at him.

Rory took off his tuxedo jacket and tossed it to the ground. Then he began to unbutton his shirt.

"Oooo, I never thought about this part," Missy grinned as she clapped her hands together a few times and settled in for the show.

All Rory could do was shake his head. He finished unbuttoning his shirt, peeled it off and dropped it to the ground.

"Mmmm, muscles and a six pack," Missy said, "I like that in a man."

Rory bent over and chucked off his black dress shoes. "Can't you at least give me some privacy?" he asked her.

Missy shook her head vigorously, "Oh no, payback is a bitch, ain't it?"

Rory had to smile as he undid his belt buckle and undid the zipper. He pushed his tuxedo pants down to the ground.

"Oh, you're a boxer man," she said as she lightly clapped her hands again, "now I know."

"Can't you at least keep watch around us?" he said as he stepped out of his pants.

"Stop trying to distract me," Missy complained. "On with the show."

Rory shook his head good-naturedly. After what she had just gone through, Rory was willing to do anything to keep her mind off the terror they were in. Even if was only temporary.

Missy whistled as Rory bent over in his boxer shorts, "Where is a dollar bill when a girl needs it?" she cooed. "Are you going to change into his shorts too?"

"No."

"Oh, too bad."

Rory laughed as he picked up the dead hunter's pants and began to redress in the camouflage outfit, staying fully alert for any sign of movement and danger in the wilderness around them.

Chapter 14

ONCE HE WAS DRESSED, Rory stood over the dead hunter's body and was deep in thought for a moment.

"What are you thinking?" Missy asked, still kneeling on the ground.

Rory finally took a deep breath and let it out, "I guess we should hide this guy somehow. I should have thought of that with the other body as well." Rory looked back upstream. "My survival training is more than a little rusty. And that's not good considering the situation we're in," He shook his head in frustration.

"What do you want me to do?" Missy asked him.

Rory rubbed the back of his neck as he looked around. He noted some dead leaves piled up close by on the edge of the clearing and that gave him an idea. He bent over and grabbed one of the dead hunter's legs, "Help me drag him over there."

Missy got up but grabbed Rory's discarded tuxedo jacket, "I'm not touching him like that." She wrapped the jacket around the dead hunter's bare leg before she started to pull. Together they got him over to the edge of the clearing.

Rory pulled the large Bowie knife from the sheath on his belt and instructed Missy to pull her own hunting knife. He cleared some leaves and together they began to dig a shallow grave. When it was deep enough they rolled the dead body into it. They shoved Rory's clothing in with it, covered it over with dirt and then camouflaged the spot with dead leaves.

"As long as animals don't dig up the body or the other hunters find it, our whereabouts will remain a mystery if anyone else comes up to the waterfall," Rory said. He stood up and brushed the dirt and leaves off his hands, "Let's go take care of the other one."

THEY HIKED BACK UP to the other dead body, making a detour to retrieve Missy's black silk dress and pantyhose. They buried her black dress along with the hunter's body, hiding the shallow grave as best as possible with more dead leaves.

As Rory finished covering over the makeshift Missy stood up and held out her hand, "Can I have your little canteen?"

He slipped his own Bear Grylls canteen from the holder on his belt and handed it to Missy, "Sure, why?"

"I'll rinse and refill them. I don't want any of their backwash," Missy explained with disgust. She took the two small canteens over to the waterfall, stepping out across two flat rocks where she emptied them, rinsed them out and refilled them with cold mountain water.When she was finished, she stepped back to shore she sat down, removed her boots. She then stood up, glanced over her shoulder and undid her camouflage pants, dropping them to her ankles. Her black silk panties peeked out from under the shirttail of the camouflage shirt as she bent over and pushed them off completely. She glanced back at Rory.

He had discreetly turned his back, waiting

Missy smiled to herself. She pulled her pantyhose back on and then redressed in the hunters pants, socks, and boots before heading over to join Rory.

He heard her footsteps and turned, "All set?"

"Yeah." She handed him one of the small, refilled canteens. "Fresh mountain dew," she announced. Just then a radio squawked with static several times. Missy looked at Rory with panic in her eyes, wondering where the noise was coming from.

Rory calmly took out two small walkie-talkies from his large side-pockets.

"Carl, Seth? You guys there?" asked a disembodied voice from one of the walkie-talkies. It sounded like the Bossman.

Missy looked up into Rory silver-blue eyes and opened her mouth but no sound came out. Her own eyes were filled with fear.

"I think you had a small role of duct tape in one of your pockets," Rory said calmly to Missy.

Missy nodded and patted a few pockets until she found the right one. She pulled out a small roll of gray duct tape and held it out to Rory. Her hand was shaking.

"I'm going to press down on the edge of this button," Rory said. "I want you to wrap some tape around it to keep it down and hold it firmly in place. Don't say anything while we're doing it, understand?"

Missy nodded silently, her eyes still showing fear.

Rory pressed down on the button.

Missy quickly wrapped the duct tape several times around the walkie-talkie to permanently lock the button down.

When she cut off the duct tape, Rory placed the taped walkie-talkie gently on the ground. Then Rory did the same with the second walkie-talkie, holding down the edge of the button while Missy taped it down to hold it in place. Rory then took the two walkie-talkies and walked off into the woods.

Missy followed him, walking as lightly as possible and not uttering a sound, even trying to keep her breathing quiet.

Twenty feet in, Rory bent down and quickly dug a shallow hole with the large Bowie knife. Gently placing the two walkie-talkies into the shallow hole, he buried them with dirt and camouflaged the spot with leaves.

Missy stood to the side, the tension evident in her taut stance.

"Okay, all set," Rory said to Missy. "You can talk now."

Missy let out a noisy breath, "Why did we do all that with the tape and the holes?"

"We taped down the transmit buttons on the walkie-talkies," Rory answered, "It's another valuable step in fighting back. While those buttons are down, nobody else can talk on the frequency. We just cut off their communications. They'll figure it out eventually and go to another frequency or a different set of walkie-talkies. But it gives us a brief edge. And we need all the help we can get. Still...."

Missy blinked her eyes when she saw the look of worry cross Rory's face, "Still what? What aren't you saying?"

Rory chewed on the inside of his cheek for a moment, "These guys are good in the woods, Missy. Even though I was watching for them, they almost caught me by surprise before sun-up this morning. It would have been difficult but *maybe* we could have stayed ahead of them and found a way out. But...the night vision goggles you found in your pocket...those are a game changer."

"What do you mean a game changer?" Missy asked. She wrapped her arms tightly around her chest.

"Hunting us in the daylight is one thing. But with night vision goggles, they can hunt us all night as well," Rory explained. "Even if one of us stays on watch while the other one sleeps, it won't be a sound rest because we know they can see us long before we see ever them. Before long we'll be exhausted and make a mistake. That means we have to get back up the hill to the compound and see if we can find a way out or call for help."

Missy's eyes revealed the terror she was feeling but she tried to remain resolute and brave. "So...how do we do that without being seen or...?"

"I'm not really sure," Rory admitted, "I'm really kind of winging it here."

"That's worked well for us so far, I guess," Missy said. "So what are odds?" she asked after a moment.

"Well," Rory said as he looked into the distance and gave her a question some thought, "they outnumber us by about 30 to 1. Well...with Frick and Frack here gone, it's only 29 to 1. But they all have powerful Longbows. And I assume they all know how to use them expertly. We have two bows but I'm the only one who can use one. And I'm not sure how good I can be with a bow without a lot of practice. They know the terrain like the back of their hand, we don't. They have night vision gear, which means they can track us 24-7. Half the hunters can track us at night while the other half sleeps. They have lots of food and can bring more in. We have berries and acorns - *when* we can find them. And who knows what else we can find? And even if we continue to avoid them, eventually winter will set in and we'll probably freeze to death. Have I left anything out?" he asked.

Missy pursed her lips and shook her head no. After some thought, she asked, "So, what's the bad news?"

Chapter 15

RORY BRUSHED THE BACK OF HIS HAND across his forehead, wiping the perspiration away and considering their next move. It was strangely paradoxical. A hot, sunny day, birds singing, the breeze gently moving through the mountain forest around them - and they had just buried two dead bodies and were now trying to figure out how they could avoid the same fate. He shook his head softly, trying to get rid of those thoughts, "Okay. If we're going to start fighting back, I guess the first thing we need to do is reconnaissance." Rory looked up at the trees around them, removing more sweat from beneath his chin with the back of his fingers.

Missy bent back at the waist, looking up as well, "What are you looking for?"

Instead of answering, Rory began to walk downstream, turning in small circles and shading his eyes from the sun. "We need to find the tallest tree. One that will give us the farthest view," he said.

Missy followed closely behind him, watching as he considered various candidates for his reconnaissance mission. At one point she leaned back and looked up, shading her eyes, "They all look pretty tall to me."

Rory stopped at the base of a tree and looked straight up through the long branches, "You're right. I guess this one looks as good as any. I'll go up there and scout out the terrain. Maybe I can find a safe path back up to the lodge." He removed his Longbow and passed it to Missy.

Missy turned, looking for a spot to set it down and then scooted across the grass and put it near another tree. She ran back to Rory and took his Butt Bucket Kit, running back across to the tree and then back again.

Rory handed her his canteen and a few other items, a puzzled look on his face.

Missy knew what he was thinking and she simply shrugged, "That way you won't break them when you fall."

"Thanks a lot for your confidence," Rory said with a chuckle.

"You're welcome."

As she scooted back across the grass, Rory tested a few of the lower branches, "If we're really fortunate, I'll be able to see where the other hunters are, so we can avoid them."

"Do you really think there are others nearby?" Miss asked as she ran back.

"Probably."

"But what if someone comes while you're up there?" asked Missy with genuine concern, her head now on a swivel.

"I'll scout around as I climb. I *should* be able to see someone coming long before they get close to us," Rory told her.

"Should?" Missy crossed her arms over her chest.

Rory gave her a reassuring smile, "We'll be fine. Don't worry."

"Uh huh. You're way up there and I'm down here. Easy for you to say," she chastised him. She jerked a thumb skyward, "Get climbing, Tarzan."

Rory began his ascent. He climbing slowly upward from limb to limb, testing each for safety as he climbed. His head was on a swivel as he concentrated on surveying the heavily forested terrain on all sides, while he also moved upwards from branch to branch. Climbing and trying to see everything in the forest around him at the same time wasn't an easy task. But he didn't want to be surprised and leave Missy vulnerable down below. The higher he climbed the farther he could see. And the forest was clear of hunters on all sides. *So far, so good.*

DOWN BELOW, MISSY LISTENED intently to every sound around her. She watched for the slightest movements in the forest around her, realizing the hunters could come from any direction, at any time. She felt very exposed and completely at the mercy of anyone who attacked now. She was amazed at how much safer she felt with Rory right beside her. Every few moments she looked up to check Rory's progress. He was moving higher, constantly moving farther away from her. If someone came now, Rory wouldn't be able to get down to her very quickly. It was all so nerve-racking and she anxiously tried to slow her breathing, afraid she wouldn't hear someone approaching.

RORY ANALYZED THE TERRAIN as he climbed. Two-thirds of the way to the top of the tree, Rory stopped and was dead still. Then he quickly began to hustle back down the tree.

MISSY TURNED SLOWLY as she waited, watching for any movement in the trees around her. Every branch that moved from the slight breeze or a squirrel skittering across was a cause for her heart rate to rise and she had to fight to get it back down, trying to stay calm and rational. She stepped back and looked up through the branches of the tree soaring overhead. She caught a glimpse of Rory high up on a limb, still climbing...no...was he? No, he was starting to move down towards her again. She felt a bit of relief that he would be down and beside her again. But...the way he was dropping from branch to branch...quickly concerned her. She wrung her hands, anxiously trying to watch the forest around and looking up, wondering what was happening. When Rory was about twenty feet above her, she put her hands to her mouth and called up, "What's wrong."

"Two hunters coming this way, fast," Rory yelled as he dropped down another branch.

Missy looked at the forest around her, then called up again, "Do they know where we are?"

"They *are* headed right for the waterfall," Rory yelled as he dropped down another branch. "The two we took out probably used their walkie-talkies to report back last night or early this morning and told them we were at the falls."

"And since they can't contact them now, they've come looking," Missy said, following his train of thought.

Rory nodded as he prepared for the last jump to the ground. "This is all my fault for screwing around with those bodies. But we have enough time to stay out of their way if we move fast."

Missy nodded and she scooted away to retrieve his Longbow, quiver, backpack and other items from where she had piled them.

"Ow!"

Missy quickly turned to see Rory limping in pain. "What's wrong!?"

"I landed on that root and jammed my ankle," Rory said with a grimace.

Missy quickly carried Rory's Longbow and backpack over to him.

Rory took a few steps and shook his head in agony, cursing, "I'm not going to get too far right now."

Standing beside him as she held the Longbow and backpack, Missy's chest began to heave with fear. Now what?

Chapter 16

MISSY CLOSED HER EYES AND FOUGHT HER FEAR. When she opened them, she did her best to remain calm. Looking around, she hunted for a hiding spot. Spotting a possibility, she held the Longbow and backpack out to Rory, "Get ready."

Rory balanced on one leg as he grabbed the backpack and slipped it on. "Get ready for what?" he asked as he grabbed the Longbow. "We can't fight out in the open. We won't last very long."

"That's not what I'm talking about." She pointed off to the left, "We can go up there. It's higher ground. That will give us the advantage if they get here before your ankle feels better. Right?"

Rory nodded, "It's as good a plan as any right now."

Missy retrieved the other items and then stood beside Rory, allowing him to put his arm around her shoulders. Once he was set, she helped him hobble towards the higher ground. It was slow going and they nearly toppled over several times. As they moved uphill Missy spotted a possible hiding spot, overlooking the clearing below, "How about hiding behind those boulders?"

Rory looked at where she was pointing, "Yeah, that's good. And it can give us some protection if they attack us."

"But how will they know we're up here...?"

Rory grimaced as he hopped over a root, "I'm leaving a bit of a trail behind."

Missy glanced back down the hill and saw the scuff marks leading up the hill. "Oh crap," she muttered.

Reaching the top of the ridge, they moved in between two six-foot high boulders. Missy took Rory's Longbow and leaned it against one of the boulders, setting his back-back and quiver down next to it.

Rory surveyed the terrain below as he hopped closer to the boulder, grimacing whenever he put weight on the ankle. With Missy's help, he gently eased himself to the ground, leaned gratefully back against the boulder and rubbed his sore ankle.

Missy looked around and scooted over to the trees twenty feet behind their hiding spot. She quickly returned with some green moss she'd collected. Propping Rory's ankle up on another small boulder, she wrapped the ankle with the moss, "It's not really that cold, but it should help to keep the swelling down."

Rory nodded, "It's starting to feel a bit better already." He took a quick peek around the boulder. "Still no sign of them. Maybe we can get moving again in a few minutes."

"You won't get far on that ankle. You need to rest it."

Rory leaned his head back against the boulder, "We can't wait too long. Just give me another minute."

Missy reached over her shoulder and drew her own Longbow. She propped it against the large boulder beside Rory's Longbow. "Can you reach it from there?" she asked Rory.

Rory looked at the bow and then at Missy, "I only need the one bow. You should keep it—"

Missy was suddenly up and running back down the hill in full flight.

Chapter 17

ALARM BELLS WENT OFF in Rory's head. He tried to rise quickly but the ankle was still too sore. He grimaced in pain and then shouted, "Mis–" He cut himself off. Any hunters nearby might hear him. He had to grit his teeth and watch helplessly as Missy run down to the bottom of the hill, crossed the small clearing below and disappear into the trees. *What is she doing?* He swore under his breath and put his head back against the rock for a moment, letting the throbbing ankle rest. *I can't just wait here. But if those hunters come and I'm caught in the open, then what? Does she think she'll save me by leading them away?* Clenching his jaw, Rory slowly and carefully struggled to rise by sliding his back up against the boulder. He made it to his feet and gingerly reached over for a Longbow and picked up a quiver of arrows, slinging it over his back. But as much as he tried, he couldn't get put weight on both feet to walk. He tried hopping on one foot but that wouldn't work either. He tried to use the Longbow as a crutch. No good. He bent over and picked up the second Longbow, trying to use the pair as crutches. That didn't work either. The Longbows bent too much under his weight to be effective. Throwing the bows down in frustration, he looked around for a log or a fallen limb to use as a crutch or cane. But he couldn't see anything near enough to get to. Leaning on one leg against the boulder, he tried to figure another way to go after Missy. But it was futile. He would have to wait until his ankle felt better or she returned. Rory slumped back down against the rock, running his hands through his black hair in frustration.

Time passed agonizingly slow as he watched the terrain below and to the left. *That's where the hunters should—*

Missy came out of the trees across the clearing below. She was moving low, holding something in each hand as she headed for the bottom of the hill.

Good. She's coming back—

But instead of climbing the hill and coming back to where she had left him, she kept on running.

Where's she going? She'll run into the hunters. He put his hands to his mouth to call to her and then decided against it. *The hunters might be too close. What is she carrying? Damn it, Missy—*

Missy disappeared out of sight, plunging into the trees off to the left.

No, no, no. Rory struggled to rise again. He slid upright against the boulder but that was it. Rory cursed. *It feels better but I won't be able to go after her. And if I run into those hunters, I can't fight hand-to-hand very effectively this way. Maybe...maybe they'll chase her back this way.* Reaching down, he grabbed one of the Longbows and pulled an arrow from a quiver. Notching the arrow, he balanced himself on his good leg, leaned against the boulder and readied himself.

Missy came back out of the trees. But this time she was moving backward on her knees and doing something in the dirt.

What is she doing now? Then it dawned on him. Missy had retrieved her black, high-heeled shoes from where she had thrown them. She was on her hands and knees, making footprints on the ground with them. Rory shook his head and marveled at her audacity.

Missy worked frantically across the clearing below, making shoe prints that led from the direction the hunters were coming from and off into the trees and away from Rory's hiding spot up the hill.

Rory heard voices to his left. *They're here.*

Missy heard them as well. She looked up the hill but it was too late. There was no way she was going to be able to get back up to Rory. There was no time and she had no choice. Missy turned quickly and slipped away into the trees.

Chapter 18

MOMENTS LATER, two men in green and brown camouflage hunting clothing appeared in the clearing below and Rory recognized them immediately. It was acne-face and whiskey-breath. Anger flared through his body and Rory lifted his Longbow, drawing back on the bowstring, his fingers right near his ear. A heartbeat later, common sense won out. At this distance and shooting off one leg, the shot was not going to be easy or accurate one for a novice. His jaw clenched as he did it, but he lowered the Longbow and eased up on the arrow. Then he muttered a curse under his breath.

Acne-face and whiskey-breath had spotted the shoe tracks Missy had made. They were hunched over them and acne-face reached down to the tracks.

Glancing off to the trees where Missy had disappeared, Rory wondered if she had found a good hiding spot or could find another way back up here. He cursed to himself. This had all gone sideways when she ran off and he couldn't do a thing about it.

The two hunters continued to converse in low voices.

Rory wished he could hear them. Reading lips would be a good skill right now.

After a few more moments of talking, whiskey-breath pulled his Longbow and stood up. He said something to his partner and then headed off at a trot in Missy's direction.

He's going after her. Rory lifted the Longbow, pulled back on the arrow and aimed for whiskey-breath as the man trotted to the bottom of the hill. But trying to track the moving target while balancing on one leg proved difficult. *Almost have him–*

whiskey-breath suddenly broke into a run.

Balanced on one leg, Rory couldn't turn and react fast enough to track the hunter and whiskey-breath disappeared into the trees. Rory cursed and swung the Longbow around to acne-face. *He's gone. Where did he go? What's going on here?* Rory had a sense of dread. *Something's wrong.* The way they had split up in opposite directions and disappeared so quickly gave him a sense of foreboding. He lowered the Longbow and struggled to move back further behind the boulder to use it as cover.

UNKNOWN TO RORY, ACNE-face had doubled back and was working his way around through the trees to the high ground and the large boulders. The two hunters had spotted the *real* tracks leading up to the high ground. The other tracks made by a woman's shoe were obviously faked. There was no weight to them. Someone was trying to mislead them. But it wasn't going to work. They had tracked too many people in these woods. acne-face pulled his Longbow from over his shoulder and notched an arrow, anticipating the kill.

MISSY SAW A HUNTER in camouflage clothing enter the trees. He was looking down, following the footprints she had made. It was working. But she hadn't planned on being trapped in the trees. She watched him move in a low crouch in her direction. She placed the shoes in her hand on the ground, figuring the hunter would find them once he got to her present spot. Crouched low, she now began slowly moving to her right. She had to stay as silent as possible as she moved out of the camouflaged hunter's path. Once he moved passed her, she would head back to Rory. It was all so easy. Missy heard her own ragged breath as she moved and grew afraid the hunter would hear it as well. Holding her breath, she moved at a pace that felt agonizingly slow in order to stay quiet. After a few minutes, she glanced back towards the hunter. She froze. *Where is he? He was right there. Did he see me? Is he circling in for the kill?* Missy squeezed her eyes shut. *No, he won't kill me right away. He has other plans for me before he kills me.* Missy's heart pounded and she was unable to control her breathing.

Missy opened her eyes and scanned the trees and bushes around her frantically. *Where is he?* Then she remembered something Rory had told her as they had walked through the forest. He told her not to focus on one spot as she watched for movement in the trees around them. She tried to relax and not focus on any one spot. She was scared and she had to concentrate to calm her breathing. She scanned the trees around her again. *There.* Movement in the trees ahead and off to the right. It was the hunter. He wasn't close after all. She felt relieved and was about to move away when her blood ran cold. He wasn't following the footprints she had made. He wasn't moving towards the spot where she had left the shoes. *Why not–?* Missy cursed. She knew exactly what the hunter *was* doing and it changed everything.

Chapter 19

ACNE-FACE SCANNED THE TREES on either side of him as he moved forward. He listened for the smallest noise. But even the birds were silent now. He could only hear the low hum of flies in the air. He stopped and turned to look behind him every few feet. He expertly walked over the ground in silence as he scanned for a target. He slowly ate up the distance between himself and the high ground. Large boulders appeared just ahead at the crest of the rise. acne-face noted the tip of a Longbow peeking up over one of the large boulders. He eased up, figuring his partner had scored the kill before he did. He cursed under his breath and wondered if his partner was now with the woman. Here he was sneaking through the bush while his friend enjoyed the pleasures of the hunt. acne-face rose but stayed alert as he surveyed the trees around him. He walked forward a little faster but still stayed vigilant. He held his Longbow at the ready. He reached the large boulder, drew back the arrow for safety and quickly darted around the boulder. He blinked his eyes when he saw the Longbow had one end lodged between several small rocks on the ground, holding it upright. He lowered his Longbow, trying to figure out what had happened.

Rory flew from the top of the large boulder and hit acne-face with the full force of his weight.

Acne-face's arrow was released with the blow.

The arrow clanged off another large boulder, ricocheting back over the two rolling men.

Coming up with a large hunting knife in his hand, the man whirled around towards Rory.

Rory lashed out with his good leg, knocking the knife out of acne-face's hand. Then he collapsed in agony as his jammed ankle gave way under the effort.

Acne-face didn't hesitate. He pounced on Rory, trying to strangle him.

Rory tried to pull the man's arms apart to break the stranglehold. But the man had too much leverage by being on top and pressing his full weight down. Rory couldn't breathe. Black specks began to appear in his vision. Rory released the man's wrists, brought both arms up forcefully and slammed the palms of his hands against the hunter's ears. It wasn't a clean blow but acne-face immediately screamed. He pushed himself back off Rory, trying to get away from the pain.

Rory did a back roll and pushed himself up to land on his feet. His bad ankle nearly gave way. He struggled to balance himself on one leg in a defensive posture.

Acne-face was back up quickly, growling as he swept out a boot, sweeping Rory's good leg out from under him.

Rory fell on his back with a hard thud. The wind was knocked from his lungs.

Grinning, the hunter launched himself at Rory.

But Rory rolled to his right and acne-face landed face down in the dirt.

Rolling once more, Rory came up onto his feet again.

The hunter scrambled around on the ground and threw a boot at Rory's crotch.

Rory countered by lifting his knee and blocking the kick. His bad ankle immediately gave way and he collapsed to the ground.

Jumping to his feet, acne-face lifted a boot, stomping down towards Rory's head.

The boot clipped Rory's ear as he rolled away and he grimaced in pain. He managed to get back up into a defensive posture, holding most of his weight on the good ankle as his hand automatically went to his ear and he felt blood. Rory cursed at the near miss.

Acne-face now attacked by lowering his head and charging with a yell of anger, trying to tackle Rory around the middle.

Rory pivoted on his good ankle, letting the charging man slide by. Placing a hand on the man's back, he used the hunter's momentum to throw him face down.

Acne-face grunted in pain as his face banged against a rock.

Rory tried to move away to get some distance but his bad ankle gave way again and he collapsed to the ground in agony. This wasn't going to last much longer. acne-face was young, strong and quick and Rory on one leg was at a great disadvantage.

Rory spun himself around on the ground with his feet towards acne-face.

The hunter was up again, his face bleeding and he bellowed in rage as he charged.

At the last minute, Rory made the only move available to him. He lifted his good leg and planted it in acne-face's stomach, using the man's own momentum to launch him up and over. He heard acne-face's body hit something and Rory spun himself around on the ground, struggling to get himself up into a defensive position on one leg again before the hunter came back at him.

But acne-face wasn't coming back. His was sliding slowly head first down the side of one of the large boulders. His neck was at an angle, obviously broken.

Rory slumped to the ground, relieved that it was over.

But his relief was short-lived. He heard a terrified scream. It was Missy! He looked down to the clearing.

Chapter 20

MISSY AMOS BURST FROM THE TREES. Her face was a mask of terror and she screamed again.

Rory struggled to get to his feet.

Missy ran for the clearing in full flight.

Whiskey-breath burst from the trees behind her and stopped dead.

Missy turned halfway across the clearing and ran hard for the high ground. Her boots slipped in her panic as she tried to scramble up the hill and she cried out when her knees banged into stones and exposed roots.

Grinning, whiskey-breath cackled and took off after Missy.

There was no doubt Missy would not make the top of the hill before the hunter caught her.

Missy grasped for grass, roots, buried rocks, anything that would give her added momentum to climb the hill and get away. Her chest was heaving and she didn't know how much longer she could go.

Whiskey-breath was now at the bottom of the rise. He looked up at Missy's shapely bottom in great anticipation. Then his face took on a sense of urgency. He quickly reached back over his shoulder and pulled the Longbow from his kit.

Missy heard something whoosh over the top of her head. The sound made her duck and cringe. She heard a gurgle behind her and turned in the direction of her pursuer.

The hunter was clutching at an arrow piercing the right side of his chest. But it didn't stop him. He looked up at Missy and pulled a hunting knife from his belt. Flipping it around to hold it by the blade, he brought his hand back to throw it.

Missy screamed.

Another arrow buried itself in whiskey-breath's chest. He dropped the knife, fell to his knees and slowly toppled over onto his face.

Missy turned back around and looked up the hill quickly.

Rory stood there, Longbow in hand, leaning back against a boulder. He gestured for her to join him as quickly as possible while he set another arrow on the Longbow. He kept watch for other hunters.

Missy was exhausted from the chase but she scrambled and clawed her way back up the rise as quickly as she could. She finally reached the top and flopped at the side of Rory's feet.

Rory finally slumped down himself and sat propped against the boulder.

Missy leaned back on her hands, her breath raspy and her chest heaving as she tried to catch her breath.

Shaking his head, Rory ran a hand through his black hair, "You cut that one kind of close this time, Amos. I almost didn't get that second arrow off in time."

"Uh huh," she nodded. "I thought I would hide and he'd go by. But when I saw he was actually trying to circle back to where you were up here, I figured I had to get him back out here in the open."

"He could have dropped you anytime with an arrow. You know that, right?"

Missy shook her head emphatically no.

"You sure about that?" he asked her.

Missy nodded "Uh huh. I played cute and I used every man's weakness against him."

Rory raised his eyebrows, "And what exactly would that be?"

"Thinking with the wrong head," she said.

Chapter 21

RORY PUSHED HIMSELF UP on one leg, gingerly favoring the other, and took a peek over the boulder. "Sorry, Missy. I wish we had some time to rest but I think we're going to have to move on," he said.

Missy sat there wearily, understanding the need to make tracks before more hunters arrived on scene, "Yeah, I know." She ran her fingers through her hair, her breathing still raspy, "Did you figure out a path back to the lodge while you were up the tree?"

Rory shook his head as he gingerly sat back down against the boulder, "No. Once we leave the trees down here, there's no safe path back to the top. Everything I could see was the same, an open killing field. The odds are not good that we can sneak back up there without being seen."

"There you go with those bad odds again," Missy grumbled.

"Well, they only outnumber us now by 23 to 1," Rory offered as solace.

Missy gave a weary thumbs-up.

"Maybe, if we get around to the west side of the compound, or even all the way around to the north, there may be more cover," Rory said.

"You think it's possible?"

Rory just shrugged, "It's worth a try." He jerked a thumb at acne-face's body, "But first we have to hide this guy. And then the one down there."

"Are you sure? If they come while we're doing that...."

"I didn't see anyone close to these two, so we should be okay for now," Rory told her as he struggled to his feet. "But you're right. They will come. But if they can't find these two guys and the first two we took out, they'll start to wonder what happened to them. And *anything* we can do to get into their heads will give us a slight edge."

"Okay. I'll take any edge we can get, any old way I can," Missy said.

They worked together as quickly as possible to bury acne-face in a shallow, hidden grave along with his Longbow and a taped down walkie-talkie. Then, Rory needed Missy's help to hobble down to the other fallen hunter. First, they stripped any items they could use from whiskey-breath. Then they buried his body in another shallow grave, hiding the burial spot under dead leaves. They also had to work to cover the blood-stained ground where whiskey-breath had fallen.

Once done, they headed back up to the crest of the hill and hiked westward beyond the boulders. When they settled down later on a strategic high spot to rest, Missy applied some more cool moss to Rory's ankle. She insisted on keeping watch while Rory rested his ankle and they both ate a lunch of protein bars and cold mountain water, all salvaged from the possessions of the four dead hunters.

"Any change in plans?" Missy asked as they prepared to move again.

"No," Rory said, "let's just keep heading west, away from the waterfall. That seems to make the most sense. That's the last place the dead hunters would have reported seeing us. And that's the first place the others will likely head for. But as we move west, keep an eye out for enough cover to make the climb back to the compound safely. We have to find some way to get back up there. Once we do, maybe we can find a radio in one of those buildings and call for help. Sound good?"

"Yeah," Missy said, "I wasn't really keen on climbing back up to the compound. But...it sounds a lot better than staying down here and just waiting for them to find us." She shook her head, "I guess it's better to go out fighting than sit on your butt and do nothing but wait for...."

Rory felt sorry for her but he had to keep her spirits up, "No more defeatist talk. We will get out of this. Let's go."

Missy blew a strand of hair from her forehead, "Okay." She rose to her feet slowly, brushing the dirt from her hands, trying not to look too worried. But it was there in her eyes.

Together they continued to move westward but it was at a very slow pace. Because of Rory's ankle, they were moving even slower than when Missy was in her high-heels. They angled up towards the compound, hoping to find cover all the way to the top. But all they found was disappointment. Every avenue back up to the compound provided the same open terrain they had slid down through on the car hood when they were first let go. The entire south hillside was just another open killing field for the hunters.

The disappointed pair continued to stay in the denser forest down lower and continued to track westward. The only good thing about having to stay lower was finding more acorns to fill their pockets. Missy was becoming quite adept at spotting white oaks. They rationed their water but it was getting low and that concerned Rory a great deal. They moved on slowly, always alert to the possibility of being spotted by hunters. The fact that they hadn't been spotted meant the hunters were probably still looking for them on the east side or back at the falls. And not being able to communicate with their missing men was probably giving Rory and Missy another slight advantage. At least, that was the theory, Rory thought.

Chapter 22

AFTER A FEW HOURS, Rory looked up at the sky. The sun was going to start setting soon. Rory knew they needed to find a campsite where they could rest and eat to keep their strength up. Missy didn't say anything but he could see that she was getting very tired. He couldn't wear her out completely. In fact, if he didn't get some rest soon himself, he wouldn't be any good to either of them in a fight. Rory considered their options and came up with a plan he felt was workable. And probably the safest plan. He kept an eye peeled for a tall tree, big enough to accommodate them both. Rory finally found a likely candidate and he stopped. "I think we can camp here for the night," he said to Missy as he slipped his Longbow and backpack off.

The obviously exhausted Missy looked immensely relieved,"Oh, thank god, finally. I was hoping you'd say that soon." She took off her own Longbow and backpack off and slumped to the ground.

Rory pulled a small stone from his pocket and handed it over to Missy, "Crack open some supper and let's eat before it gets dark."

Missy took the rock, dug into a pocket and began to crack open several acorns. She handed the rock back over to Rory and then started to eat as she watched Rory cracked a handful of his own acorns. It was an exquisite meal for two nearly famished hikers.

Missy reached for her canteen.

"Try to keep water consumption to a minimum, if you can," Rory asked her.

Missy nodded as she undid the cap, "I will. Just a little sip. It's a good thing these acorns are moist. I'm surprised we haven't seen any more berries."

Rory nodded, "I know. I've been watching for them as well. But that's the problem with wilderness survival; you never know when you can come across food without specifically hunting for it. And we don't have the time to go foraging, with maniacal hunters on our trail."

They ate the rest of their meal in silence, took a few sips of water and buried the acorn shells. They wanted to leave as little trace of themselves as possible in case hunters ever came this way.

"Should we just bed down here for the night?" Missy asked as she looked around for a soft spot.

"No," Rory answered. He pointed a thumb upwards.

Missy looked up, "In the tree? Really? Is that safe? I mean, if they come by and we're up there, we'll literally be stuck up a tree. Won't we be trapped? And what if I fall out?"

"All very good questions," Rory answered as he dug into his backpack. "Just stay calm, everything will be fine. I saw something we can use."

Missy's body shook and her eyes betrayed her fear as she looked up again.

"Just trust me. Getting caught up there by the hunters isn't a good idea, you're right about that," he admitted. "But if they *do* show up...they probably won't be looking for us up a tree. But we also don't know what kind of wildlife could pass by here in the middle of the night. We need to be safe."

Missy's eyes widened as she looked at the wilderness around her, "Wildlife? What kind of wildlife?"

Rory shrugged as he shifted over to rummage in her backpack, "Oh, I don't know...mountain lions, grizzly bears, coyotes–"

Missy held her hands up, "Okay, stop, stop stop. I don't need to know anymore." She got to her feet quickly, "Let's just get up this friggin' tree before I crap my pants."

Satisfied they both had what they needed, Rory handed the backpack to Missy, "Put this and your Longbow and stuff back on and start climbing."

Missy complied, although she looked extremely concerned.

Rory donned his own gear and started to follow her up the tree.

Missy was obviously nervous as she climbed, moving from limb to limb but she persevered.

They had to move forty feet up the tree to reach the two branches Rory felt they could use. He was happy when those branches turned out to be perfect perches. He told Missy to stop and began to dig into her backpack again.

When he jostled her a bit as he looked in the backpack, Missy's eyes widened and she applied a death grip on the tree as she looked down at the ground far below them, "P-please be careful, Me and heights don't work well together."

"Sorry. Just keep your eyes up. Missy?" Rory gently touched her shoulder, squeezing a bit and he spoke gently, "Just keep your eyes up. C'mon. That's it. Now take a look at this." Rory pulled out a bundle of rope and showed it to her, "We are going to tie ourselves to the tree to make sure we don't fall, all right?"

Missy licked her lips and nodded, "O-okay." Then an eyebrow flickered, "I never...thought...we'd be into bondage in a tree."

Rory had to laugh. Then he instructed her to move carefully and sit on one of the branches on the south side of the tree. Once she was sitting on the wide branch, Rory threw the rope around Missy and the tree and fastened it with a bowline knot.

Missy touched the rope, gingerly feeling the tension in it, "You're *sure* I won't fall out of the tree?"

"I'll let you know in the morning," Rory answered.

Missy rolled her eyes but she relaxed a little as she laughed.

Rory pulled out his own bundle of rope. He settled himself on a branch a little higher than Missy's but on the other side of the tree where he would be facing northward. He reasoned he should be able to see anyone coming from the west, the north or the east. That left the south and he hoped he would hear someone trying to sneak up from behind or Missy would see them. He tossed the rope a couple of times back around the tree before he was finally able to catch the end and tie himself in.

As the sun finally set, Rory dug into his pocket and pulled out a pair of the night vision goggles. Everything lit up green when he put them on. He could actually see a raccoon toddling through the forest down below. He hoped he would see any hunters coming this way just as easily.

Chapter 23

RORY HEARD HIS NAME BEING CALLED. He was tired. He didn't really want to wake up. It was summer. He wanted to sleep in. But someone persisted in calling out his name and he slowly opened his eyes. The early morning light was painful! It was brighter than he could ever remember. Suddenly, Rory knew where he was. And what he was wearing. Damn! He had fallen asleep on watch. He ripped off the night vision goggles. He had a hard time focusing his eyes because of the sensory overload.

Missy screamed his name.

A very agitated Rory turned his head, desperate to see, "Is there someone nearby? Missy?"

There was no answer.

Rory shook his head, his vision beginning to clear from the sensory overload. Twisted his body on the limb, he leaned over to look at where Missy was tied to the tree.

Missy screamed his name again.

Rory suddenly realized she wasn't on the tree limb. He could see the rope dangling from the spot where she had been sleeping.

Another scream. It was coming from somewhere below!

Rory tried to focus his eyes as he looked at the ground far beneath him. Damn, he still couldn't see very well. He fought feverishly to untie the rope binding him to the tree.

Missy screamed his name again but this time it sounded farther away.

Rory felt like panicking but he knew he couldn't. He swung his feet to the right, scanning the forest below in the direction he thought the scream was coming from. He was desperately looking for any signs of movement. He forced himself to relax, to not focus in on the forest too sharply. He saw movement. There. Rory could see two camouflaged hunters moving away through the trees. One of them was carrying something over his shoulder like a sack of potatoes. They had Missy.

Rory hastily coiled his rope and stowed it in a side pocket. He kept the hunters in view as long as possible as he climbed down to the ground. He made mental notes of the various landmarks between the hunters and this tree. He couldn't afford to make a mistake in the direction of the path they took as he tried to chase them down.

Rory hit the ground running. He ran from landmark to landmark, always keeping an eye on the forest ahead for a trap. His lungs started to burn as he reached the spot where he had last seen them in the trees. He pushed on. He felt responsible. It was his fault he had slept fallen asleep. *Damn. I let her down. I can't let them do things to her. I can't let her die.* He pushed on harder, looking and listening for any sign of the hunters and Missy.

Rory suddenly realized he was running blindly, now far past the last landmark. They could have changed direction after the last spot and he wouldn't know it. He had forgotten to watch for their tracks. Dumb! Stupid! Falling asleep on watch was bad enough. Now he was running blindly through the woods like an idiot. He had no choice now. He had to keep on going. This was turning into a total screw up. *And it's all my fault.*

After a few more minutes of hard running, Rory stopped dead in his tracks. His chest was heaving. He licked his lips, his mouth dry, his breathing raspy. He could see Missy through the trees. She was tied to a tree in a small clearing dead ahead. Rory sank to a low crouch. He couldn't see anyone else. *Where are the hunters?* Then he realized what they were doing. Missy was being used as bait to lure him in. He moved slowly to his right, settling into a denser patch of bush and tried to slow his breathing. He listened for the slightest sound around him but it was difficult because the blood was pounding in his head. There were no bird sounds. No squirrels chattering. Just the buzzing of flies. He closed his eyes, concentrating on the air. There was the smell of pine...damp earth...a light but sweet vanilla smell...probably sweet clover. What he was hoping for was the smell of a wood fire that had lingered on a hunter's clothing. Or something that would give him an idea where they were. But there was nothing. He felt his blood pressure rise and his breathing increase under the tension and Rory concentrated on calming himself down. He had to think the situation through. He couldn't afford to make a mistake. His life and the life of Missy depended on the next few minutes.

Chapter 24

RORY WENT OVER EVERYTHING IN HIS HEAD. Where would they hide? Are they both in the bush around the clearing? Is one hiding overhead in the trees? Are there more than the two I saw? His breathing slowed. The pounding in his head ceased. Rory knew moving ahead in any way was a losing proposition. He had to do something they wouldn't expect. Rory thought about the hunters and what he had learned about them so far. They were probably excellent in tracking and wilderness survival. They were used to tracking an easy prey. They expected people to fight back. They were ready for it and they relished it. But maybe, just maybe, they were not expecting someone to consider *them* as the prey. At least, that was the theory.

Rory pulled his Bowie knife and the coiled nylon rope from his pocket. He looked around for several young, supple trees. Using the Bowie knife, he went to work cutting off as many thin, Y-shaped branches as he could. He cut all three sides of the Y-shaped sections to sharp points, piling them at his feet. He kept watching for any signs of movement around him as he worked. Then he took a sharpened Y section and used a piece of nylon rope to tie it about knee height to another sapling. Then he cut a small notch higher up on the sapling and bent it around like a spring, anchoring the notch against another branch. If someone brushed the lightly anchored sapling, the sharp Y sections would spring out and stab like small spears. He didn't need death from this weapon; he only needed to inflict pain. Rory set as many as he could to cover a small area. Then he slowly backed away from where Missy was tied, staying as low as possible to avoid detection until he was ready. He searched for more small saplings as he moved back, cutting small Y-shaped spears and setting them up. He moved back and forth, leaving a wide path of booby traps as he moved back and away from the clearing. He was fearful that someone was working their way around behind him but he had to keep working. He felt he owed it to Missy after falling asleep on watch.

Finally, Rory felt he had something he could work with. He put the Bowie knife back into the sheath on his belt and moved over to a large tree. Rory pulled the Longbow from over his shoulder and laid it on the ground. Next, he pulled the home-made sling from a pocket along with the last two small smooth stones he had kept from the falls. He loaded the two stones and whirled the sling above his head. He aimed over the wide patch of booby-traps and fired. One stone hit a tree some distance away and bounced off the bark. The other stone passed through some leaves and made a rustling noise. He put the sling back in his pocket. He picked up his longbow, notched an arrow and knelt on the ground. With his back against the large tree for protection from the rear, he now waited for *his* prey.

Chapter 25

IT DIDN'T TAKE LONG for him to spot some movement in the trees ahead on the left. It was subtle but it was there. Someone was definitely heading for the area where the stones had made noise. The movement ceased for a moment. But he knew the hunter would still be moving in for the kill. Rory had to stay patient. These guys were good. Under normal circumstances, they would be extremely difficult to spot. But he had set up abnormal circumstances for them. But would it work well enough?

Rory got his answer. He heard a howl of pain from the direction of the booby-traps and a form popped up. He stood and fired his arrow. The howl of pain was cut off. Rory immediately dropped to the ground. Sure enough, he heard a hard thunk in the tree above him. He looked up and saw the arrow had come from ahead and to the right as he had expected.

Rory rolled over and scooted low into the forest to his right. He stayed as low and as silent as possible as he weaved his way through the trees. He figured the hunter would probably move in this direction as well. He was gambling the hunter would want to avoid the area where his partner had cried out in pain, not knowing what had happened there. He would also be trying to outflank Rory. And Rory was counting on it. All he had to do is move faster than the hunter.

Rory kept looking up, searching for his next weapon. He saw it in a tree just ahead. Moving to crouch behind the tree, Rory looked up at the wasp nest. It was built around a finger-thick branch. A few wasps were coming and going. It would work nicely. Rory looked around and found a fallen branch about 2 inches thick. Using his Bowie knife he cut a two-foot long section. Then he found a number of small stones on the ground and dropped them into a pocket. Returning to the tree with the wasp nest, he pulled the homemade sling from his pocket and placed the small stones in the pouch. Then he laid the sling on the ground, with the cords set to let him pick them up and fire in one motion. He set the stick beside the sling. Then he set his Longbow and an arrow beside the stick. Rory took out the knife again and took a quick look around. So far, so good. He stood up slowly and as close to the tree as possible to hide his movements. He reached up and gripped the wasp-nest branch where it joined the tree and carefully cut through it. He had to be careful or this would backfire on him. He gently held the branch when it came free and he sank to his knees. Rory carefully switched the wasp branch to his left hand. Using his right, he carefully reached down and picked up the sling, making sure he didn't jostle the wasp nest. He was now ready. Raising the sling over his head, he whirled it three times and fired the stones into the trees ahead of him. The small stones hit tree leaves and bushes, giving the impression someone had passed through the spot. Rory returned the sling to his pocket and picked up the stick. He now waited in a low crouch.

Sure enough, before long Rory sensed movement in the trees ahead of him. He waited. Someone was moving up on the spot where he had fired the small stones. Rory waited for a moment. He had to stay patient.

The movement ceased.

Rory waited another moment. Then he tossed the stick as far as he could off to his right where it brushed through leaves and branches. Would the hunter take the bait? A moment later, he saw movement in the bush ahead of him again. The hunter was moving a little quicker now, with less stealth. He was moving directly to the spot where Rory had thrown the stick. The hunter no doubt felt he was moving in on a dumb city slicker who had just made a fatal mistake. Rory carefully passed the wasp branch to his right hand and readied himself for the next step.

As the hunter moved into view and was close enough, Rory tossed the wasp nest at him. As the wasp nest arced towards the hunter, Rory reached down for the arrow and Longbow.

The wasp nest landed near the hunter's feet.

The hunter looked down, startled. He suddenly realized what was happening. The hunter turned around and ran as a yellow and black swarm funneled into the air. The mass of wasps undulated and then the mob mentality of the wasps kicked in. The furious swarm attacked the fleeing hunter and he began screaming as the wasps stung him with a vengeance.

Rory stood up, drew the Longbow back smoothly and then released the arrow, ending the man's agony.

Wasps formed a thick cloud over the body, still attacking.

Rory shot another arrow into the cloud to make sure the man's agony was over.

Chapter 26

RORY RAN AS FAST as he could back to where Missy was tied. He'd only seen two men running with Missy so he was gambling there were no others moving in for the kill right now. He had to take the chance. He had no choice. As he neared the tree where she was tied, he could see the relief in Missy's eyes.

"I'm so sorry," she said, pleading with her eyes for forgiveness as he approached her.

"Were there only two hunters?" Rory asked her as he glanced around nervously.

"Yeah. That's all I saw."

Rory felt some relief as he placed the Longbow on the ground, pulled the Bowie knife and knelt beside her. "What happened?" he asked as he cut through the nylon rope.

"I had to pee," she explained with some embarrassment as the ropes fell away, "and they caught me before I went back up the tree. I'm so sorry, Rory."

Rory just shook his head as he sheathed the Bowie knife.

Missy wrapped her arms around Rory's neck, hugging him tightly, "Thank you. I did something stupid and it could have...."

"No. It was my fault," Rory told her, "I fell asleep on watch. That was the real problem." He hugged her back for a moment, "You're fine now. We have to get going. Okay?"

Missy stepped back, nodding as she rubbed her wrists, "Right. Okay. I'm fine."

Rory looked around, "Where's your bow?"

"I'm not sure. They took everything off me, including the knife and canteen." Her lip curled in anger, "The pigs took turns searching me and feeling my body...everywhere."

Rory grit his teeth, imagining the liberties they must have taken. *It's my fault.*

"I'll look around for the bow."

"Not a good idea. We have to move fast," Rory said as he picked up his own Longbow.

"What about the bodies?"

"We can't take time to bury the bodies either. Let's go before someone else shows up."

They ran hard back westward through the trees. Passing their camping spot, they kept on running. They were breathing heavy but kept working hard to put distance between themselves and any other pursuing hunters. When they were too exhausted to run, Rory kept them moving - even at a slow walk – trying to put as much distance as possible between themselves and the dead bodies. Finally, Rory felt safe enough to stop.

Missy slumped to the ground with her back against a large tree, her breathing raspy from the long, hard flight from danger.

Rory set his Longbow against the tree and sat heavily beside her. His chest was heaving and he pushed his fingers through his black hair in frustration. His voice was low and filled with anguish, "I can't believe I fell asleep. That never happened in the army."

"You were tired," Missy said between heavy breaths, "it's understandable."

"You're right," Rory admitted, "But that mistake could've gotten us killed. That's what happens when you fall asleep in battle."

"But it *didn't* get us killed," Missy countered.

Rory shook his head, "It doesn't matter. We're in a fight for our lives and that kind of thing can't happen."

"Look, This was entirely *my* fault. Next time, I'll just drop trow, hang my butt over the limb and let her go."

Rory had to laugh at that, "I believe you. But maybe the next time one of us makes a mistake, we're not so lucky."

Missy didn't say anything. She just sat with her hands between her knees for a long moment as her chest heaved. Then she shook her head and spoke in a small voice, "I thought I was going to be raped and murdered."

Rory pushed his fingers through his hair again, still agonizing over the fact it was his mistake that was responsible for putting her in that situation—

Missy cocked her head, "What was that?"

Rory didn't say anything. He just sat there, listening.

"Rory—?"

He raised his hand for silence and turned his head, straining to listen.

The slight scrape of something moving against bark came from their right. But it was the sound somewhere to the front that worried him more. It was the soft creak of a Longbow being drawn back—

"Down," he yelled as he pushed Missy to the ground.

A hiss was followed by a sharp thud sound above them.

Both looked up to see an arrow buried in the tree, the shaft still vibrating, just where Rory's head had been a moment before.

Chapter 27

RORY ROLLED AND GRABBED Missy's jacket. Turning her, he lifted her to her knees as he urged, "Move, move, move. Get behind the tree."

Missy scrambled across the thick roots on her hands and knees–

Another sharp hiss split the air.

An arrow just missed Rory's neck. The triple, razor-sharp broadhead point buried itself in the thick bark, the shaft vibrating violently from the force.

Missy let out a cry of fear at the sound and she started to crouch in cover, not yet quite behind the tree.

"No, no, keep moving," Rory urged her. As she rose, Rory put his hand on her bottom and pushed her, "Stay low and run for those trees."

Missy took running in a low crouch.

Rory took off behind her.

Someone began crashing through the trees in hot pursuit behind them.

Missy pushed her way through a stand of dense bushes and then began weaving through the trees beyond it.

Rory crashed through the bushes, tumbled to the ground but rolled to his feet and kept moving.

The forest around them was a blur as they pushed hard to stay ahead of their pursuer. Branches whipped at their body. The crashing sound behind them disappeared.

After several more minutes of running, Rory let out a low curse, reached for Missy's hand and stopping her run, pulling her to her knees.

"What's wrong?" she asked in a hurried whisper.

Rory turned on his heels and looked back, "I left my bow back against the tree."

"Can we go back and get it?" Missy asked as she turned to look back.

The sound of someone moving closer through the trees from behind and to their right reached them.

Rory shook his head, "No. I doubt we'd make it." He listened intently.

Someone moved through the bush towards them on the left

Missy looked at Rory, fear filling her eyes.

Rory took her hand and pulled her to her feet again and they ran. Hard. The trees were a blur again as the two fled through the forest. The trees and bushes were denser in some places and they had to push their way through to keep ahead of their pursuers. Others spots were more open and left them vulnerable to an arrow attack. But it never came. Their breath was coming in raspy gulps now and their run became a tortured jog.

Rory decided they had to rest. They had no choice. At this pace, complete collapse was inevitable. He placed a hand on Missy's arm and urged her to slow to a walk. He listened for the sounds of pursuit above their own raspy breaths but there was nothing. That didn't mean the hunters weren't close but they had to stop, at least for a few moments to catch their breath. Bringing Missy to a stop, he put a hand to his lips to make sure she stayed silent. Then he crouched down, breathing heavily and scanned through the trees, watching for movement and listening intently for the slightest sound of danger.

Missy did the same, trying her best to control her heavy breathing.

But the only sound around them was their own raspy breath mixed with the steady buzz of insects.

The hollow knock-knock-knock of a woodpecker busy at work echoed through the trees.

But everything else was still. Deadly still.

After a few moments of rest, Missy glanced at Rory and whispered, "I can't hear them anymore. Do you think we lost them?"

Rory shook his head no, positive it wouldn't be that easy.

There was the slight crack of a dry twig underfoot somewhere off to their right.

Missy sucked her breath in and turned on her heels to look for movement. She pivoted a little more–

Rory placed a hand on her knee to keep her from moving...because there was the sound of fabric sliding against bark off to their left.

Missy's breathing began to increase with fear.

Rory couldn't blame her. His hand began to drift towards his knife–

Missy's eyes were filled with terror at what might come at any moment. But her shaky hand slowly moved to the knife on her belt as well. She was going to fight to the death, if necessary.

Someone began moving through the bush on their right.

Rory grabbed Missy's hand and pulled her to her feet and they began running in a low crouch again.

Noisy movement on their left now.

Rory and Missy ran hard. They skirted large trees and jumped fallen logs in their attempt to put distance between them and their pursuers. Their breathing began to labor again and Missy stumbled on tree roots several times. She was having a hard time staying on her feet now.

Rory felt his own legs tiring as well.

But noise behind them and on either side kept them moving. They couldn't stop.

Rory tried to swing them to the left but the hunter on that side kept pace and moved them back.

He tried slipping away to the right, just ahead of the hunter on that side, but that didn't work either.

It suddenly dawned on Rory what these two hunters were doing. At least, he thought he did. He pulled Missy back to the left but the hunter on that side thrashed through bushes and moved them back–

Rory pulled Missy sharply to a stop and crouched down between two larger bushes that offered some cover.

Missy crouched beside him, her breathing heavy and raspy.

Rory put a finger to his lips

Missy's chest was heaving and she closed her eyes tightly. She opened them after a moment and looked at Rory and whispered, "What is it...?"

"These guys are too good to be so noisy in the bush like that," he whispered. "They're herding us into something up ahead."

Missy's eyes took on a look of concern, "What do you mean? Herding us where?"

He shook his head slowly as he peered through the trees, "I don't know. But we can't just keep running blindly like this."

"So what do we do?"

"I don't know," Rory answered as he clenched his teeth.

"But if we stay here...." Her voice trailed off with fear.

She was right. The hunters would start moving in when their prey refused to run anymore. Rory put a hand over his eyes, trying to think. He began looking around them, trying to figure out how they could fight back against the two hunters. He had an idea. A crazy idea but what else could he do? "Keep a sharp eye out and warn me if you hear or see any movement," Rory whispered as he drew his knife.

Missy drew her knife as well, her voice filled with fear, "Why–?"

Rory moved a few feet away from her.

"You're not going to leave me are you–?"

"No," he assured her as he knelt beside a small tree about one inch thick and three feet high.

"W-what are you going to do?

Rory put a finger to his lips and then gestured for her to keep watch.

Missy's hands shook as she kept one eye on Rory while trying to scan the trees around them.

Rory worked as quietly as possible as he pushed the edge of his hunting knife into the bark at the bottom of the small tree and cut into it deeply. He then held the knife at a 45-degree angle to the first cut and made a second one. He worked his way around the small tree, cutting it free and slowly lowering it to the ground. He held his breath as he waited to see if the movement attracted any attention.

Missy moved in a low crouch across to Rory, to see what he was doing.

A twig snapped off to the right and Missy froze.

Chapter 28

RORY SAW MISSY FROZEN in her tracks and his heartbeat rose. He listened intently. But when no one came in after them, he realized it meant the hunters were trying to get them to run again. And if they didn't run, that meant time was running out. *They'll come after us if we don't give them a hunt.* Rory went back to his task, working feverishly on the tree, cutting all of the branches away except the lowest one.

When Missy realized no one was coming after them as well, she turned her attention back to Rory, whispering, "What are you doing? Shouldn't we be running?"

Rory didn't answer, not wanting to take the time to explain.

But Missy's panic began to rise, "Rory, please. I don't understand. Why aren't we–?"

"I'm making an Atlatl," he whispered as he worked away, hoping to keep her from doing something foolish.

"A what?"

"It's an ancient spear-throwing stick," Rory whispered. He cut the top of the tree off, leaving him with a two-foot long piece with one lower branch.

"But we don't have a spear," she whispered back in confusion.

"No, but we do have arrows." Rory cut the lower branch down to a one-inch stub and then whittled the stub down to accept the notch in an arrow.

Missy blinked her eyes as she looked at Rory's creation, "Will it work?"

"I don't know," Rory admitted after a moment. "It'll be crude but–"

Missy turned on her heels to the right again, "I think I heard something. I think they're moving in...."

"Almost done," Rory whispered. He pulled an arrow from his quiver and tried to slip the notch over the stub. But it was still too thick.

"I'm not sure they're going to wait."

"I hear you," he said as he calmed his nerves to make sure he didn't ruin the throwing stick as he worked to shave the stub just a bit more.

"Hurry–"

Rory knew they were going to start moving in but he had to stay calm and do it right.

"Rory–"

Finally, the notch in the arrow fit perfectly over the stub.

"I'm sure someone is not far over there," she whispered urgently as she pointed dead ahead through the trees.

"Almost done," he assured her. He now worked hard to make a long, shallow v-shaped trench in the length of wood to rest the arrow in.

Missy listened intently, her eyes wide in fear as she licked her lips.

Rory slipped the knife back into its sheath and examined his handiwork. It wasn't perfect but it would have to do. He set the notch in place and then lay the arrow in the shallow groove along the stick. Holding them together with his right hand he pantomimed a few throws.

"That's like taking a knife to a gunfight," she whispered skeptically.

"Not if I catch them by surprise," he answered. He turned on his heels in the direction she said the sound had come from.

"And how do you expect to surprise them...since they already know we're here? And there are two of them...at least."

Rory didn't really have an answer as he watched and listened intently.

Missy looked at Rory, took a deep breath and made a decision, "Okay. But you better be ready with that At-lanta thing."

Rory turned in alarm, "Ready for–?"

Missy was slipping away low around the bush to his right.

Rory reached for her but he was too late. He cursed under his breath as the arrow dropped off his throwing stick with the movement. He had to stop to retrieve it. When he looked up again, Missy had disappeared into the trees.

Rory cursed as he set himself on one knee and picked up the arrow. Her impulses were going to get them killed. He set the arrow back in place against the throwing stick and prepared to go find her–

"Rory, where are you?" It was Missy, calling in a low voice somewhere off in the trees.

Fear struck Rory's heart when he heard her. *What is she doing? These hunters work in pairs. They could attack her from two sides–*

Movement about thirty feet to his left.

Rory rotated to the left and slowed his breathing. Were they coming for him? Or going after Missy?

A large hunter dressed in brown and green camouflage stepped out from behind a tree twenty-five feet away. He carried a Longbow loaded with an arrow.

Rory froze on the spot.

Chapter 29

RORY SLOWLY RELEASED HIS BREATH when he realized the hunter wasn't looking at him.

Instead, the big man was moving swiftly but silently in Missy's direction.

It was now or never. Rory reacted quickly, springing up and forward, throwing the arrow as hard as he could.

The hunter turned in Rory's direction, bringing his Longbow up fast. Rory's arrow hit the hunter's shoulder and bounced upward. But it created enough of a surprise that his own arrow shot high over Rory's head.

Rory didn't have time to notch another arrow. And he was sure the man's partner would be taking aim from somewhere any moment now. Rory ran hard, directly at the large hunter, fully expecting to feel an arrow penetrate his back at any moment.

The hunter was reaching back for another arrow when he realized his prey was almost on top of him. He dropped his Longbow and reached across his body, pulling a large Bowie knife.

Rory deflected the knife thrust with his right.

The hunter braced for a collision but it never came.

Rory stepped around behind the hunter and slipped his right arm up around his neck, using him as a shield.

There was a whooosh and the hunter grunted as an arrow penetrated his chest.

Rory felt a sharp pain in his lower chest. A fearful thought flashed through his mind. Did the other hunter's powerful Longbow drive the arrow through both of their bodies?

The dead hunter fell over backwards, his heavy bulk landing on top of Rory and pinning him underneath.

Rory groaned as he felt more pain in his chest. Was the dead weight of the body driving the arrow deeper? Rory struggled to push the dead weight to the side but the huge man must have weighed 350 lbs. Rory cursed–

Missy appeared above him, her face reflecting the fear inside her. She grabbed at the dead body on top of him and tried to pull it off, "He's coming–!"

A large blur hit Missy's body with a dull thud and she disappeared out of sight.

Rory tried to lift and turn his head to see where she was. *What's happening?* He heard a man's laughter, the dry, stupid cackle of someone pleased with himself.

"Rory," Missy screamed. "Rory." Her voice sounded like she was being carried away.

Rory felt a surge of adrenaline as he struggled to get out from underneath the dead body. He pushed harder and the dead body slowly rolled to the side. Rory saw the arrowhead and one inch of shaft sticking out the dead hunter's back. He put a hand to his chest and he realized he was bleeding. He wondered what kind of damage had been done but there was no time to think about it. Pushing it to the back of his mind, he spun around on the ground and grabbed the dead hunter's Longbow. Scrambling to his feet, he took off at a run through the trees in the general direction where the laugh and the scream had come from. His eyes desperately scanned the trees, trying to spot either the hunter or Missy.

"Let me go!"

The yell had come from a spot to the left. Rory turned in that direction and jumped over a large fallen tree. He stumbled as his foot sank into dead leaves on the other side and he fell hard on his right side, the Longbow underneath him. He rolled over and lifted the Longbow. *Damn.* The silk bowstring had been snapped by his body. Throwing the Longbow to the ground, he took off in a frantic run. Weaving his way through the trees, Rory hoped his fall hadn't let them get too far ahead. And what if they changed directions–?

Missy's scream sounded off to the right.

Rory quickly moved in that direction. Pushing his way through a stand of large evergreens, he spotted the back of another large hunter. He was just beyond the trees and crossing a small, grassy clearing.

Missy's head hung down over his shoulder as he carried her and she was beating on his lower back with her fists.

The hunter stopped and threw her to the ground.

Missy landed hard on her back.

The hunter threw his Longbow to the ground on his right. Then he reached down to his belt buckle as he stared at the woman.

Missy dug her heels into the earth and pushed herself away from him.

Rory drew his hunting knife as he burst out of the trees and ran hard for the hunter.

The hunter turned and moved deftly to the side.

Rory felt himself being flipped in the air and his back landed on something softer than the ground.

Missy's breath was knocked from her body and she grunted.

Rory realized he had landed on Missy. But there was no time to check on her. He had an upside down view of the hunter drawing his own knife. Rory rolled to the right and came up on his feet in a defensive stance. Not daring to take his eyes off the hunter, he stole quick glances around to see where his own knife had gone. But the foot-high grass was going to make that impossible without a concentrated search. And he didn't have time for that right now.

The hunter grinned and got into a low knife-fighting stance.

Rory realized the man had military training; he was holding the knife underhanded with his thumb locked.

"I thought I got both you and Moose with that arrow," the hunter said in a low, husky voice. He glanced at Rory's bleeding chest, "I guess he was a lot thicker than I thought."

Rory didn't reply. He had to concentrate. Moving slowly to the left, he glanced at Missy. He could see her lying in the grass but he couldn't see her face.

The hunter mirrored Rory's move, "Looks like she's out. It'll still be fun though." He gave Rory a grin and a wink.

Rory knew the hunter was trying to bait him into impulsive anger. He did feel anger, but he had to keep it under control. He took another step to the left and then stopped, thinking. He couldn't let the hunter get near Missy and use her as leverage against him. Or maybe even as a shield to limit Rory's attack. He stepped back to his right.

The hunter mirrored Rory's move, moving low and cat-like.

Rory watched the man's movements, looking for a weakness. *I have to end this quick. There's no telling how many other hunters are nearby. Better to deal with one wolf than the entire pack.* Rory took a quick step back to the left.

The hunter took a quick step to his left as well, looking for a chance to attack.

Rory studied his opponent. *He's nimble on his feet, so I don't have the advantage in speed.* The large hunter didn't have a large gut hanging over his belt either. So his size suggested an advantage in muscular strength and power. Rory moved back to his right, watching and thinking.

The hunter did the same, performing his part in this deadly dance.

Rory's mind automatically clicked through all the Special Forces training and experience he had, looking for a solution to this particular problem. He moved two steps to the left.

The hunter did the same and was deadly serious now, looking for an opening.

Rory decided to give him one. *Maybe I can use one of his assets against him. But I'll only get one chance.* Rory took a breath and readied his muscles...he took a step to the right and then one backwards...and pretended to stumble.

The hunter moved fast.

In fact, the speed surprised Rory enough that he barely moved back to his left in time.

The hunter thrust with his hunting knife.

Rory grabbed the hunter's right wrist and then the elbow with his left and used the large man's momentum to put the arm in a straight arm-lock. Then he waited for the expected countermeasure.

The hunter growled and pulled his arm hard back toward himself to break Rory's hold.

Rory obliged. He slipped his hand to the inside of the hunter's elbow while letting the wrist go.

The hunter's arm hinged and the knife plunged deep into his own chest, driven by his own strength. The hunter's eyes shot wide open in surprise. He fell to his knees, looking down at his own hand holding the knife hilt against his chest, where his heart was.

Rory took a couple of steps back.

The hunter looked up at Rory and sneered. Then his eyes rolled back in his head and he fell over, face down in the grass.

Rory moved quickly to Missy. Kneeling beside her, he tapped her lightly on the cheek, calling her name and trying to get a response. Nothing. Rory swore under his breath. *Maybe I'll have to carry her and that will slow us down to a crawl.*

Chapter 30

RORY TAPPED HER CHEEK AGAIN, calling to her in the depths of the blackness. He scanned the trees around them and swore. He didn't have much of a choice. He reached down to her arms–

Missy's eyes fluttered and she opened them.

Smiling, Rory touched her cheek, "Welcome back. Are you okay?"

Missy nodded and she closed her eyes. Then she opened them and looked up, her voice a bit weak but the annoyed tone very strong, "You big lug. You fell on me–" Suddenly, she shot to a sitting position, looking wildly around her, "The man–!"

"He's dead," Rory said. He indicated the body lying not far away.

Missy relaxed. Then concerned crossed her face again, "If more come...."

Rory nodded, "Can you move? Or do you need to rest–?"

Missy shook her head and she scrambled to her feet, "No, no. Let's go."

Rory got up and went over to retrieve the dead hunter's Longbow. Slipping it over his back into his kit, he went back to the body to get the dead hunter's quiver and arrows.

Missy walked over to him, still unsteady on her feet, "Now what?"

Rory didn't say anything as he patted the man's pockets.

"You're bleeding!" she said in alarm as she spotted the blood staining the front of his jacket.

Rory looked down, "Oh yeah, forgot about that. The arrow went through the other hunter back there and...."

"Sit down over here and take your jacket and shirt off," she said quickly.

"I'm fine—"

"Just do it," she insisted as she moved him away from the body

Rory slipped off the jacket and then the shirt.

"Sit down," Missy said as she pulled her hunting knife and went back to the dead body.

"But if someone comes—"

"Don't make me go over there and knock you on your ass," she said as she cut strips off the dead hunter's clothing. Taking his canteen as well, she went back to Rory and washed the wound off.

Rory grimaced in pain.

"It's not too deep," she announced.

"Feels like it," groaned Rory as she pressed a folded piece of cloth over the wound.

"Hold that," she instructed. She wrapped strips of cloth around his body to act as homemade bandages, tying them off at the back. Then she helped him put the shirt and jacket back on before broaching the subject again, "Okay. So what do we do now? Where do we go...?"

Rory took a deep breath and made a decision "I'm afraid we can't stay down here any longer."

"You...you want to try and go up there now?" Missy asked, the fear evident in her voice. "But we still haven't found a safe way back up. We need to keep looking, right? That's what you said."

Rory grimaced as his chest throbbed, "No. We can't wait. Remember how the first two hunters found us after we escaped?"

"They tracked my high-heel shoe prints," Missy answered after a moment of thought.

"Right. Your high-heel shoe prints led them right to the waterfall–"

"I said I was sorry before, didn't I?" Missy said, obviously miffed he had brought it up.

"No, I'm not blaming you," Rory countered. "They could have just as easily tracked my dress shoes. Yours were more distinct but...."

"But...we're not wearing those shoes now, so they can't," Missy countered.

"Exactly. So...the men who caught you when you came down that tree...how did they find us? Or these last two hunters? How?"

Missy blinked, not sure of an answer.

"They should have been looking up at the falls. Not over here," Rory reasoned.

"I'm...I'm not sure...."

"Neither am I," Rory conceded. "But these guys strike me as expert woodsmen. And they're probably expert trackers as well. Maybe they found those dead hunters we buried in those shallow graves, stripped of their clothes and boots. To an expert, each boot leaves a distinctive print...."

Missy nodded in understanding, "They must have tracked us over here."

"That's what I'm assuming." Rory shook his head, "I should have thought of that. But I didn't."

Missy licked her lips as looked at the forest around them, "Do...do you think there are more around here?"

"There will be...sooner or later," Rory answered as he scanned the forest as well.

"Maybe we can change boots again," Missy said as she looked at the dead body.

"It might buy us a little time...but eventually, they'll figure it out."

"Maybe we can find some place to hide," Missy whispered. "Maybe if we go to the mountains, we could find a cave...."

"And once they track us there, then what?"

Missy looked frustrated as she looked for some way out, "Maybe we just keep moving–"

"It still won't work–"

"You don't know that!" she said sharply.

"Yes I do," Rory said calmly. "Think about it. We have to rest at some point and they know it. They can work in pairs with one pair resting while the other tracks us. They can work 24-7 in shifts with those night vision goggles. We have to take time to search for food and water. Especially water. They probably know where all the water sources are and they'll come across us at some point. Or they'll simply wait for us to show up. They *will* find keep finding us and the odds of always beating them aren't good–"

"So what do we do then, give up?" Missy said with anger in her voice.

Rory took a deep breath and let it out, just looking at her.

Missy looked at him apprehensively.

"We have to take a chance"

"Take a chance at what?"

Rory waited for a heartbeat and then said, "If we're going to survive we have no choice. We have to head straight up, crossing the killing field as quickly as possible and getting back to the top of the plateau."

Missy let out a small gasp of fear. "Are you crazy?"

"Probably. But I'm sure those hunters would expect anyone who escaped and got down here like we did, will keep running and hiding down here. They probably won't expect us to be up there."

"Probably?" Missy asked in a small, shaky voice.

"At least that's the theory," Rory said.

Chapter 31

MISSY AND RORY KNELT SIDE-BY-SIDE in the protection of the dense forest, barely noticing the warm sun, the birds singing overhead or the exquisite scent of pine surrounding them. They were too busy scanning the open killing field dead ahead

Missy nervously fidgeted on her knees, "If we get spotted out there, I don't see any places to hide. We'll be so exposed...."

"I know," Rory agreed. He reached over and adjusted Missy's Longbow in the Butt Bucket Kit on her backpack. They had picked up the one he had left leaning against the tree. She still couldn't pull it back and fire an arrow but it seemed to make her feel better to be armed.

"It's just like you said," Missy whispered as she wrung her hands, "they made the whole thing so open. I can see a lot of places where it *looks* like you could hide but...it wouldn't take much searching to find you. Everyone they send over the hill doesn't really stand a chance."

Rory gave a slight nod as he considered the rising terrain ahead, "You're right. But...." Rory shifted to his other knee, "Consider the fact we're going to be going *up* the hill–"

Missy grimaced, "And that's a good point?"

"Actually, for our purpose, it is." He pointed at different spots going up the hill, "If we move from tree to tree and bush to bush to maximize our cover as we climb, we can make it harder for anyone higher up to see us coming."

"Are you sure they won't see us?"

"I said make it *harder*. There's no guarantee they won't."

Missy opened her mouth to say something and then she closed her eyes tight. A moment later she opened them and gave a slight nod of understanding as she considered the climb again.

Rory looked up the hill again himself and then added quietly, "Of course...the fact it's all uphill is also a negative. It could take us quite a while to get to the top. In fact...considering we have to keep an eye open for hunters searching for us as we climb...the going will be slow. Very slow. It could take us half the day...maybe a full day. I have no idea. That leaves a lot of time to be spotted. If you have a better plan, speak up now."

"Or forever hold your peace?" Missy asked. "Is this a wedding or a planning session?"

Rory smiled at her, "As long as it's not a funeral—"

"Not yet."

THEY BEGAN RUNNING for the protection of the first large tree. They sunk behind it, checking in all directions to see if they had been spotted. When everything looked okay, they moved out from behind the tree and began their long, dangerous journey uphill through the killing field. They worked in tandem to keep an eye peeled for movement on three sides. Every so often they would stop, with their back to a tree or a clump of bushes, and check the denser terrain below them. So far, so good.

IT TOOK THEM SEVERAL hours of this stopping and starting to reach what they estimated to be the halfway point. They stopped for a quick sip of water and a brief rest while they kept their eyes and ears open for any sign that would tell them they had been seen. So far, everything seemed okay. After a few moments of rest, they began the final climb to the top through the open killing field.

BARELY FIVE MINUTES had passed when Missy froze and she clutched Rory's sleeve. He had been looking in the other direction and he immediately dropped to a knee beside Missy.

"What's wrong?" he asked in an urgent whisper, scanning the terrain around them for danger.

Missy pointed a shaky finger up the hillside.

Between the trees, Rory could see a hunter moving down the hill. He was several hundred yards uphill and off to their right.

"I don't think he's seen us," Missy whispered in a shaky voice.

"Doesn't matter," Rory said with a shake of his head.

"What do you mean?"

Rory pointed straight up the hill.

Almost dead ahead of them were two other camouflaged hunters. They were several hundred yards uphill as well, but it wouldn't be long before they were right on top of Rory and Missy.

Rory gripped Missy's sleeve, "Lie down."

Frozen in position, Missy didn't move or acknowledge the request.

"Missy, lie down," Rory urged her, tugging on her sleeve harder.

Startled, she looked at Rory, fear in her eyes.

"Lie down," Rory whispered as he sank to the ground.

She finally moved woodenly to lie down and the two lay on the grass side-by-side, watching the hunters work their way down through the trees. Missy's body was shaking and her breathing was ragged.

Rory watched the hunters using hand signals to work in unison down the hill, "They're using a search line to try and find us." He watched the hunters for another long moment, thinking. "I bet they're doing the same thing over on the eastern side. The Bossman is probably sending everyone out."

"H-how do you know that?"

"I don't for sure, but it makes sense. These guys are getting their thrills from hunting men and women and doing what they want to them–"

"They're sick and perverted."

I agree. But right now - you and me -we're giving them a thrill-hunt they haven't had before."

"What do you mean?"

"Think about it. We're the two hostages who eluded capture. That's what one of the men said to me, that it hadn't happened before. They couldn't kill me and they couldn't–"

Missy grimaced, "Don't even say it."

"Sorry. But those guys - Seth and Carl, was it? - anyway, they said anyone finding us would be rewarded in some sick way. That's why they're *all* coming."

Missy cursed and pressed her body flatter against the ground, "So what do we do now?" She turned and looked back down the hill, "Should we run?"

"Not just yet." Rory put a hand on her arm to keep her in place. He watched the hunters checking spots where someone could be hiding.

"Crap."

"What?"

Missy slowly moved an arm, afraid the movement would be seen, pointing up the hillside to their left, "Look."

There were more hunters, several hundred yards higher, working their way down that side. Rory and Missy were trapped in the middle of a long line of hunters moving down the hillside, closing in for the kill.

Rory looked back down the hill - then looked over at Missy. "If we run now," he whispered, "they'll spot us for sure. We'll be done. We'll have no chance."

"But we have nowhere to really hide," she whispered urgently, "they're going to find us eventually and–"

"Not if we hide in plain sight," Rory said as he looked at her.

"What the hell does that mean?"

"Just trust me–"

Fear filled her eyes and she shook her head, "No, we should run."

Rory repeated himself slowly, "Just trust me." He turned and pointed to a tree behind them, "Side back to that tree. C'mon."

Rory started to shimmy on his stomach backward towards the tree.

But Missy stayed frozen in place.

Rory reached up to touch her boot.

She jumped at his touch and looked back at him.

"It's okay," he said as he tried to reassure her, "this will work. Trust me."

Missy tried to calm her breathing. After a few agonizing seconds, she finally nodded. She began to shimmy on her stomach backward down to Rory. Together, they shimmied further back down to the tree. Then they shimmied into cover behind it.

"Okay. Now we're going to move over to that larger tree," Rory told her. When she didn't acknowledge the instruction, Rory put a hand on her shoulder.

Missy's body jumped.

"It's okay." Rory pointed at a tree over to the left and a little more downhill. "Just stay low again and move slowly over to that tree. Okay?"

Missy nodded but her hands were trembling.

It was slow going as they shimmied on their stomachs across the grass and over behind the other tree.

Once there, Rory had Missy sit up and place her back against the tree and then he sat beside her with his back to the tree as well.

"We can't do this. They'll see us here!" Missy said in a frantic voice.

"That's what I'm counting on," Rory replied calmly.

"What? You're crazy!" Missy whispered harshly.

"I can't dispute that," Rory said.

That comment made Missy shake her head. But it also made her try to calm down and she shrugged, "Then again, I thought you were crazy with the upside down hood thing."

"That you did. And I'm still hurt by that."

Missy gave him a half-smile, doing her best to stay calm.

Rory took Missy's shaking hand and gave it a reassuring squeeze. Then he looked off to the right, wondering if this one chance *would* work or if he was just blowing smoke up his own butt.

Chapter 32

THE WAIT WAS NERVE-RACKING. Rory tried to keep watch on both sides. Time passed agonizingly slow. The sun beat down on them and sweat began to trickle down his neck. Rory did his best to ignore it. Any unnecessary movement could give them away. He glanced at Missy and could see her shaking but doing her best to stay still. When Rory finally felt it was nearing the time to act, he whispered to Missy, "When I tell you, I want you to stand up with me."

Missy's voice was a tight squeak, her eyes were wide with fear, "What? They'll see us for sure."

"That's what I'm counting on, Rory told her.

"You're crazy."

"You keep saying that and I keep agreeing." He squeezed her knee, "Just trust me."

Missy closed her eyes tightly and then opened them, giving him a nod of agreement, "Okay." She pulled the cap lower over his eyes.

"Good. Now we need to time it just right." He checked the hunter's positions again, then whispered, "When we stand up, start walking down the hill like they are. Try to imitate how they're moving. Remember, we're dressed like them. We look like them. They're expecting to see somebody in a tuxedo or a dress, right?"

Missy was shaking but she began to comprehend. She nodded her head yes.

"Okay, get ready," Rory said as he looked left and right, trying to time their move. It had to be just right for this to work. Two camouflaged hunters suddenly appeared off to their right. It was now or never. "Stand up," Rory whispered.

Missy was shaking but she rose to her feet to stand beside Rory.

"Look down as we walk," Rory instructed her. He began to walk forward.

Missy stayed frozen in place.

Rory reached back and touched her elbow to get her moving.

Missy's eyes startled and she sucked her breath in.

"Start walking."

She placed one wooden leg in front of the other and started to walk.

Rory watched from the corner of his eye, gauging the pace of the hunters. "A little faster," he whispered.

Missy complied, looking down, but her eyes were moving from side to side, wondering....

Looking to the left, Rory saw other hunters on that side now. The pace he had set with Missy was working. They were staying roughly in line with the advancing line of hunters. He turned his head slowly, looking back to the right. The groups of camouflaged hunters on both sides continued to search as they moved down the hillside. Rory took a chance and glanced back. He didn't see anyone behind them. So far, so good.

Rory noted Missy now had her eyes looking over to her right, trying her best to imitate the hunters. She was walking in the same hunting crunch. It was working, they were blending in. But how long could they continue to do this without being caught? *Great plan, Steele, now what do we do?*

Chapter 33

TIME PASSED AGONIZINGLY SLOW as Rory tried to figure out how to get out of this mess he had put them in. The line of hunters kept moving down the hillside with a methodical approach. Each bush, tree or outcropping of rock that offered a potential hiding spot was checked as the line slowed. Then they continued on with their steady search down the hillside.

Rory shook his head. *The Bossman isn't stupid. He's trying to think like us. He knows we'd have to come back up to the compound if we're going to have any hope of survival. We can't underestimate him. But if we don't get away from this line, we're going to find ourselves back at the bottom of the hill. And then what?* He realized Missy was looking at him, wondering if he had a plan to get out of this situation. He gave her a brief nod of assurance.

"So what then?" she whispered.

Good question. Rory glanced in both directions along the line. No one was paying much attention to them. It was now or never. "Start to walk a little slower," Rory whispered after a few minutes.

"What?"

"Start to walk a little slower," he whispered again.

Her brows pulled together hard - her eyes darted to the hunters on her right - and Missy slowed her pace grudgingly, "I hope you know what you're doing?"

"Me, too."

Gradually, the line of hunters began to move ahead of them. It was slow, like the creep of a glacier, but it was working.

After a few more minutes of them slowly dropping back, Rory dropped to a knee, pretending that he had found something.

Missy stopped - eyes darting to the hunters - afraid to even look down at Rory, "What are you doing?"

"Just play along. Pretend you're watching me." Rory placed his hand on the ground as if he was examining something.

Through clenched teeth, Missy looked down, "You have a crazy sense of playtime."

Rory took a quick peek and noted one of the hunters over on the left was looking back and watching him. A moment later, Rory up and shook his head no. He looked straight ahead but spoke low to Missy, "Start walking ahead again. But go slow."

Missy complied, walking woodenly step by step with Rory as they went into their hunter's crouch-walk again as if watching the ground for signs.

The hunter who had been watching them turned and resumed his own march down the hill. After a few more long, agonizing minutes, the line of hunters slowly drifted ahead of Rory and Missy again.

Rory touched Missy's arm to get her attention and then angled their walk off to the left, heading for a small clump of trees. None of the hunters paid any attention to their slight drift off-line. Reaching the clump of trees, Rory put his hand on Missy's shoulder and they both sank to the ground. From here they couldn't be seen by the hunters now moving in the terrain below them. Rory took a quick look uphill, checking for hunters anywhere from left to right. Everything looked clear. He looked back downhill. *Now, we just need to stay patient.*

Missy was looking at him, fear and apprehension in her eyes.

Rory gave her hand a light pat of assurance. His plan seemed to be working but you never know. Rory visualized the hunters walking down the hillside, trying to gauge the time that passed and where they would be in their sweep down the hill. After an agonizing wait, he slowly rose, peeking over the grass that stood a couple of feet high around the clump of trees, checking downhill.

The line of hunters was just over hundred yards downhill now.

Missy tapped him on the shoulder and pointed off to the left.

There were more hunters in the distance, moving in a line down the hill.

What the–? Rory looked back behind him quickly and then off to the other side. He couldn't see any others, but the new line of hunters could easily spot them once they got lower.

Missy's leg bounced nervously as she watched the line of hunters.

Rory couldn't blame her. He tapped her lightly on the shoulder and gestured for her to move with him to the far side of the small clump of trees. Once there, they were exposed to the group downhill. They had to hope no one down there turned around.

Settling in a crouch, Missy's eye took in the group below and fully understood the danger. She glanced to her left at the second line and shook her head softly, "Son of a...."

"Yeah." Rory watched the second line of hunters as well as they drifted down the hill. "Okay, we can't wait any longer," he said finally as he glanced downhill. "Let's get going uphill again. Just keep your eyes open for more hunters."

Missy nodded, visibly grateful to be moving uphill again and away from the lines of hunters scouring the hillside for them.

Chapter 34

IT TOOK THEM NEARLY another two hours before Rory and Missy finally reached the brow of the hill. The sun beat down on them as they knelt down and slowly lifted their heads to peer over the crest. About 300 yards dead ahead were two rows of large hangars. The problem was those 300 yards were without any type of cover. They would be exposed all the way to the hangars.

"I don't see anyone," Rory said. "Do you?"

"No," Missy answered as she scanned the flat terrain ahead of them.

"I think most of the hunters are behind us now, working down the hillside."

"You *think...*?"

He looked at Missy, "Okay, I hope, then."

"Not much better, Steele," she grumbled. "But I know we can't stay here."

"Are you game to make a run for that first building?" Rory asked, pointing straight ahead.

Missy braced herself, took a deep breath and nodded to Rory.

"Okay then," Rory said as he took a deep breath himself. "Let's run low on - three-two-one."

They were up and running over the crest of the hill, moving as fast and as low as they could, heading straight for the shelter of the hangar closest to them.

Running in the heavy, hunting boots was a challenge after a long, tiring climb. Missy stumbled to the ground halfway across the open terrain.

Rory stopped and went back to grab her hand. He pulled her up and they were running again. They pushed on and finally reached the first building. Turning and dropping on their butts, they pressed their backs up against the wall of the hangar. Both were breathing heavy and they fought to control their breathing, listening for any sound to indicate they had been spotted.

After a few moments of rest, Rory rolled to his right and peered around the corner of the hangar. He didn't see anyone. He looked over at Missy. She was sitting with her head against the hangar, her chest still heaving. "There's a window right here," he whispered. "I'm going to take a quick look inside. Keep an eye peeled."

Missy just rolled her head and nodded, still too spent to really move. Then she rolled her head back the other way, pulled a foot in and struggled to get to her knees to keep watch. Her voice was raspy, "Okay. Go."

Rory slipped around the corner and crept forward along the wall of the hangar. Reaching the spot just below the window, he slowly lifted himself to look inside the building. *It looks empty.* There was a door next to the window and Rory checked the knob. It wasn't locked. Crouching low, Rory slipped back to the corner. "It's empty," he said to Missy. "Follow me and keep low."

Missy nodded, struggling to her feet and then following him around the corner of the hangar.

Rory took a few quick steps back to the door, turned the knob and slipped inside with Missy following him. Once they were inside, he slowly closed the door behind them, trying to stay as silent as possible. They sat side-by-side with their back against the door, trying to catch their breath.

The inside of the hangar was huge and empty. The floor was dark and gleaming. The ceiling was filled with exposed steel beams. Several rows of unlit fluorescent lights spanned across the ceiling. There wasn't a single sound.

"What is this place?" Missy whispered.

"It's an airplane hangar. Or more likely a helicopter hangar for these guys," Rory said. "When we were first up here, I saw what looked like a large helicopter landing zone out there to the west."

"A helicopter?

Rory nodded. "Probably a big one as well, considering the size of landing zone out there *and* the size of this hangar. You couldn't put a landing strip out there long enough for any large airplane to land. But even the largest helicopter would have enough room to land. That's probably how these guys get in and out." He thought back to the sights and sounds he vaguely remembered before waking up in the room in the lodge. "In fact, that's probably how they got us all here, by a large cargo helicopter."

"You can just go around buying big helicopters?"

Rory nodded, "Yeah. There are commercial models of the Chinook that are used by oil companies, firefighters, construction companies and loggers. In fact...this whole thing is starting to make sense."

"It does? You're kidding, right?"

Shaking his head, Rory said, "No, I mean in the sense of understanding why they targeted that fundraiser put on by Trent and Emily Corrigan. As you probably know, Trent Corrigan runs TG Capital, an investment banking firm that specializes in working with heavy industries like mining and logging to fund projects. You were there because your father owns coal mines–"

"Don't remind me," she grumbled.

Rory carried on, "There were some people like me there, but everyone else was with a company that Corrigan deals with or has dealt with in the past. They're all companies that could use large cargo helicopters as part of their operation. I imagine the Bossman or someone with him was invited–"

"*Why* would Trent and Emily Corrigan invite someone like that? That's crazy."

"Consider where we are, Missy. These guys are probably making a lot of money through logging. They probably built this whole compound out of redwood logs they cut and hauled up here. These guys could fly cargo helicopters back and forth up here without anybody thinking about it twice. I bet they've dealt with Corrigan at some point, were invited and got their hands on the list of others who were going–"

"And they just decided to kidnap and rape on a whim?" She shook her head, "No, I can't–"

"Who said it was on a whim? Or even their first time?"

Missy's eyebrows knit tightly together.

"This whole sick *game* they created is too highly organized to be a whim - or even their first time."

Scowling, Missy refused to believe it.

"Think about what we've seen. The way they've worked to create the killing field they send the couples into. The fact we're on a plateau, surrounded by mountains with no real way out." Rory shook his head as he pushed his fingers back through his hair, "I'm not sure how he did it, but the Bossman assembled a real crew of–"

Her lips curled and Missy spit out, "Psychopaths."

"Actually, I was going to say sadists."

"Sadistic psychopaths then. Does it matter?"

"Probably not. But these guys are sadistic sexual psychopaths. They will never see us as human - we're just a playtoy to them–"

Missy cursed under her breath, "I'm not going to be any playtoy - I'll die first."

Rory put a hand on her arm, "All I'm saying is reasoning won't work with them - negotiations won't work - we won't be able to talk our way out of this."

Frowning, Missy nodded her head in understanding, "Yeah." Shaking her head in disbelief, she said, "I can't believe there are that many sadistic psychopaths in the country."

"25% of males in our federal prisons are said to be psychopaths. I heard that at a seminar. Wouldn't take much to find a pile of ex-con, misfit psychopaths looking for work. Or maybe he just found a bunch of serial killers running around the bush, I don't know."

Missy gave a visible shudder.

Rory decided to change the subject and he looked across the large open space, "Okay. It looks like there are some small rooms and offices on the other side of this hangar. Let's take a look and see if we can find a radio or a cell phone. Maybe we can find something to contact the outside world." He shifted around to his knees. "Try not to make too much noise. I don't think there's anyone here or nearby outside. I imagine everyone is out looking for us, but you never know."

Missy shifted around to her knees as well and then rose in a crouch beside Rory. Side by side, they moved across the hangar floor. They tread as quietly as possible but their footsteps still echoed lightly in the large, empty space. Reaching the other side of the hangar, they found a number of small offices and a lunchroom. Exploring each one, they found nothing they could use to call out for help. The only good thing they did find was a small washroom with water and they filled their canteens before stepping back into the hangar area.

Rory pointed to the corner, "There's another exit door over there. Let's go check the next hangar."

Missy followed him, glancing behind every so often to make sure someone wasn't sneaking up on them.

Reaching the exit, Rory slowly opened the door to check outside. Not seeing anyone, Rory led Missy outside and over to the edge of the hangar where they pressed their backs against the building. Rory edged forward to peer around the corner of the hangar. The coast was still clear but there were fifty yards of open space before they reached the next hangar. He whispered to Missy, "We're going to run to the next hangar. Okay?"

Missy nodded reluctantly.

"Stay right behind me." Slipping into the open, Rory led her at a run across the open ground to the next hangar.

They reached the hangar unseen and settled below a window ten feet past the corner. A door was a few feet ahead.

Rory slowly lifted his head up and peeked through the window. He let out a low whistle.

Chapter 35

MISSY'S BODY WENT RIGID from the sharp whistle, "What is it?" What did you see?"

"Sorry about that. Follow me and I'll show you." Rory crept tried the brass doorknob. It was unlocked. Rory slipped inside with Missy right behind him. Closing the door as quietly as possible, he crouched with his back to the door.

Missy crouched beside Rory and let out a sharp whisper, "Wow."

Looming dead ahead of them was a huge, black helicopter. It was a little over fifty feet long, more than twelve feet wide and almost twenty feet high. It had twin sixty-foot rotors on top.

"It's a Boeing CH-47 Chinook," Rory explained. "Like I said, a large, heavy-lift cargo helicopter."

"It really is big."

"Uh huh. Depending on how it's configured inside, they could probably carry 30 people and their equipment easily."

"Can you fly it?" Missy asked hopefully as she looked at him.

Rory looked at it pensively, "I've been trained to fly smaller ones in a pinch...but one this size...I don't know. It would be dicey. But then I guess we're in a dicey situation."

"Does it have a radio? To call out maybe?" she asked hopefully.

"Let's take a look," Rory said. He moved cautiously to the side of the helicopter, with Missy following right behind him. The back door ramp was closed and Rory slipped towards the nose and the first round window in the body. He carefully peeked inside and found it empty. Moving low, he slipped by a door without a window and up to the copilot's door, where he peeked inside.

Missy was right behind him, leaning over his shoulder to look inside the helicopter herself.

Rory whispered back over his shoulder, "Keep watch while I take a quick look inside."

Missy nodded and looked around apprehensively.

Rory opened the flight cabin door and slipped up into the large helicopter. After a few minutes, he slipped back out, "Looks like they're working on this one. The radio and other instruments are missing. So is a critical fuse, which means we can't fly this one unless we could replace it."

"What about in the back of the helicopter?" she asked, "maybe there's something back there."

"Good thinking, I should have thought of that when I was in the flight cabin," he admitted. He moved back to the solid passenger door and opened it up. He slipped inside the helicopter with Missy right behind him. There was a row of seats towards the back, but most of the cabin was open space with thick, rubber mats on the floor.

Missy glanced at Rory, "Do you smell that?"

"Yeah."

There was the light but definite fragrance of perfume.

"*That* is an expensive perfume, not some cheap men's cologne," Missy said, "a girl knows."

Rory bent down and picked something up, passing it back to Missy.

Missy took the item in hand. It was a pearl earring. She cursed under her breath, "And *this* is an expensive piece as well. I guess that confirms your theory." She glanced around the space, "They used this to transport us here."

"Or some of us. There are other hangars. Let's see if we can find a radio or cell phone. Maybe one of the victims lost one here or the kidnappers left one behind."

Missy shook her head, her anger evident but she worked with him to check every nook and cranny. They came up empty and Missy cursed again. She looked out a small window on the other side of the helicopter body and pointed at some work benches and a small office area on the far side of the hangar, "Maybe we can find something to communicate with over there."

Rory took a look out the window and agreed. They slipped back out the passenger door and moved around to the front of the massive helicopter. Not seeing anyone, they ran across the hangar floor. Rory went right to the workbench area and the mixed scents of degreasers, cleaners, gearbox lubricants, and turbine oils. He examined the electronics strewn across a workbench against the wall, hoping to find something to use to communicate with the outside world. He was surprised when he found some of the missing pieces for the Boeing helicopter. But he was disappointed when he realized the communication board and that critical fuse were not here. *The Bossman probably has those locked away somewhere else, being extra cautious.* He glanced around the work area. *They have to be here somewhere.* He headed to another workbench loaded with parts, hoping to find what he needed.

Missy looked at the items on top of two large dirty desks and opened all the drawers. Not finding anything, she wandered over to one of the office doors. Pressing both hands against the glass, she looked into the dark interior. Not seeing anyone, she reached down and tested the doorknob. It was unlocked. Pulling the door open slowly, she peered through the crack and then slipped inside without Rory noticing it.

Rory moved over to a line of gray lockers to the right of the workbenches. *Maybe the parts we need are in here. Or maybe someone has a cell phone in here.* He opened one and looked inside. There was nothing they could use. He closed the locker door and opened the next one. Nothing. He checked the third one. Two boxes on the top shelf caught his attention. He pulled them down. Each box contained electrical fuses. Rory noted each box was for a different type of helicopter. The labeling said one of them was for the Boeing helicopter. The other one was for a Sikorsky helicopter.

Rory took a look over at the Boeing CH-47 Chinook and thought for a moment. Then he took one of each type of fuse and slipped them inside a top pocket of his camouflage jacket. He closed the boxes and looked around. Heading back over to the long workbench, he bent down and slid the two boxes of fuses as far underneath the workbench as he could. Even if someone finally found them, they would have to rip the entire workbench off the wall to get at them. Another possible advantage for his side of the fight.

"Have you found anything?" he asked Missy as he stood up. When there was no reply he jerked around to see where Missy

was. *Where is she?* He took several steps, looking around frantically, "Mis–"

The sound of items crashing loudly onto a floor came from
behind him. He spun around. More crashing sounds. It was coming from the office with the partially open door. He sprinted
across the hangar floor and pulled the door open.

A mountain of a man in coveralls was bent forward, holding
Missy down on the top of an office desk. He was standing between her flailing legs and his huge hands were wrapped completely around her throat.

Chapter 36

MISSY'S LEGS KICKED VIOLENTLY as she clutched desperately at the man's hands, trying to tear them away from her throat. The cap from her head went flying across the desk as she fought. Her right hand reached out to grab something...anything...she tried to lift a lamp but it slipped from her hands, tipped and crashed to the floor.

Rory moved forward across the room, pivoted sideways as he lifted his foot, and brought it down violently on the back of the man's right knee. The knee gave way partially, but the man didn't tumble to the ground as Rory had expected.

The man cursed loudly and swung his left arm around, smashing it against the side of Rory's head.

Rory grunted from the force and crashed to the floor. The man was not only big but immensely strong. Rory could feel it. He got up, trying to ignore the pain in his head. He drew his fist back and punched the man in the kidney.

This time, the man roared and swung around to smash Rory in the head with his right hand.

Rory tried to duck but the big fist struck the top of his head and he dropped to the floor again.

The only good thing about Rory's last attack was that Missy was able to roll over the desk to the edge where she tumbled to the office floor.

With his original target gone, the large, 6 foot-10 inch hunter turned on Rory. He growled as he picked up Rory's body. Handling Rory's weight with ease, like a sack of potatoes, he threw him across the room towards a desk.

Rory slid right across the desk and crashed to the floor on the other side. The wind was knocked from Rory's lungs and he groaned in pain.

The big man turned, emitted a low growl and went after Missy again.

Missy was skittering across the floor towards the door leading out to the hangar floor.

The man reached Missy just before she could reach the door. He grabbed the back of her jacket, lifting her up in the air.

Missy squealed in fear, her arms and legs flailing.

Rory rose from the floor, shaking the fuzzy feeling from his head. He stepped up onto the desk, took two large steps and launched himself towards the big man's back.

But the big man caught the move from the corner of his eye and he was quick. He bent forward, using Rory's momentum to throw him over his shoulder.

Rory landed hard upside down against the wall beside the door, groaned in agony and sagged to the floor.

The movement allowed Missy to break free and she skittered back across the office floor.

The big man picked Rory up again. This time, he turned and threw Rory to his left, towards several tall, gray filing cabinets against the back wall.

Rory grunted in pain as he landed hard on top of the cabinets. The cabinets banged and clanged together under his weight.

Man Mountain wasn't finished. He headed across the room in huge strides in Rory's direction again.

But just as Man Mountain reached Rory, Missy attacked from behind, hitting the big man across the shoulders with a small metal chair.

Man Mountain bellowed with pain and rage as he turned around to face his attacker.

That move by Man Mountain gave Rory an opening. He spun around on the cabinet and lifted his legs, wrapping them around the big man's neck, trying to strangle him.

Man Mountain pulled Rory off the filing cabinet and whirled him around the room like a windmill, trying to dislodge him.

Rory was banged against the wall several times but he fought to stay on the bucking bronco, squeezing his legs hard around the big man's neck.

Man Mountain whirled around the room again in the opposite direction, trying to dislodge Rory with the momentum.

Rory squeezed desperately with his legs, trying to cut off the man's air.

But Man Mountain's neck was enormous and Rory's efforts were largely ineffective.

Man Mountain whirled in the other direction and banged Rory hard against the wall. Pivoting away from the wall, he yelled with rage as he banged Rory's body back against the wall with all his might. Seeing that it still didn't dislodge the smaller man, Man Mountain now whirled around in a circle, trying to gain more momentum and power. After five turns, he slammed Rory hard against the wall once more.

Rory opened his mouth in a silent scream of pain. But he hung on.

Missy had ducked under a desk to avoid being hit by the massive hunter or Rory's body as it was whirled around the room. She looked at a broom in the corner. Scooting out on her knees, she grabbed the broom and scooted back under the desk. The next time Man Mountain stepped backward, getting ready to slam the body on his back again and came close to her, Missy stuck the handle between his legs, just above his ankles.

Man Mountain tripped backward and fell heavily on several office chairs before crashing to the floor.

Rory fell with him, landing heavily on his back.

The room was now silent as both men lay dead still on the floor.

Chapter 37

MISSY FEARED FOR THE WORSE and she scrambled on her knees and knees over to Rory. His legs were still wrapped around Man Mountain's neck. She cradled Rory's head in her lap, "Rory, are you okay?" She tapped his cheeks a few times, "Rory, wake up."

Rory's eyes fluttered open. He looked around for a moment and then shot up to a sitting position on the floor, looking for his opponent, "Where–?"

"I tripped him and you both fell," Missy said.

Realizing he was still sitting partly on the big man's shoulders, Rory quickly checked for a pulse in the large neck.

"Is he...?"

Rory nodded, "Yeah. He's dead. When my butt hit the floor, my legs forced his head forward. Probably broke his neck."

Missy stood up, looking down at the dead body. "I'm sorry, Rory. I made a mistake again. He came in from that door and caught me by surprise. I...I should have waited for you to come in here with me."

Rory simply nodded as he began searching the body of Man Mountain.

"How in the world do we get rid of this body? He's so...big," Missy whispered.

"Maybe we don't," Rory mused. He pulled a few items from the dead man's pockets.

"But if they find him—"

"Maybe we hide him in plain sight," Rory said, lost in thought as he looked at what he had found.

"There you go with that stuff again," Missy complained with a shake of her head, "I don't understand what you mean."

Rory turned to Missy, "Can you get everything back on the desks in here? Get the furniture back in place? Can you make it look like nothing ever happened in here?"

Missy looked at Rory with a puzzled look on her face, "Of course, but I don't understand. Once they find him, they'll know we were here for sure."

"Maybe not," Rory replied, "get started and I'll be back in a minute." He got up and disappeared out the doorway leading to the hangar floor.

Missy turned to her task of cleaning up the office. She made sure to avoid the dead body and kept one eye on it, just in case he wasn't dead. She was just finishing up when Rory rushed back into the office. He helped to get the last few displaced items back in place around the office and then turned to the dead body.

"Now what?" Missy asked.

"Help me get this big lug out of here and into the hangar." Rory knelt down, grabbed the dead hunter's two arms and placed them back over his shoulder, maneuvering the body into a fireman's lift. Missy pushed and Rory groaned as they worked to lift Man Mountain off the floor. Once up, Rory staggered under the weight. He had to take small steps as he worked to get the body through the open doorway into the hangar. He turned and car-ried the body over towards the long workbench. With Missy's help, he slowly propped the body face-first over one end of the workbench. "Can you hold him up here?" Rory asked her.

"He's big...but I...I think so," Missy said as she reluctantly placed her hands on the back of the dead man. When she was sure she could do it, she finally nodded yes. She held the body propped in place as she watched Rory move further down the workbench, "What are we doing?"

"Those items I found in his pockets suggest he's a helicopter mechanic working on this helicopter. That's probably why he came into this hangar, to finish working on it." Rory started working on the inside of a large piece of equipment on the bench. He did something to it and then quickly jerked his arms away, holding them in the air as he turned to look at Missy, "At least, that's the theory."

Missy watched Rory walk back to her, shaking her head in confusion again, "I still don't get it."

"I just turned that good piece of equipment into a faulty piece of equipment. And we're going to use it to cover our tracks," Rory explained. "Help me move the body down to that piece of equipment. But...whatever you do...*don't* touch that piece of equipment as we slide him down there. Do you understand?"

Missy's eyes went wide as she looked at the equipment on the workbench. And she kept her eyes glued to it as she helped Rory get the massive dead body upright off the bench.

Rory put the dead man's right arm across his shoulders, hold-ing him upright. Then he and Missy struggled to slide the body to a spot just a foot in front of the rigged piece of electrical equip-ment. "Okay," he said to Missy, "lean the body against me. Good,

good. Now...when I say 'go'...I want you to move back quickly
away from the body. You need to move back 15 to 20 feet. Understand?"

A nervous Missy nodded, "Yes," as she eyed the rigged piece
of equipment.

Rory braced himself, "Okay. 1. 2. 3. Go!"

Missy jumped back out of the way while Rory lifted the dead
man's right arm up. Then he gave the body some momentum to
fall forward. Jumping back out of the way himself, he watched
as the body fell forward slowly, while the raised right arm came
down on the machine part at a faster clip. There was an immedi-
ate *flash and crack* when the arm connected with the rigged part.

Missy let out a small scream and the dead body of Man
Mountain shot backward and crashed to the floor.

The sickening smell of burnt flesh hung in the air.

"What...what happened?" asked a shaken Missy.

"He just electrocuted himself," Rory told her. "At least, that's
what I'm hoping they'll think when they find him."

"Won't they notice the broken neck?" Missy pointed out after
a moment.

Rory shrugged, "Probably not. At least, I'm gambling they
won't. And I doubt they'll do an autopsy, so we should be safe."

"Always *should* and *hopefully* and *maybe.* Can you try and be
more positive the next time we do something?"

"Maybe."

"Very funny. So what do we do now?"

Rory looked around the hangar, "We can't stay in here, that's
for sure.

"Do we go back down the hill?" Missy asked, fearful of the
answer.

"No," Rory said after a few moments of reflection. "We're probably safer up here for now. This will probably be the last place they look for us. And maybe...like this guy," he said as he looked at the dead body with the charred arm, "we're better off hiding in plain sight."

"You just used probably twice and maybe once. Can you at least try and make a girl feel safe?"

Rory opened his mouth–

Missy held a hand up, "I know...maybe."

Chapter 38

MISSY CROSSED HER ARMS, "Okay. If we're better off hiding in plain sight, *where* exactly would that be?"

Rory closed his eyes and ran his hand through his black hair, "I'm not really sure yet, I'm still trying to figure that out."

"Oh great," Missy mumbled. "So much for my pep talk."

Rory had to admit she had a point. "Let's go check out the other buildings first before it starts getting dark." He headed for the exit, Missy following closely behind. Reaching the door, he slowly opened it and peered outside."I don't see anybody. Ready to go Ke-mo sa-bee?"

"Pardon?"

Rory looked back at her blank expression. "Ke-mo sa-bee? The Lone Ranger?"

Missy's blank expression stayed on her face and she shook her head no.

"I guess I watch too many old movies," said a bemused Rory as he looked back out the door.

"I guess that's what happens when you get old.".

Rory looked back at her and complained, "I'm not that much older than you, young lady."

Missy gave him a grin.

Rory shook his head, turned back to the door and slowly stuck his head out to check both ways. Then he said, "Let's go. Remember to keep low."

Together, they slipped out the door, closed it behind them and headed for the edge of the hangar where they checked to see if everything was clear. There was still no sign of anyone. A quick run across the open ground brought them to the next hangar.

Moving low, Rory peeked into the hangar window. Not seeing anyone, he edged over to the door and tested the handle. It was open. "Good thing they don't lock anything up here. Probably don't get a lot of visitors...or escaped hostages." Opening the door a crack, he slipped inside, Missy following closely.

Inside the hangar were two more large helicopters. But these two were painted in camouflage colors.

"This one looks like the one back in the other hangar, except it's painted different," Missy said. "That one on the other side of the hangar is totally different."

Rory nodded, "This one is another Boeing Chinook, but it's the MH-47G model. It's bigger in the body than the one in the other hangar. That other one on the far side is a Sikorsky CH-53E Super Stallion. Let's check this first one. Stay here and keep an eye peeled for visitors," he whispered. He sprinted across to the helicopter and looked through the window in the Chinook's body, checking to make sure no one was inside. Then he cautiously moved forward until he reached the cockpit area. It was empty as well. He motioned for Missy to join him.

Missy sprinted across to the helicopter.

Rory opened the cockpit door and slipped up inside with Missy right behind him.

"I'll check in the back," Missy said.

Rory nodded as he checked out the instrument panel and communications.

Missy appeared back beside him after a few moments, "Nothing back there we can use. No cell phone or radio left behind. How about up here?"

"No. The communications area is also missing an electrical board. We can't do a thing without it. It's also missing a fuse so it won't fly. Let's go check the Sikorsky."

Missy followed Rory out of the Boeing MH-47G helicopter and across the hangar floor to the Sikorsky. Their footsteps echoed lightly inside the large hangar.

Rory slipped up inside the cabin-crew door of the huge Sikorsky.

Staying close behind, Missy watched him search for a moment and then she slipped into the back of the large cargo helicopter. After a few minutes, she appeared back beside Rory. "Nothing back there either. You find any way of calling out?"

"Nope. Communications are disabled just like the other choppers. The Bossman is either very cautious or a control freak. He's made sure no one has a way to call out through these helicopters. Let's check out the rest of the hangar."

Missy and Rory slipped out of the Sikorsky and methodically explored the rest of the hangar. They were not surprised when they came up empty-handed once again. Rory led her back across the hangar floor where he stopped, running a hand over the dark stubble on his chin, thinking. "These guys are very organized. The entire place has been sanitized of communication devices. The Bossman runs a very, very tight operation."

"*Anal* tight, from what I remember of him," Missy added.

Rory gave her a slight grin, agreeing with her assessment wholeheartedly.

"You said there were a number of other hangars. Maybe we can find something in one of those?"

Rory nodded. "Possibly, but not right now." He looked over at the window at the edge of the hangar, "Besides, it's getting dark. We need to eat and rest to keep our strength up."

"That sounds good. But...where should we go?" She looked around the large hangar. "It's so open in here."

Rory looked at the 88 foot long Sikorsky helicopter just across from them, "Hide in plain sight. We can use that helicopter as our campsite."

"The Super Stallion? Isn't that a little Freudian?" asked a bemused Missy.

"What you talkin' bout Willis?"

"Huh?

Rory just shook his head.

"What's that? Another old movie reference–"

"Old television," Rory corrected. "Doesn't really matter. Let's go." He took her arm and headed around for the passenger door of the Sikorsky. It was situated just behind the flight crew area. He opened the door and gestured for Missy to get inside and then he slipped in behind her. The main cabin of the Sikorsky was fitted with canvas seats along the sides and down the center of the craft.

"I was amazed how big this thing was when I searched back here," Missy said, "you could carry a lot of people."

"You're right." Rory moved down to the first window in the body, "It could probably hold 50 to 60 people." He took off his backpack and Longbow, laying them on the center seats.

Missy did the same with hers. "How do we know they won't use this?" Missy asked as she sat on one of the seats.

Rory took a deep breath and let it out, "We don't. But it's not likely right now. That long line of hunters we went through tells me they are out in full force, hunting for us down in the trees. And with the night vision goggles they're carrying, they could be looking for us down there all night."

"So it makes more sense for us to be up here," Missy said, nodding in understanding. Then she held up her hands up, "I know, I know. At least, that's the theory."

Rory had to smile. "Let's not worry about it right now. Let's eat." Rory pulled some acorns from his pocket and spilled them on a canvas seat.

Missy pulled acorns from her pocket as well and added them to Rory's pile. Then she pulled out a small, four-inch-long hammer, "I'm ready to eat."

"Where did you get that?" Rory asked her as he sat down to eat.

"It's a toffee hammer," she said with a smile. She held the hammer up to show "Toffee" embossed on the handle, "I found it on the workbench and I figured I could use it to break the acorns."

"As long as no one misses it," Rory replied.

"Well, knowing a workplace, they'll probably blame a workmate," she replied, "and maybe they'll kill each other over an argument about it. At least, that's the theory."

THEY ATE IN SILENCE, each lost in their own thoughts. After a bit, Rory noticed Missy was turning one of the acorns around and around in her fingers, only vaguely looking at it. Her brow was furrowed. "Penny for your thoughts," he said quietly.

Missy broke out of her thoughts and looked at Rory, "What?" She realized he had asked her a question "Oh. I was just...thinking about my father...."

"What about him?"

She just looked down, giving him a slight shrug, "I don't know. It's just...," her voice trailed off. She sat there in silence, looking at the acorn in her hand again, rolling it a few times in her fingers. Then she popped it into her mouth after a moment and chewed slowly, still thinking.

Rory let her sit in silence.

Her voice was quiet when she spoke again, "I always thought of my father as...not really evil, you know? But...I don't know...I thought of him as doing bad things. Being responsible for digging up dirty coal and...," her voice trailed off again. Then she shook her head slowly, "But when you really meet evil like we have up here? He doesn't seem so bad. Just a man providing for his family. Giving good jobs to men and women with families of their own. Trying to create a cleaner industry and...and he did, you know? But I would never give him credit for it. I was more worried about my friends and what they thought...."

"Something we all do in one way or another, I imagine," Rory reasoned.

"Maybe that's why we're in this mess. Payback," she offered.

"No," Rory said firmly. "Neither of us is responsible for what those men are doing. Or for what they've done," he insisted.

"Maybe," she replied in a soft voice.

"Why don't you get some sleep, while I keep watch," Rory offered gently.

Chapter 39

MISSY WOKE UP WITH A START and cold fear stabbed her heart. Someone was in the helicopter! She felt a hand on her shoulder and lashed out hard–

"It's okay, it's me," whispered a low voice.

Her eyes narrowed - trying to focus in the dark - Missy realized the form above her was Rory. "What's wrong?" she asked in alarm.

"Nothing," Rory said. "I just don't want to be in here when it gets light. Someone might come in."

Missy's shoulders relaxed. She rubbed the sleep from her eyes, "What time is it?"

"I think it's about 4 o'clock. Gather your stuff up and let's get going."

"But won't it still be dark out?" Missy asked as she reached out for her backpack. There was barely enough moonlight to see anything.

Rory nodded and then handed something to Missy, "Remember these?"

Missy took the item and looked at it, "The night vision goggles?"

Rory nodded again. "It's not likely they'll be using their own night vision goggles up here on the plateau. This should give us the advantage while we explore the other buildings up here. Maybe we'll find something we can use yet to get us out of this mess."

Missy took her pair of night vision goggles and put them on. "Yuck," she complained, "everything is a puking green. Remind me never to buy a dress in this color."

"I'll keep that in mind," Rory said as he put on his own goggles.

Once Missy was ready, they left the helicopter, heading for the back door.

Rory cracked the door and checked outside. Everything looked clear. Slipping outside into the crisp, early morning air, they moved quietly over to the corner of the hangar. The scent of a wood fire still lingered in the air.

Missy and Rory crouched against the side of the building as they scouted around for signs of any hunters.

"Stay behind me and stay as low as possible," Rory instructed her, "they might see our movement in the moonlight. We want to stay as low as possible as we run. Ready?"

Missy nodded and adjusted her goggles, "I hope I don't trip. Everything looks so strange through these things."

Rory took a quick peek around the corner of the hangar again. "Okay, let's go," he whispered.

They moved low and quick as they ran across the open space to another large, log building. This was the one Rory had first noted when they were escorted from the lodge. Crouching against the western wall they scanned the terrain around them and listened carefully. Everything was dead still.

Then a low sound caught Rory's attention. He stretched his neck and peeked around the edge of the building. He pulled his head back in quickly.

"What's wrong?" Missy whispered urgently.

"Four hunters coming from the front of the lodge. They're walking slowly our way," Rory whispered.

"This way? Why are they out at 4 o'clock? Did they see us?"

Rory didn't answer as he took a quick peek again.

"What do we do?"

Rory pulled back and held put a finger to his lips.

Missy opened her mouth, fought the urge to ask more questions and pressed her lips tightly together.

Waiting for a moment, Rory took a slow peek around the corner again.

Two more hunters had joined the other four from somewhere and were definitely headed in their direction.

Rory pulled back fast.

"Two more," Rory whispered. He took another quick peek.

The six hunters were moving at a quicker pace now.

Missy started shaking, "Did they...?"

Rory turned and grabbed Missy's arm, "They're coming fast. Move, move."

Missy was frozen with fright and she stumbled as she turned.

Rory pulled her to her feet and urged her to run northward down the side of the log building.

Missy stumbled and fell against the log wall twice more as she struggled to run.

Rory tried his best to keep her up and moving as he watched behind them. Reaching the end of the building, he pulled Missy hard and sent her around the corner. She stumbled and fell, cursing in a low grumble.

Rory followed right behind her, "Shhh."

"Tell a girl when you're going to–"

"Shhh." Rory pressed his back against the log wall and peered back around the corner.

The six hunters were stopped at the far corner of the building now, talking.

Rory pulled his head back. *They must have seen something.*

Missy got to her knees and tugged at his arm, whispering urgently, "Rory, Rory!"

Rory ignored her, peering back at the hunters.

Missy tugged at his arm again.

Rory turned to look.

Missy gestured behind her. The back of the lodge was visible across open space on the far side of the log building. A light was burning on the veranda. They were now exposed to anyone who stood back there. "What do we do?" Missy whispered in a shaky voice.

Rory shook his head. *This is not going well.* He heard a scuffle and peeked back around the corner. Two of the hunters were heading in his direction. Rory turned back to tell Missy to move but she wasn't there. His heart froze for a minute until he realized she had moved down along the wall, looking for a way into the building. He saw her stop and place her hands against the logs.

Missy had found a door at the center of the log wall. She tried the doorknob. It was unlocked. Missy pulled the door open and peered inside. It was dark. She turned and beckoned Rory.

Rory took off at a run, trying to run as quietly as possible in the hunting boots. Missy disappeared into the building. Reached

the door quickly, he followed her inside, shutting the door behind him.

"What now–?"

Rory put a finger to his lips.

Missy froze in position, her back against the log wall.

Rory slowly twisted the thumb-turn and the door's deadbolt
slid into place with a small, hollow thud. He held his breath and
listened.

Low voices sounded on the other side of the door. The doorknob twisted.

Rory looked into Missy's eyes. She trembled as someone
pushed and pulled on the doorknob.

Then silence.

Rory slowly let his breath out but continued to listen.

The voices moved away.

After a number of long, agonizing minutes, Rory relaxed just
a bit, letting his heart rate begin to fall. He took a look around.

They were in a long, dark hallway with several doors on the
left.

Missy looked around as well. "Now what?" she whispered.

"Take it slow. Maybe we can find a radio or a cell phone in
here," Rory said in a low voice. "Let's start down there at the far
end of the hall and we'll work our way across these rooms."

Missy nodded and she moved down the hallway. The upper
half of all the doorways had wired, tempered-glass windows.
Reaching the end of the hallway, she tried the doorknob. It was
locked. Missy pressed the goggles against the tempered glass,
looking through the window. It was a small room filled with
shovels and pickaxes, some hanging on the walls and others just
leaning against them.

Rory pressed his goggles against the glass as well.

"That stuff will work if we need to shovel our way out of here," Missy said.

"Yeah, right. We'll keep that in mind if we have to build a tunnel. Let's try the next one."

Missy frowned at his dismissal of her idea but she led the way down to the next door and peered through the tempered-glass window. "This looks like a better bet of finding something," she said. She tried the doorknob. It was unlocked and she opened the door cautiously, slowly moving into the room.

Rory moved in behind her, pulling the door shut behind him There were several workbenches against one wall of pegboards that held a wide variety of tools. A number of large cabinets and lockers were lined up against another wall.

Missy headed over to the lockers.

"Look for anything we could be used to communicate with the outside world," Rory whispered to her as he headed for the workbenches.

"I know, I know."

The search was quick and there was nothing of interest on the top of the benches or in the drawers and cupboards below. He moved over to the cabinets and began a methodical search there. Closing the last cabinet door, Rory looked around. Missy wasn't there. *Where did she go now?* There was a partially open door on the far side of the room and light was spilling through the crack.

Rory hustled across the room, removed his goggles and stuffed them into a side pocket as he pushed the door open and stepped through. He found himself in a large room that was lit up from end to end under bright, fluorescent lights that ran completely across the ceiling.

Missy was standing a few feet away. She had removed her night vision goggles and held them by her side.

"Please don't do that again," said a relieved Rory as he walked up behind her. "*Let me know* if you're going to go exploring without me."

"Okay," Missy said, only half listening.

"Don't forget what happened the last time you wandered off," Rory said a little sterner.

Missy gave him a slight nod, "You're right." She wrinkled her nose at the sickly-sweet smell that hung in the air.

That caused Rory to sense the smell as well and he looked at where she was staring.

Thirty feet ahead and to the left were three large stainless-steel boxes. Each gleaming box was about 10 feet tall by 8 feet wide, had a control panel with a large round gauge sitting above four rows of white, black, blue and red buttons and a reinforced, glass door. Below each glass door was a ten foot long, live-roller conveyor.

Missy slipped her goggles into a pocket and walked over to the end of the conveyor for the nearest box. Her hand played along the conveyor, rolling over the wheels as she walked forward to the glass door.

Rory watched her bend sideways over the conveyor and peered into the glass.

"Everything inside is made from brick," Missy said after a few moments. "And it looks like there are some ashes inside." She looked back at Rory with a questioning look, "It looks like a big stove or a fireplace." She ran her hand over the conveyor rollers again, "They must pile the logs on here to push them inside. Although that doesn't make sense...."

Rory walked to the control panel and examined it. As Missy stepped back, he put the side of his hand on the reinforced glass door and looked inside.

While Rory was checking that one out. Missy stepped over to another one of the gleaming boxes and looked in the glass door. "More ashes in this one as well," she said.

After a long look through the glass, Rory had the answer. He took a step back, his face holding a dark, somber look as he considered all three stainless-steel boxes. He now knew what the sickly-sweet smell was from.

Missy watched Rory with curiosity for a moment and then asked, "Do you know what these are?"

Rory took a moment to answer, not really wanting to believe what he was seeing. "Each one is a crematorium," he finally answered in a low voice.

Missy took a few steps back and looked at all three gleaming boxes, "A crematorium? What would they need these for?"

"This is probably how they get rid of the bodies," Rory said. His voice was strained. "The hunters place the bodies on the conveyor and roll them inside. I wondered...."

After a heartbeat, Missy turned to him with wide eyes. She pointed a trembling finger at the gleaming stainless-steel boxes, "That smoke we saw after those screams...and all the single people they killed when we were up here...."

"Nothing left but ashes," Rory whispered. "They probably take the ashes up with one of their helicopters and scatter the remains over the mountains. No DNA. No evidence left behind for anyone to find."

Missy's eyes glistened with tears. "That would've happened to us," she said in a small voice, "if we hadn't escaped."

Rory nodded. "No one will ever know what happened to them. Or to us if we get caught again."

Chapter 40

MISSY LOOKED ABSOLUTELY STUNNED as she stood there looking at the three stainless-steel boxes. "We have to stop them," she whispered. She turned to Rory and pleaded, "We have to stop them, Rory. We *have* to."

Rory nodded in sympathy.

"We have to burn this place down," she added with more forcefulness. "Maybe we can find a lighter or some matches," she said as she turned, looking around the open space, "they must have something here they use to start those things."

Rory looked at the gleaming boxes, "I doubt they would need matches. It's probably electronic ignition—"

"Who cares!" Missy yelled in rage. "We need to burn the building down *now* so they can't use it again."

"If we do," Rory answered in a quiet voice, "then they'll know we're here for sure. The Bossman will bring every hunter back up her to search for us. If there *are* any other kidnap victims alive, how do we help them if the hunters capture or kill us?"

Missy blinked back hot tears and crossed her arms tightly over her chest. She knew he was right but it still didn't make things any easier. Her body was shaking with anger and her voice was tight, "All those innocent people...what they did to them...."

"I know, I know. I feel the same way," Rory said as he placed his hands on her shoulders to calm her. "Let's just keep looking for some way to let people on the outside know what's happening up here. Okay?"

Missy took a deep, sobbing breath and then nodded.

Rory gave her shoulders an encouraging squeeze and then led her on a methodical exploration through the rest of the building. They slowly went from room to room in the log crematorium, looking for a phone or radio they could use to contact the outside world. But they found nothing. There wasn't a single way to send a message or get word out on what was happening.

Rory led Missy out of the last side office and back into the main room.

"This is getting ridiculous!" said Missy, clearly frustrated as they walked past the three gleaming boxes. "That...Bossman!" She cursed a blue streak.

Rory didn't say a thing but he felt the same way. "Let's head to the back door–"

Missy's eyes took on a look of alarm, "Look out–!"

The warning was too late. Rory had the breath knocked from his lungs as he was tackled from behind. He hit the floor face down.

The attacker straddled Rory's back and started throwing blows at his head.

Rory instinctively reached back over his head, grabbed a handful of greasy hair and yanked hard.

A deep voice uttered a painful cry and a sandy-haired man, dressed in camouflage clothing, fell to his back on the floor.

Rory rolled away to the left

Missy screamed.

Rory turned his head and caught a glimpse of her a few feet away.

A large man with glasses and dressed in camouflage clothing had Missy by the hair and was dragging her across the floor. Her hunting knife lay on the floor a few feet away.

Missy grabbed frantically at the man's hand, trying to free herself.

Rory realized it was the same two men who had been looking around the outside of the building earlier.

The man holding Missy's hair laughed as he looked at the sandy-haired man lying on the floor, "C'mon Cash. You gonna let that little pip-squeak play with you like that?"

Missy twisted around and kicked glasses-man in the shins.

The large man sneered at her effort and swung Missy by the hair against the side of one of the gleaming boxes.

Missy grunted as she slammed into the stainless-steel and slid to the floor.

Rory jumped to his feet and started for glasses-man.

But Cash hit him from behind with a punch to the lower back.

Rory fell to his knees in agony, clutching at his kidney area with his right.

Cash snaked his right arm around Rory's neck and cut his wind off.

Rory brought both hands up and struggled to break free.

Cash choked harder.

Rory jabbed back over his head with a thumb to the man's eye.

Cash screamed and released his hold as he dropped to his knees.

Rory fell to the floor, struggling to get his breath back.

Yelling in rage, Cash sprang to his feet and lunged for Rory.

Flipping around, Rory caught Cash in the stomach with his feet and used his momentum to throw him over.

Cash grunted in pain as he landed hard on his back.

Rory rolled over and got part way to his feet when a hunting boot caught him in the stomach. His breath left him in a sharp blast of air and he crashed to the floor.

Glasses-man laughed.

Rolling slowly away in agony, Rory's diaphragm was paralyzed and he brought his knees up into a fetal position, fighting the sense of panic at being unable to take in a breath.

Glasses-man enjoyed watching his opponent lying in agony as he walked to the end crematorium. He pulled open the glass door, "Why don't we just see–"

"No! He's mine," Cash yelled as he struggled to his feet. He snickered, "Besides, your girl is getting away, Dirk."

Dirk swung around.

Missy was scrambling across the floor on her hands and knees, heading towards the knife.

Dirk laughed and went after her.

The tension in his diaphragm beginning to ease, Rory took in a partial breath, rolled to his back and tried to bring his feet up to trip the man as he passed. But he was too slow.

Cash took several stumbling steps to Rory, stood straddling his body and began to rain hard blows down on his head, cursing at Rory with every strike.

Rory did his best to deflect the blows, still trying to get his full breath back. His instincts told him to watch for an opening to strike back but his body still wasn't cooperating under the relentless attack.

Missy screamed and began fighting as Dirk caught up with her.

Dirk grabbed Missy's hair and flipped her onto her back.

Cash stopped punching, dropped to sit on Rory's body and placed his hands around his neck, grunting as he squeezed.

Rory clutched at his attacker's hands and then heard Missy yelling. He strained to look in her direction.

Dirk savagely undid Missy's belt as she slapped at his hands. He laughed and ripped open Missy's camouflage pants at the zipper.

Missy screamed and pounded harder at the big man's hands, twisting her body away from him.

Dirk yanked her back around, lifted her hips off the floor and pulled at Missy's camouflage pants until he got them halfway down her thighs, exposing her black panties.

Cash grinned maniacally as he squeezed hard on Rory's throat, "Normally we want the man to watch his wife getting nailed. But in your case, I'll make an exception." He leaned his body down to apply more pressure.

Missy screamed again, "No!"

Rory's heart beat wildly. The man was going to rape Missy while he fought here on the floor.

Chapter 41

MISSY YELLED AND KICKED and beat her hands against the big man but she was like a rag doll in his hands and her eyes were filled with terror.

Dirk only laughed as she slapped and fought against him, relishing the fight he was engaged in with the beautiful woman.

And in the other fight for life and limb, Rory felt the adrenaline rush through his body. *I can't let it happen. I can't.* He reached up, grabbed Cash's right wrist and elbow and twisted and rolled in one motion.

Cash tumbled over, fell to the floor and rolled. He came up with a knife and lunged with an underhanded thrust.

Rory stepped to the side - deflecting Cash's knife arm with his left - then threw a vicious blow to the man's throat with his right.

Dropping the knife and clutching his throat, Cash's eyes were wide open in fear - his mouth opening and closing like a fish.

Rory spun on his heels and darted across to Missy as Cash dropped face down, trying to breathe, his windpipe crushed.

Dirk had Missy's bare legs in the air - he had one pant leg off and he laughed cruelly as he worked to pull the other one over her hunting boots.

Missy screamed, twisting her body away from him and slapping at his legs.

Rory wrapped his right arm around Dirk's neck and choked him hard as he pulled him away from Missy.

Swearing, Dirk placed his hands on Rory's arm and pushed back with his legs, propelling both of them backward and crashing to the floor - Dirk lifted his legs at the last moment and landed with his full body weight on top of Rory.

Missy scrambled away on the floor, the camouflage pants around on ankle and flapping behind her

The body blow hurt and Rory lost his grip on Dirk.

Rolling to the side, Dirk spun around into a crouch and attacked.

But Rory was already rolling the other way - he got into a defensive crouch and did his best to ward off the blows as he tried to recover from the body slam.

Seeing he had lost the advantage - Dirk pulled a knife from his right hunting boot - his eyes now gleamed as he advanced on Rory.

Rory looked for an opening but Dirk was more patient than Cash had been.

Circling Rory like a big cat, Dirk looked for an opening. He thrust and fainted underhanded at Roy's chest - thrust and fainted for the heart- then he fainted to the abdomen and thrust the point of the hunting knife at Rory's face.

It almost worked. Rory felt the side of the man's hand brush his ear as he got his head out of the way and moved to his left.

Dirk grinned - he thrust the knife at Rory's crotch this time.

The move caused Rory to shuffle back awkwardly his right ankle rolled. He winced in pain. He staggered back and bumped into the end of the live roller conveyor set against the end crematorium.

Seeing his opening - Dirk changed to an overhanded grip and attacked.

Rory just managed to step aside and used the man's momentum to push him past.

Dirk landed face down on the roller conveyor, slid along its length and right through the open glass door into the crematorium.

Stepping quickly forward, Rory slammed the glass door shut. "Thank you, Dirk. Or is that Dork–?" Rory froze as flames erupted inside the gleaming box.

The air was filled with Dirk's screams and he beat the bottom of his hunting boots against the inside of the glass door.

Rory jumped at the door and tried to pull it open. It was locked shut and wouldn't budge.

Dirk's screams were soon muffled by the roar of the flames burning at 2,000 degrees Fahrenheit. He beat against the sides of the crematorium with his fists as his feet kicked frantically at the glass.

Staggering back a step, Rory felt numb as the screaming and pounding and kicking lessened until the only sound was the dull roar of the flames. His legs were wooden as he turned and walked over to Missy.

She was sitting still on the floor, staring at the crematorium, her pants still only part way up, revealing her bare thighs and underwear.

"Here," Rory said softly as he reached to the waistband of the camouflage pants to pull them up.

She screamed and slapped at his hands.

Rory held his hands out to her and spoke gently, "It's okay, it's me. It's me, Missy."

Missy blinked several times, finally recognizing the form over her, "I'm...I'm sorry." She looked at the crematorium, "You...you threw him in there...."

Rory looked over at the still roaring box, "He just...slid in. And I just wanted to trap him...it must be set to fire up when the door closes...."

"T-the screaming," Missy whispered.

Rory just nodded. He still couldn't believe it had happened either.

They both became aware of the sickly-sweet smell becoming stronger.

After a moment, Missy got to her feet and began pulling her pants up. Her hands were shaking. "I guess he was going to do it to you - to us - and like you said - there is no negotiating or reasoning with these sadistic psychopaths - some would call it justice - but...."

"Still not easy having to kill someone like that," Rory admitted as he averted his gaze.

Missy nodded as she pulled her zipper up.

Rory looked over at Cash. He was lying face down, hands still at his crushed throat, obviously dead. "I guess we could try and hide him."

"Or - or we do the same as his partner," Missy offered quietly as she pulled the belt tight again and buckled it.

Rory looked at her.

Missy tilted her head at one of the other gleaming boxes, "You know? That way they won't find him."

Rory swallowed as he understood her meaning.

"I'll help," she said quietly as she walked across the room.

They carried the body to the conveyor, opened the glass door and slid it inside. The flames ignited as soon as they closed the glass door.

"Hopefully, no one sees the smoke this early," Rory said.

"They'll be ashes before long," Missy said in a soft voice as she stood back with her arms crossed.

Rory nodded as he glanced at her. The light from the flames flickered across her face. She had stood up well to this point but there was no doubt the ordeal was wearing on her. He clenched his jaw, wishing this was all over for her, but knowing full well it wasn't.

Missy asked quietly, "Now what...?"

"We need to find a way out of this nightmare, we need to find a way to escape with anyone else still alive," Rory said with iron in his voice. He put an arm around Missy's shoulders and pulled her close, "Just like when you got us out of here in the first place, right?"

She nodded in agreement after a few minutes. But her body was still shaking as she looked at the stainless-steel boxes and what they represented.

"Let's keep looking, okay? We keep on looking for a way to escape or we find some way to communicate with the outside world. We don't give up. We keep fighting back. We *never* stop fighting. Ever. We make them pay for all of this. We make them pay hard!"

Chapter 42

RORY TURNED MISSY away from the flaming stainless-steel boxes and across the floor, heading for the back door of the crematorium again. He was quiet as they moved into the next room.

It was Missy who spoke up, her voice quiet, her thoughts obviously still on what had happened, "So what do we do now?"

"There are a couple more hangars behind this building. Let's check them out and see what we find. Do you feel up to it?"

Missy nod was wooden, "Yeah."

When they reached the back door, Rory cracked it open and slowly poked his head out. He then closed the door softly, looking back at Missy, "Okay. The way is clear. I don't see anyone. The sun is just coming up and we won't need the goggles."

Missy nodded woodenly again and then her eyes flickered, "But...that means we'll be easier to spot. Right?"

Rory didn't reply.

Her jaw tightened and she closed her eyes, "I know. We don't have any choice." She let out a soft breath, "Okay. Let's go."

Rory was going to reassure her but knew the words would just sound hollow. He just clenched his own jaw in frustration, cracked the door open wider and slipped outside.

Missy moved out behind him, staying close as they ran north to the next camouflaged hangar.

Rory stopped just past the corner of the hangar and motioned for Missy to step past him and flatten herself against the wall beside him. He then peered back around the corner of the hangar to make sure no one had seen them from the back of the lodge. *So far, so good.* Rory then turned and stepped past Missy to the hangar window. He peered inside, making sure the hangar was vacant. Ducking under the window, in case he had missed someone inside, Rory moved across to the door and twisted the doorknob. Like all the others, it was unlocked. He pulled the door open a crack and waited for an attack. It didn't come. Everything was quiet. He peered inside, then pulled the door open and moved into the hangar.

Missy slipped inside behind him, closing the door quietly.

In the center of the hangar floor was another huge Sikorsky CH-53E Super Stallion helicopter. A heavy scent hung in the air.

"What's that smell? Kerosene?" Missy whispered.

Rory put a finger to his lips.

"Sorry." She winced.

"It's aviation fuel," Rory whispered to her. "Stay here."

Missy grimaced lightly but nodded.

"You'll be fine." Rory ran in a crouch across the floor to check the helicopter. His footsteps echoed lightly in the large space.

Missy turned and opened the door a crack, listening for movement outside more than watching.

Rory peeked into the round windows in the body of the huge helicopter to make sure no one was inside. Then he cautiously crept along the body towards the nose and peeked into the crew cabin to make sure no one was working on it. It was clear. He motioned for Missy to come over.

Closing the door, she took off at a run, wincing as her own footsteps echoed in the large hangar. "Sorry," she said as she arrived next to him.

"No problem. I want you to stand here. Let me know if you see or hear anything. Okay?"

Missy looked scared but whispered, "Okay."

Taking a quick scan of the hangar himself, Rory then moved to the door and slipped into the helicopter to check out the flight cabin.

Within two minutes, Missy was inside the flight cabin with him, "Anything we can use to call out?" she asked with some anxiousness.

Rory was sitting in the pilot's seat, checking out the communications panels and the other instruments. He slowly shook his head no as he reached over and tapped his finger on a gauge. Next, he bent over and checked underneath a lower panel.

Missy was fidgeting and became impatient, "Let's check in the back." She turned in her seat and disappeared back into the fuselage area.

Rory clenched his jaw and quickly followed her back, "You *do* realize one of us should be outside watching, liked I asked you–?"

"I know, I know," Missy admitted, "I just want to find something so bad and get away from this place."

Rory was going to say something but he held his tongue.

Missy started looking.

Rory began to explore the insides of the huge Sikorsky himself. At one point, he realized this Sikorsky had no seats down the center. There were only outside rows of seats against the body of the helicopter. There was also an empty space, free of seats, in the back third of the body on the right side. Rory went to check it out and found a large, sliding door on this side of the Sikorsky's body.

"Is that a doorway?" Missy asked as she moved up behind Rory.

"Yes, it is," Rory said as he pondered this find.

"Why would someone need a large door like that?" Missy asked, "I didn't see one in any of the other helicopters."

"No, there was, including the Boeing that we first saw. They just weren't as prominent as this one."

"Oh. So why would they have one this big in this one?"

Rory thought about it for a moment, "Well, for one thing, the main users of large helicopters like this are armies. When they go into battle, soldiers flying aboard the helicopter could use a doorway like this to mount some type of weapon, like a machine gun."

"I remember seeing that on old newsreels of Vietnam," she said, "they would shoot at the enemy on the ground."

"Exactly," Rory confirmed. "Or they could have a number of soldiers in here and use this for a quick exit or entrance to the helicopter," he added, "army medics could also use a large doorway like this to efficiently evacuate soldiers wounded in battle."

Missy shook her head, "It still doesn't make sense to me. I know from that first one that they probably used these things to kidnap us...." She seemed to feel the bitter taste of the words on her tongue, "But it's almost like they're playing soldier."

Rory took a deep breath as he considered the doorway, and then he shook his head as well, "No. I don't think they're just playing. Maybe not all of them but...I think a bunch of these guys are ex-military as well."

"You're kidding?"

"I wish I was." He gestured to the center spot without the seats, "They *could* lay some of the hostages along there. But the fact this one has seats, while a couple of the others didn't, tells me this one was used to lead the raid to get us. This one would carry the men who were trained in military tactics. They could move in and out of this helicopter pretty quickly through that doorway. Using one or two of the other helicopters, in combination with this one, would make a hostage raid quick and effective. They probably landed on the roof of the building we were in, took us captive and were gone in a heartbeat. Everything was done with military precision."

Missy's body visibly shuddered at the thought.

Rory grimace, "I'm afraid to say this - but - this tells me they're escalating in the chances they're taking and the number of people they're taking to participate in the sadistic game—"

"We have to find some way to stop them, Rory," Missy pleaded, "we just have to."

"I know. I agree." He rubbed his hand over the stubble on his chin for a moment. Then he said, "You keep looking back here. I'm going to check something out."

"But—"

"Just keep looking." Rory headed back to the crew cabin at the front of the Sikorsky. He had a tentative plan and wondered if it would work.

Missy continued her meticulous search of the helicopter, looking in every nook and cranny for a cell phone or radio.

After a few minutes, Rory came back to the passenger area to find Missy cursing and kicking a few things. "I take it you didn't find anything?"

Missy shook her head no. She was obviously very frustrated. Her hands were formed in tight fists like she wanted to punch something.

"Don't give up yet," he encouraged her. "Remember, a winner never quits."

"I don't want to quit," Missy growled. "I just want to kick somebody's ass!"

Rory had to smile, "I guess I'm not turning my back on you right now."

Missy stuck her tongue out at him. Then she gave him a faint smile as she tried to relax.

"Let's go check out the rest of the hangar. Maybe we'll find something yet."

Chapter 43

THEY LEFT THE SIKORSKY and moved across to search the small office on the far side of the hangar. But there was no telephone, no cell phone, no radio or any other communications device lying around. Like all the other buildings, this one was sanitized of every single communications device.

"What now?" Missy asked as they exited the office and stepped back into the hangar.

"There's one more hangar behind this one," Rory said, "last chance to find something, I guess."

"Okay, let's go," Missy said as she headed eagerly for the exit on this side of the hangar.

"Not too fast," Rory said as he trotted a few steps to catch up to Missy, "we've been fortunate so far, but we need to make sure the way is clear."

"You're right." Missy slowed down, "I just want to find something so badly."

"I know, but let's keep our guard up." Rory made her stay back while he made sure there was no one outside. He then led her out of the hangar and over to the corner. He peered around the edge of the hangar, making sure the way was safe. Setting out at a low run across the open stretch, they headed to the last camouflaged hangar. They crouched at the window of the hangar and Rory peered inside. Everything looked clear. He checked the doorknob and it was unlocked. Rory and Missy slipped inside the hangar.

There were no helicopters inside. This one was empty and their footsteps echoed lightly as they moved across the hangar floor to three small office cubicles on the far side. But once more they were disappointed. They exited the last small cubicle. Their search of the last hangar had turned up nothing of any use. There were no cell phones, no radios, no communications devices of any type. It didn't surprise Rory anymore. The Bossman was taking no chances. He had taken every precaution possible in case a hostage escaped their clutches temporarily. He had made sure there was no way to escape and there was no way to call for help. And even if someone did escape, it simply became part of the thrill-hunt for them. They would eventually find a hostage and do whatever they wanted to do. Everything was thought out to the last detail. The entire compound was a killing field.

"What's that?" Missy asked. She was pointing to a small vehicle near the large hangar door.

"That's basically just a glorified golf cart," Rory explained as they walked over to it. "It's electric, runs on a battery. See that hook-up on the back bumper? The golf cart hooks up to the front of a helicopter and moves it in and out of the hangar."

"That little thing can move one of those big helicopters?" Missy asked in surprise.

Rory nodded, "The front wheels on the helicopter allow it to move fairly easily on the ground. You could actually use a hand-lift dolly to move it. But this golf cart will do it so much faster and easier. Especially if you're moving a large helicopter back and forth to the landing zone away over on the western side of the plateau."

Missy walked around to the driver side, reached up to the visor and pulled it down. A key dropped down and she caught it in her hand, "Walla!" she exclaimed with a triumphant smile.

"You mean Voilà," Rory corrected her.

"Huh?"

"Voilà," repeated Rory, as he attempted to explain, "It's French. You pronounce the v and w together - never mind, it doesn't do us any good anyway. We can't just go running around up here in a golf cart."

"What about leaving the compound and driving away? Go for help...?" Missy asked hopefully.

"We're surrounded by mountains, remember?"

Missy's shoulders slumped.

Rory took the key from Missy and put it back up in the visor.

"Are we going to check out those small buildings behind this hangar?" Missy asked. She was now pointing to the back of the hangar and to the east.

Rory shook his head, "No. There's too much open ground between us and them. We can't chance it. They could easily see us from the back of the lodge. We'd be tempting fate a little bit too much."

"Even if we use the golf cart?"

"It sounds good. But what if they only use this golf cart to pull the helicopters? If that was the case, driving it around in other areas of the compound where they don't use it normally would attract suspicion immediately. We can't chance it."

"Okay. Then what do we do next? We don't give up, right–?"

A rattling sound came at the door on the far side of the hangar. Someone was coming into the hangar.

Rory grabbed Missy quickly and pulled her roughly into the last small office cubicle. He pushed her behind him and they crouched low against the wall inside. There was no place to hide. And there was no door to shut. If anyone came close, they would be easily spotted. Rory silently pulled his Bowie knife.

He heard a slight whisper as Missy pulled her knife from its sheath as well.

They could hear the far door close.

Heavy footsteps echoed on the far side of the silent hangar.

Rory felt like his breathing was so loud it was going to give them away.

He could tell Missy was trying to calm her breathing as well.

The heavy footsteps came closer.

Rory tensed himself, ready to thrust the knife upward.

"Hey, Roger."

The voice was coming from the far side of the hangar. The speaker sounded like he was Cajun.

"What?" answered a deep voice not far outside the cubicle.

"Whatcha you doin'?" the Cajun asked.

"Moving the chopper out to the landing zone, like I was told," grumbled the deep voice.

"No, no," the Cajun said, "the boss want to talk to you and me a half hour ago. He's pissed some you haven't shown up."

"Ahhhhhh, this damn new walkie-talkie isn't working," grumbled the deep voice, "what does he want?"

"We found Big Vic dead," replied the Cajun speaker.

"What happened?" the deep voice asked. Rory could hear the heavy boot steps start to walk back to the other side of the hangar.

"Don't know me," complained the Cajun speaker, "but the boss don't like it none. He's calling everybody back up from the hunt. He's gonna tell us what we lock down till they come. I'm still tryin' to find Cash and Dirk. Allons!"

"I'm comin', I'm comin', keep your pants on Vieux!" grumbled the deep voice.

Rory could hear the footsteps fading away across the hangar. The far door banged shut and there was silence.

After a few moments, Missy whispered, "Are they gone?"

Rory moved forward gingerly and peered around the corner, "Looks like it," he whispered. Then he moved a little farther out to make sure.

Missy slid into the doorway behind him, her boots scraping on the floor.

Rory turned back and put his fingers to his lips, asking her to stay quiet.

Missy froze in position.

He lightly stepped to the left of the cubicle, listening intently.

Not wanting any distance between them, Missy moved out of the cubicle.

Hearing her light footsteps, Rory turned and motioned for her to go back in.

Missy reluctantly stepped back into the cubicle, fear etched onto her face.

Rory turned and moved slowly over to the next cubicle, checking inside, Bowie knife at the ready. He then checked the next cubicle. Finding it empty, he quickly went back to the small cubicle where Missy was waiting.

She was crouched just inside the doorway, eyes wide in fear.

He gestured for her to come out.

Missy carefully stepped out of the cubicle and they stood silently side-by-side for a moment.

"Sounds like we're going to be in trouble pretty quickly," Rory said in a low voice.

Missy's voice was low and sounded afraid, "What should we do?"

Rory gave it some thought. "If they're coming back up, that means we can't head back down into the trees to hide. That will leave us only two choices. One - we can take that golf cart and make a fast run back to the helicopter in the last hangar. Remember that smell you mentioned? The aviation fuel?"

"Uh huh."

"That's what I went to check on while you searched. The gauges indicate it's fueled and ready to go. But it's also missing a fuse, like the other ones. *If* I replace the right fuse *and* can get the helicopter over there working, we can pull it out as fast as we can with the cart and try to escape. No guarantees I can fly it though."

"What about the other hostages?" Missy asked him. "We can't just run away and leave them behind."

Rory looked right into her eyes, "That would be choice number 2."

Missy looked at him for a few moments. Then she began to shake as she realized what he was talking about.

Rory took a deep breath and let it out. "Are you willing to make a visit to the lodge?"

Chapter 44

RORY AND MISSY stood in the large, empty hangar, looking at each other. They had a decision to make. Or at least, Missy did.

"Do we have to go to the lodge?" Missy asked in a scared, shaken whisper.

"As I said. We can take a chance and try to fly the helicopter out ourselves. Or we can see if we can help the others. To do that, we need to go into the lodge. I don't see any other way. I'll leave the decision up to you."

Missy was obviously scared but after a moment she said in a shaky voice, "The thing is...we have no idea why they're getting ready to take that helicopter out. Right? Maybe they plan on looking for us that way. But...they could be getting ready to just kill all the hostages and get rid of the bodies."

Rory's eyebrows knit together as he considered the possibility.

"Since they can't find us, the Bossman may be getting ready to eliminate as much evidence as possible."

"Maybe."

"Either way, I'm tired of being the little girl, running scared around the mountain in her underwear."

"I didn't mind it."

Missy stretched her neck and kissed him lightly on the lips, "And I didn't mind you seeing it. If we get out of this, I'll show you a lot more."

Rory opened his mouth.

Putting a finger to his lips, Missy said, "No more talking. I want to try and help the others."

"Okay. The first thing we can do is move as quietly as we can over to the other side of the hangar. Let's make sure those two guys are gone."

"Do you think they saw us and are just waiting for us to come out?"

"No, but we can't afford to take a chance. Keep your eyes and ears open."

"Right. And my butt tight, because I'm liable to crap my pants."

Rory had to stifle a laugh as he led the way across the quiet hangar. He kept watching the window on the far side of the door for any movement outside. They couldn't afford to be caught off guard in the open.

Reaching the door without incidence, Rory stepped over to the window, placed his shoulder against the hangar wall and checked outside. It didn't look like anyone was waiting for them. Stepping back to the door, he gripped the doorknob and pulled his Bowie knife, holding it at the ready.

Missy did the same, her hands shaking as she held her knife up and ready.

Rory gave her a nod and slowly opened the door a crack. Placing his body against the opening, he watched for movement outside. Nothing came. Opened the door wider, he slipped outside quickly and went into a defensive crouch. There was no one there. He motioned for Missy to join him outside the hangar door and then Rory slipped over to the corner of the hangar and placed his back against the wall before taking a quick look around the corner.

Missy moved quietly up behind him.

Rory pulled his head back in and turned to look at Missy, "Okay. As we move back to the hangar, you try to keep watch to our right side and behind us. I'll watch ahead and to the left. Understand?"

Missy nodded in understanding, "I'll keep watch to the right and behind. You keep watch ahead and to the left. Sound good to you?"

"Sounds good to me," Rory agreed in a low voice. He took a quick look around the corner again, "Okay. I don't see anyone. Ready to move?"

"Yes," Missy answered. Her voice was quivering, showing her fear.

Rory couldn't blame her. He slipped the Bowie knife back into the sheath on his belt.

Missy watched him and did the same with her knife.

Rory took a deep breath.

Missy looked into Rory's silver-blue eyes and readied herself as well.

"Let's go," Rory said finally.

They moved quickly, keeping watch on all sides as they ran back across the open space to the next hangar. There was no sign of the two hunters. Reaching the corner, instead of running straight across the front of the hangar to the other side, Rory had them press themselves against the wall to allow Rory to check through the window. The hangar looked empty. Rory cracked the door open and looked inside again to make sure. Confident it was safe, Rory led Missy back inside and they ran quickly across the hangar floor to the far door. Their footsteps echoed loudly as they ran. Reaching the far door, Rory and Missy slipped out and moved quickly to the edge of the hangar where Rory peered around the corner. He pulled his head back in quickly.

"What's wrong?" Missy asked fearfully.

"Two men going into the back of the lodge," Rory told her. "It's probably the two that were back there in the hangar." After a few moments, Rory peeked back around the edge of the hangar. The way was clear this time and he whispered back to Missy, "Okay. Let's run to the back of the crematorium instead of going straight for the lodge."

"Okay," Missy whispered in agreement. Her voice sounded nervous and raspy.

Rory motioned for Missy to run. They scooted across the open space to a spot against the back wall of the log building. From there, Rory led Missy towards the corner closest to the lodge. Squatting at the corner of the crematorium, they got a closer look at the back of the lodge across the open space. The veranda swept right across the back of the lodge, with four massive redwood-log pillars holding up the roof. A wide set of stairs was set dead center at the back of the massive log building.

Missy stretched her neck to look, "Is the back wall all glass?"

Rory nodded, "It looks like a huge sunroom. I didn't notice that before."

"Is that where the two men went in?"

"Yes," Rory confirmed.

"If they're still standing inside there, if we go up those stairs, they'll see us for sure."

Rory took a deep breath and nodded.

"Is there another way in?"

Rory pondered the situation as he scanned the building, "There are a number of windows along the side, but they're too high up. I doubt we can use them to climb inside without being seen. And we have no way to climb up to the second story to gain access to those second- floor windows either. Besides this back door, there are only two other ways in that we know of right now. One is the front door. The other is that side door that they took us out. And that one would lead us back into the holding area where they killed those people."

"That would be like going into the teeth of the lion. So, we don't have much choice, we have to use the back door," Missy concluded.

"It looks like it."

"And we can't tell from here if someone's inside the sunroom," said an obviously scared Missy. "If they see us coming up those stairs...."

"Then we're dead," Rory said simply, "but...."

"I know, I know," Missy said, "but what are the alternatives? I wish you would stop saying that."

Rory smiled as he looked at the back of the lodge.

"Okay, Scaramouche," Missy said, "let's go."

A puzzled Rory looked back at her, "Scaramouche?"

"You're not the only one who can reference old things," Missy retorted with a smug look.

"Scaramouche was a roguish clown," Rory complained.

Missy just gave him a 'what can I do' shrug.

"In a Punch and Judy puppet show," he complained further.

"Hey! I was a kid," she complained back to Rory, "we went to England...."

Rory just shook his head and turned his attention back to the lodge. He peered around the corner of the crematorium and didn't see anyone between the two buildings. "Okay," he said finally, "the coast is clear as far as I can see. Let's just hope no one's inside."

Missy looked at him and nodded. There was fear in her eyes but she was ready.

They each took a deep breath.

Then Missy and Rory were up and running across the open ground between the back of the crematorium and the back of the lodge. So far, so good. They moved across the back of the lodge and hit the wide staircase at a run. They bounded up the stairs and across the veranda to the glass, double-door back entrance to the hunter's lodge.

Rory notched an arrow in his Longbow while Missy put her hand on the door handle. He gave her a nod and without hesitation, Missy pulled open the door. Rory moved past her and quickly inside.

Missy moved through after Rory, letting the glass door slowly close behind them.

Chapter 45

THEY WERE INSIDE a large sunroom that swept right across the back of the lodge. The scent of pine floated across the air. This room incorporated stone and glass into the rustic redwood log theme of the other rooms. The floor was laid entirely with marble, accented by expensive Persian rugs. On the other side of the large sunroom was a massive stone fireplace that dominated the space. The stonework rose two stories high and exited through the ceiling. A door with glass on the upper half sat on either side of the fireplace.

Rory realized the entire length of the sunroom was open to the second-floor ceiling and there were railings sweeping around the entire second floor. *Just like in the first holding room.* His mind signaled the word *trap* and he immediately lifted his Longbow. Scanning all around the railing, he searched for anyone who might be looking down. He was relieved to see it was empty.

Missy stood nervously waiting, her eyes scanning across the large open area for signs of any hunters.

Rory lowered the Longbow but remained at the ready, keeping an eye on the two doors, "I'll keep watch while you take a quick check around. See if you can find a cell phone in here. Maybe someone's left one behind. Also keep an eye out for a ham radio, a walkie-talkie, anything we can use or modify to call the outside world."

"I'm not even sure what a ham radio is," Missy said as she nervously moved across the floor to begin her search.

"Just look for anything electronic and we'll figure out what it is," Rory suggested.

Missy headed straight for several tall cabinets filled with books. She methodically checked out the drawers and lower cabinet doors of each one. There were a number of easy chairs situated across the room and each one had a small side table. Missy diligently opened and closed the little drawer on every single side table. She even checked under every seat cushion, searching for something they could use.

As she searched, Rory moved across the room to check the door on the right side of the fireplace. Peeking through the upper glass, he could see a long hallway with a number of doors on either side. He moved across the front of the fireplace, pausing a moment to reach a hand out over the ashes and then touch his fingertips to the stone. He didn't feel any warmth, which meant no one had been in here recently. Continuing on to the door on the other side, he checked through the glass. Another long hallway with doors on either side. He glanced over at Missy.

She was still searching.

Rory was getting the sinking feeling that the room was entirely clean of electronic devices. He looked across the back wall of the lodge. The large, sunroom windows made him feel uneasy. It was like being on the inside of a fishbowl and he expected the sharks to appear on the outside at any moment.

Missy joined him by the door after a futile search. "I couldn't find a single thing," she whispered, "nothing."

"Not entirely surprising," Rory whispered in return, "the Bossman is one cautious creature."

Missy stepped up to the door and peered through the upper glass, "Are we going down there?"

Rory didn't answer. He was deep in thought.

"What are you thinking?"

"I was thinking about the room they were holding me in and trying to orient myself. They dragged me out of that room and down to the area where the Bossman told everyone about his plans. About why we were here. Then they took you and me out a door on that side of the building," Rory said as he pointed to the right. Rory made some motions with his hand as he tried to trace the path from the holding area back to the room he first woke up in. "I think I was on this side, on the east side of the building," concluded Rory as he pointed to the left. "Do you remember the route they took when they brought you to the room with the other hostages?"

Missy looked down as she thought about it. She nodded after a moment, "Yeah. I think I was held on the east side of the building too. Why?"

"I'm thinking maybe all the other hostages are on the eastern side of the lodge as well," Rory said hopefully. "It would make sense to have a specific part of the building set up to hold their hostages. I would imagine this hallway could lead us to them."

"Then let's go find out," Missy said with conviction.

Before Rory could speak, Missy slipped through the doorway and into the hallway.

Rory followed behind her quickly. He kept the Longbow low but still kept the arrow ready to fire, just in case.

Missy led the way down the hallway, moving as quietly as possible. They did a quick check on each door along the way. Missy would put her hand on the doorknob to a room. Rory would ready himself to shoot and Missy would open the door quickly. Unfortunately, despite the fact all the rooms were unlocked, they were also empty. The search was long and slow and they eventually came to a junction of hallways.

"Which way?" Missy whispered.

"Let's keep going east, to the left."

Nodding, Missy took the turn. As they moved along this hallway, they found a number of empty rooms, including a large, linen closet, a broom closet, and a few small washrooms. What they didn't find was any sign of the hostages, any cell phones or any other kind of communication device.

They reached a long stretch of hallway that only had one door on the left. Further down they could see the hall met another hallway running lengthwise along the building. Missy stepped up to the door on the left.

Rory readied himself.

Pulling the door open, Missy looked inside, "Wow. This one is a big workshop of some kind."

Rory touched her arm and had her step aside. Then he moved through the doorway, ready to fire as he scanned the room quickly. It looked empty and he took a couple more steps inside.

Following him, Missy let out a low whistle. The room was indeed a very large workshop.

The first thing that struck Rory was the large variety of equipment situated around the large space. He saw wood lathes, band saws, beam saws, panel saws and large table saws. He recognized a Wadkin mortiser, a Sedwick tenoner and a Casadei planer among other makes and models. And each piece of major equipment was serviced by large exhaust fans to remove the wood dust. The walls were made of gleaming, redwood logs and everywhere they looked, pegboards of every size were nailed to the logs. And hanging from the pegboards was every kind of woodworking tool you could imagine. Rory noted there were also a wide variety of hand tools, sheet metal tools, cutting tools, abrasive tools and machine tools as well as some for electrical work.

Missy wandered off and began searching the room.

Rory slipped the Longbow into his bucket kit and checked out the workbenches and what they held. He came across an interior door and slowly and cautiously opened it. He gave a low whistle as he slipped inside the room. Inside were a number of Longbows and a large quantity of wooden hunting arrows. Some of the Longbows looked to be finished, while others were in various stages of completion. Rory noticed there were also a large number of hunting knives. Some of them were only half finished. *Handmade bows, arrows and hunting knives.* These guys were definitely building their own weapons as he had surmised. Considering the wide variety of tools and the equipment he saw so far, these hunters could probably build and maintain just about anything they needed while they were here. Deadly and self-sufficient was a hard combination to fight against.

He went back into the main workshop area and joined Missy in her search. She told him she had checked out all the workbenches, and any cabinets and drawers around the room. She couldn't find anything in the workshop they could use. There was still no way to communicate with the outside world. They were still on their own.

Moving on, Rory led Missy back to the door, where he set an arrow in the Longbow again, keeping it low and ready to fire. She opened the door and he slipped back outside into the hallway, leading her down to the cross hallway. He checked both ways and then decided to turn right. As they moved along, they continued to check each door as they looked for signs of the other hostages.

Missy suddenly found a door that was locked. She jiggled the doorknob and they heard movement on the other side of the door.

Missy froze.

Rory lifted the Longbow, drew back the arrow and was ready to fire.

When nothing happened, Missy gave Rory a questioning look.

Rory thought for a moment and then gestured for her to move away from the door. Once Missy did, Rory moved slowly away from the door as well, keeping his weapon at the ready and aimed towards the closed door, just in case.

"What do you think?" Missy asked in a low voice as he stepped beside her.

Rory shrugged just a little, "If it was the hunters, I would imagine they'd be on us right now."

Missy thought for a minute and nodded in agreement.

"In for a penny, in for a pound," Rory said, "let's go back to that workshop and see if we can find something we can use to open that door."

Chapter 46

MISSY AND RORY MOVED QUICKLY and quietly back to the workshop door and peeked inside, in case someone had come along after they had left. Not seeing anyone, they slipped back inside and began to search for something they could use to pry open the locked door. After a brief search, an idea struck Rory and he went over to a section of pegboards he had noted previously. This whole section held a wide variety of hand tools.

Missy joined Rory and stood behind him, watching. "Would they have anything like a skeleton key? You know, like they have in the movies?"

Rory shrugged, "I'm not even sure what one would look like."

"Me neither," Missy admitted. She began to look around again.

Rory looked over a number of cases on the pegboards that held wood files, wood rasps, screwdrivers, punches and every other sort of hand tool you could imagine. Rory had previously noticed a leather case holding a collection of L-shaped Allen wrenches and he was looking for it. *There they are.* He ran his hand over the items and then selected one he figured would fit into the slot of the keyhole in the locked door.

Missy was opening every drawer she could see, also searching for anything she felt they could use to open the door.

Rory went back to the collection of wood awls he had seen. He looked them over and then finally selected a thin, 8-inch long wood awl with a wooden handle. Slipping both items into a long side pocket in his jacket, he buttoned it closed. *Hopefully, my skills at–*

Missy heard a loud crack and a groan of sheer pain behind her. She swung around.

It was Bossman!

Chapter 47

BOSSMAN HAD HIT RORY across the back with a 2 x 4 and clubbed him to the floor. The 2 x 4 had snapped completely in half, broken across Rory's back.

Missy saw Rory's Longbow lying on the floor.

Bossman dropped the broken 2 x 4 and kicked the Longbow across the floor. Then he grinned wickedly and kicked Rory in the stomach.

Rory groaned in pain as he curled into a fetal position, desperately trying to take in a single breath of badly needed air.

"Well, well, well," Bossman mocked in his rough voice, "don't you two have balls, walking right back into this place. I *knew* there was something wrong when we found Big Vic dead. I've called all the men back up, but you two will be dead by the time they arrive."

Missy didn't hesitate. She took a full run at Bossman, yelling at the top of her lungs.

Turning, Bossman took a step backward and began raising his hands.

Fueled by her sheer rage, Missy's full weight hit him and took Bossman by surprise. He was powered back against the wall where he hit his head. Missy bounced back a foot with the force and nearly fell.

Bossman growled in pain. He stepped forward, savagely grabbed the chest material of Missy's camouflage jacket, lifted her to her tip-toes to look at her face to face - then hurled her away from him with full force.

Missy desperately tried to get her legs under her. But her backward momentum was too strong. She landed hard on the floor and slid several feet, banging into a piece of equipment with her head. Her Longbow clattered to the floor.

"I'll get back to you in a second," Bossman growled to Missy. He rubbed the back of his head, "First, I gotta take care of your husband." There was a ringing hiss as he pulled a full-size KA-BAR hunting knife from a sheath on his belt. He turned and stepped purposely in Rory's direction, "You cost me a lot of good men, son."

Rory struggled to lift himself off the floor.

"*And* a lot of time and money recruiting ex-cons fresh out of prisons across the country," Bossman growled. "You know how hard it is to find men willing to work hard *and* who love to play after work like I do?"

Getting to his hands and knees, Rory sucked in air, started to form a fist, intending to bring it around to the Bossman's crotch–

But the Bossman lifted a boot and slammed it down on Rory's back, "Sorry, but you gotta pay for what you've done. Then I'll enjoy your wife - if you know what I mean."

Rory collapsed to the floor with a groan.

Bossman stood over Rory and lifted the KA-BAR for a killing blow, "I just wanted you to know that...'cause you're gonna to be *dead*–"

"Hey, jackass!" Missy yelled at the top of her lungs.

Bossman whirled around.

Missy was lying on her back. Her legs were up in the air and her Longbow was strung across the bottom of her boots. Missy had notched an arrow - the adrenalin was pumping hard through her veins - she pulled back hard on the powerful bowstring with both hands as she forced her feet towards Bossman.

Bossman instinctively took a large step back as he brought his hands up in a defensive position.

"This is for not being a gentleman and grabbing my chest," she yelled in rage. Missy released the arrow.

The hunting arrow penetrated the middle of Bossman's torso and nailed him back against the redwood log wall. His head dropped to his chest a moment later.

There was silence as Bossman hung, pinned against the log wall, head down.

Missy placed her feet back on the floor, looking at the Bossman's pierced body.

Blood was staining the center of his camouflage shirt.

Suddenly Bossman's head jerked to life. He slowly lifted his powerful arms, grabbed onto the wooden arrow sticking through his body and raised his head. He spat out blood as he looked vengefully across the room at Missy. "Now you've made me really mad," he growled.

Missy's body shook as she stared. It was like looking at the resurrection of evil.

Chapter 48

BOSSMAN SNAPPED OFF THE BLOODY SHAFT from his chest and threw it aside. He closed his eyes and raised his head, summoning his strength. With a yell of sheer pain, he pulled himself off the hunting arrow, leaving the bloody, broken shaft stuck in the redwood log wall behind him. He staggered around the floor as he looked down for his KA-BAR hunting knife.

That's when Rory hit him with a fierce tackle. Rory carried Bossman right over the top of a multi-rip saw.

They both landed hard on the floor on the other side.

Bossman did a tuck and roll and came up screaming, holding his back. His camouflage jacket had been ripped open by the sharp protruding saw blade and blood poured out of a gash across his back.

Rolling forward, Rory got to his feet, turning to strike a blow

But Bossman spun on his heels first - his teeth bared - and he violently clubbed Rory on the side of the head with the back of his left hand.

Stunned, Rory's legs went out from under him and he crashed to the floor.

Missy attacked, hitting Bossman's head with a large wooden mallet.

He dropped to a knee, blood oozing from a wound in his scalp. But he wasn't out. The Bossman growled, swept his right arm out and took Missy off her feet.

She landed hard on her side and the breath was knocked out of her lungs.

Sneering, Bossman got to his feet over her - reached down and grabbed the back of Missy's jacket and the seat of her pants, lifting her off the floor. Swearing at her - he heaved her over a piece of machinery.

Missy grunted with pain as she landed hard and rolled across the floor on the other side.

Taking advantage of her attack, Rory had gotten to his feet - he hit Bossman with a tackle in the midsection and drove him back against a piece of woodworking machinery.

His nostrils flaring - Bossman clasped his hands together and raised them over his head - he brought them down on the small of Rory's back.

Sickening pain shot through his kidneys and Rory collapsed in agony to one knee. He did his best to roll over several times, putting distance between him and the big man.

Bossman was in a rage now. He turned, his powerful arms ripping the 4-foot metal guard off a piece of equipment. Then he turned back and advanced on Rory, raising the metal guard over his head.

Looking up just in time, Rory managed another roll just as Bossman brought down the metal guard. The metal banged on the floor where Rory had been. Turning, Rory got to one knee, trying to ignore the painful throb in his kidneys as he looked for a way to fight back.

Bossman lifted the 4-foot metal guard over his head again and moved forward to club Rory.

Getting to both feet, Rory backed up in a crouch - he ran into another piece of wood working machinery - he spun to his right as Bossman brought the metal arm down. It landed on the machine and bright sparks shot into the air.

Bossman swung his weapon to the left.

This time Rory ducked - gathered his feet under him- and drove his shoulder into Bossman's midsection.

The metal weapon flew out of Bossman's hand as he was carried backwards against a tall, floor drill press.

The drill press rocked from their weight, allowing Bossman to use Rory's forward momentum to flip him sideways.

Rory fell on his back, sliding across the floor. He grabbed the leg of a machine and stopped his slide. He squeezed his eyes shut for a moment, then turned around and got to his unsteady feet. Bringing his hands up in a defensive posture, he was ready to do battle to the death.

A very nasty sound echoed through the room.

Bossman was beside one of the workbenches with his back to Rory. He slowly turned and looked at Rory as he revved an 8.5 horsepower gas motor. In his hands was a Husqvarna chainsaw with a 6-foot long whirling blade of death!

Chapter 49

RORY'S HEART SKIPPED A BEAT as the roar of the heavy chainsaw ripped across the room. *Damn, this doesn't look good.*

Bossman advanced purposely towards Rory. He was immensely strong and handled the huge chainsaw with ease. He swung the chainsaw from side to side in a menacing arc, intent on cutting Rory in half.

Rory jumped back and narrowly missed being cut in two by the sharp, whirling teeth. He found himself trapped against a piece of woodworking machinery again. He jumped to his right as Bossman brought the chainsaw down from over his head. The chainsaw roared and bounced off the equipment, sending a shower of red sparks into the air.

Bossman turned, quickly lifted the chainsaw up over his head again and brought it downward at Rory, trying to cut him in half from shoulder to hip. Rory banged up against a wooden workbench as he avoided the roaring chainsaw. He barely moved in time as Bossman brought the chainsaw down from over his head again. The chainsaw hit the top of the workbench. Wood splinters exploded in a cloud as the teeth slashed their way through the thick redwood!

Bossman pulled the chainsaw from the shattered workbench and pursued Rory. He thrust the blade at Rory's stomach.

As Rory jumped back, Bossman went low, swinging the chainsaw from left to right as he tried to cut Rory's legs in half at the knees. Rory managed a forward roll over the blade. The sharp teeth barely missed his feet and Bossman cut savagely through a section of pegboard, carving a deep gouge into the log wall behind it. Small tools went flying everywhere.

Rory barely had time to get to his feet and turn before Bossman was closing in again. Rory dodged the roaring chainsaw twice more before he found himself trapped against a wide piece of woodworking machinery.

Bossman brought the chainsaw down from over his head again. He barely missed Rory, creating another shower of red sparks as he cut a shallow, angry groove into the metal.

Rory nimbly moved around behind the piece of equipment, using it as a temporary buffer between him and Bossman. For the first time, Rory noticed Missy's body on the floor. Her head was lying against a piece of machinery. Her neck was tilted at an ugly angle. Did she break her neck in the fall? Rory felt both fear and anger.

Bossman fainted to the right around the piece of machinery. Then he fainted to the left, the angry chainsaw roaring in his hands. Then he quickly moved back around to the right, swinging the chainsaw low out in front of his body. He was trying to cut off Rory's legs off at the ankles this time.

Rory jumped at the last minute and the roaring chainsaw just barely passed under his boots. That was too close. Rory was tiring. He was barely keeping ahead of the chainsaw now. He moved back and bumped into the tall drill press again. He spun to the right, moving quickly around behind the drill press, putting it as a shield between himself and the rapidly advancing Bossman.

Bossman fainted a move to the left.

Rory reacted by moving away to Bossman's right.

Bossman countered by swinging the saw in an arc from that side, trying to cut off Rory's head.

Rory barely ducked out of the way in time. The deadly blade bounced angrily off the upper end of the vertical guidepost of the drill press. The force of the impact created another shower of angry, red sparks. The blow caused the drill press to tilt like it was trying to escape the wrath of the menacing chainsaw teeth.

Bossman swung the saw over to his left and took a step to attack Rory on that side.

Rory sprang forward, using the momentum of the tilting drill press to topple it over.

As Bossman swung the saw with full force towards Rory, it banged into the falling drill press, resulting in another shower of burning sparks. The force of metal against metal knocked the chainsaw out of Bossman's hands.

The chainsaw dropped and the whirling chain cut viciously into the floor. The chainsaw bounced back up and ricocheted off the falling drill press, angrily spinning up into the air. The motor continued to roar, driving the deadly blade between the two men. Then gravity took over and the chainsaw fell straight down. A shower of splintered wood erupted as the chainsaw clattered to the floor. Bossman had not engaged the lockout switch and the engine throttle of the chainsaw sputtered to a stop.

Bossman bent to retrieve the chainsaw and Rory flew over the top of the fallen drill press. He angrily slammed his body into Bossman, catapulted both of them away from the silent chainsaw.

The two men fell hard to the floor where they began grappling, each trying to get an advantage. They rolled over several times, grasping for each other's throat, throwing punches and trying for a knockout blow.

Bossman was finally on top, trying to strangle Rory.

Rory had one chance. He sagged as if his strength was gone.

Bossman straightened his arms to put more effort into finishing off his opponent.

Rory had his chance. He quickly flipped Bossman over and was now on top. Rory finally had the advantage–

And that's when Missy hit him on the head with the broken 2 x 4.

Rory immediately sagged to the floor.

Missy stood stock still with the broken 2 x 4 in hand. A look of horror crossed her face as she realized she'd taken out the wrong man.

Bossman lashed out with his foot, connecting with both 2 x 4 and her flesh.

The broken 2 x 4 flew out of Missy's hand and clattered to the floor across the room. Missy howled in pain as she held her hand.

"Thanks, bitch," Bossman growled. He lifted a heavily booted foot and kicked out, catching Missy with a powerful blow to her midsection.

Missy staggered back, lost her footing and fell backwards onto the floor, groaning and clutching her stomach in agony.

Bossman struggled to his feet.

Rory lifted his head and put his hands under him, trying to rise.

The Bossman kicked him in the side.

The blow lifted Rory up and over in a roll, where he collapsed to the floor again, his mouth open as he screamed in silence from the pain.

Bossman staggered towards Rory, his face a mask of rage.

Rory tried to move out of the way but Bossman caught him in the side with another vicious kick to the kidneys. Another solid kick to the stomach caused Rory to vomit.

Bossman turned to Missy. "Now it's your turn," he hissed with a vengeance, "nobody puts an arrow in me." He moved across the room, his eyes filled with rage, "I'll snap your neck like a twig." He threw himself on top of Missy, hands at her throat.

Missy gurgled and her eyes bulged as he shut off her air.

Rory rolled around in pain and agony, trying desperately to get up. He called Missy's name. He made it to his knees and began crawling across the floor, trying to get to Missy as soon as possible. Rory held his arms around his midsection as he rose to a half-crouch, shuffling his feet, knowing time was running out.

There was no sound from Missy now.

As Rory reached them, Bossman still had his large hands still around her neck. Rory wondered for an instant if he was too late to save her this time. Rory grabbed the back of Bossman's camouflage shirt with his right hand.

Bossman slowly rolled over to the left and collapsed onto his back on the floor. A full size, black handled KA-BAR hunting knife was sticking out from his lower belly, jammed to the hilt.

Missy clutched her throat in agony and coughed. Her voice was barely a raspy whisper, "Th-thanks. His...his weight was still...choking me."

Rory looked down at Bossman, then back at Missy. "What happened?"

Missy whispered with a grimace, "I...I fell down near his stupid knife. I almost didn't pick it up in time." She glanced at the dead body, "Hoisted by his own petard, isn't that the expression?"

"Something like that."

Struggling to sit up, Missy said, "We...we have to get to the others...."

Rory put a hand on her shoulder, "Not so fast. You're still not– "

Missy shook her head, "No. Didn't you hear him?"

"Hear what?"

After he hit you with that 2 x 4, he said he'd called all the men back up."

Rory cursed.

Chapter 50

RORY AND MISSY RETRIEVED THEIR LONGBOWS and slipped back out of the workshop. Both were incredibly sore but they couldn't stop now. The hunters could all be back at the lodge any minute. And once those hunters came across the body of their leader, they would track down Rory and Missy with a vengeance. Rory knew they had to get moving fast. It was now or never.

They moved back to the locked door and Rory inserted the Allen wrench into the bottom of the keyhole. He then inserted the thin wood awl into the keyhole above the Allen wrench up and began to manipulate the two. After a minute he received a satisfying click. Rory placed the tools back in his long pocket. He pulled his Longbow from over his shoulder and notched an arrow. "You open the door. If it's the hostages, it's better if they see a woman."

Missy nodded. She knelt on one knee to stay clear of Rory's arrow. She reached for the doorknob. Opening the door slowly, she peered inside. Back against the inside wall was a young blond couple holding onto each other. "It's okay," she said in a low, reassuring voice as she opened the door wider. She held out her hands to show she had no weapons. "We're friends," she added.

The couple inside immediately recognized her. "You're the woman who volunteered," the blonde, trim woman said.

"Yea. And little did I know what that would get me into," Missy said.

Rory moved into their view, "Are there other hostages along here?"

"Yes," the blond man said, "after you left, they locked us in the rooms all along this corridor, except for one other couple." He looked over at his wife, "I don't know if they were brought back...."

The woman shook her head slowly as tears formed in her eyes.

Missy looked at Rory. They both remembered the screams they had heard. And the black smoke.

Rory clenched his jaw but there was no time to grieve over anyone now. "We don't have much time," he said. "It looks like most of the hunters were out looking for the two of us...but they were called back by their leader. They could be back here in full force any minute."

The trim blonde let out a little cry. Her husband put his arms around her.

"Just keep calm," Rory said, "we're going to get out of here. We're going to see how many other couples we can free along here. Close this door, but don't completely shut it. I don't want anyone out in the hallways just yet. If anyone comes along they won't hesitate to kill you. Once we get as many freed as we possibly can, we will come back and get you. Okay?"

The couple nodded and the man moved forward to partially close the door.

Rory put the Longbow and arrow away and pulled out his lock picking tools. He and Missy moved to the next door, unlocked it and gave the same instructions to the scared couple inside. They moved as quickly as possible but it seemed to take forever to move down the corridor and find all the locked doors. There were 15 locked doors in total which meant there were 30 hostages they had freed. Rory instructed the last couple to leave their room and follow behind them. There was to be no talking unless someone spotted a hunter. They did the same thing at the next 14 doors, asking each couple to file it out behind them as they moved down the hallway.

Chapter 51

ONCE THEY WERE ALL OUT OF THE ROOMS and strung out in a line behind him, Rory headed back for the large sunroom where he and Missy had first entered at the back of the building. Rory threaded his way back through the lodge hallways, leading the conga line of freed victims as quickly as he could without making too much noise. The passage of time was nerve-racking but they didn't meet anyone en route. Once they reached the last hallway, Rory made sure there was no one in the large sunroom. It was still empty. He couldn't see anyone standing on the back veranda where they could spot them through the wide expanse of glass either. *So far, so good.* He opened the door and quickly urged them all to move into the sunroom and to gather in a loose group around the large, stone fireplace. He put a man on guard at each doorway looking back down the hallways. He asked another couple to keep an eye on the back veranda. Finally he and Missy stood in front of the hostages. With all the others standing there, still in their black tie attire, this looked more like a fancy party than a hostage reunion. But every single hostage had the look of fear in his or her eyes.

"Was anyone taken anywhere else?" he asked the hostages in general.

"I don't think so," answered a tall, distinguished man in his late 30s. "Everyone was taken into that hallway where you found us. There was one other couple but...." His voice trailed off.

"We know– "

A glamorous looking redhead stepped forward, "How do we get out of here?" We need to leave quickly if they're coming back or we could be like them!"

Panic started to set in as the couples began to talk all at once.

Rory held his hands up, trying to get them to lower their voice and keep calm, "Listen to me. Listen to me Look, I'm not going to mince words here. From what Missy and I have seen out there, they've taken us into an isolated valley surrounded by mountains. There's no way we can get out of here on foot. Not unless someone has climbing gear on them."

A couple of the women began to cry.

"We have two options," Rory told them. "One - we found a number of bows, arrows and hunting knives in a room not far from here. We can make a stand and fight...or we can flee down into the trees with the weapons and take our chances."

All of the hostages looked scared. They looked at each other as they considered the option of fighting the hostage takers.

"Two - it appears they used helicopters to get us in here. Maybe we can use those helicopters to get us out of here. There is one inside a hangar not far behind us that looks to be ready to go."

"Then what are we waiting for," said a younger man, "let's go."

Rory took a deep breath, "The other problem is that I've only flown a small helicopter. The ones they're using here are large, cargo helicopters. I've never flown one before and I'm not sure if I even can. Even if we can get airborne, we may crash before we get too far. Unfortunately, those are our only options. Unless some-one else has a better suggestion...."

A man in his 80s took a step forward. "What type of heli-copter is it?"

"The one I'm talking about is a Sikorsky CH-53E Super Stal-lion," Rory told him. "One of the men was about to take it out to the landing zone, so it would appear to be fully fueled and ready to go. There are several other helicopters in the hangars out there, but they've all been disabled in one way or another. The Sikorsky is our only choice."

"Okay. I *should* be able to fly it–"

"Should?" grumbled one of the men at the back.

The man turned and shrugged apologetically before looking back at Rory, an uncertain look on his face, "My name is Myron Connors and I own Well Firefighters Incorporated. We fight oil well fires around the world. I started the business from scratch all by myself 60 years ago. My company owns a number of large, car-go helicopters. I learned to fly on an old Boeing Vertol CH-46 Sea Knight years ago. I haven't done much flying myself in years and I'm an old man now...but...I *should* be able to fly a Sikorsky–"

"Again with the should," grumbled the man at the back again. "Look at his hands. They're shaky. Do we trust our lives with that?"

Conners shut his mouth and looked apologetic.

"He *can* fly a helicopter," interrupted a young, gorgeous plat-inum-blond in a fancy gold dress. She stepped forward to stand beside the older man, "Myron took me up in one–"

"That was some time ago. And it was just a small one– "

"But you did it." She looked at the others, "I.even joined the mile high club in one of his larger helicopters on our very first date!"

"Now why did you have to go and tell them that?" complained the older man with a little mirth in his voice.

"It ain't bragging if you can do it," she replied, "isn't that what you always say?"

The older man could only shake his head, "That's *not* how you apply that statement, Muriel. And I'm afraid I can still handle *that* joystick with a little more confidence...."

Rory noted everyone else was smiling like he was at the well-dressed couple.

Connors shrugged his shoulders as he looked around, "But...unless someone has a better idea, I can at least *try* to fly us out of here...."

Another man in his 80s stepped forward, "I'm Harald Schumacher. I worked on radar when I was in the reserve. And I started my own electrical company years ago as well so I *should* be able to help with the instrumentation." He glanced back at the man who had been grumbling, "Unless...like he says...someone has a better idea."

When no one else stepped forward with an alternative plan, Connors turned to Harald and shook his hand, "Pleased to have you as my co-pilot, sir," he stated.

Rory nodded, "Okay. But the Sikorsky is parked inside a hangar facing inward. There's no way we'll have time to pull it out and get it started up."

The two men who had volunteered to pilot the Sikorsky turned white as they looked directly at Rory.

Rory nodded in confirmation of their worst fears, "We have to start it up, open the hangar doors and fly it right out. Otherwise, we could be sitting ducks for the hunters. This whole thing is going to be very dangerous," he added, looking at the entire crowd of hostages.

After a few minutes of silence, Missy spoke softly. "As someone once said so eloquently, what are the alternatives?"

Everyone in the crowd of hostages looked at her for a heartbeat. Then they nodded silently in agreement. The look on their faces said they wished there *was* another choice.

Chapter 52

"**OKAY GOOD**," Rory said as he reached into a top pocket of his camouflage jacket. He pulled two items out and tossed them over to Myron. "You'll need one of these. I noticed every helicopter we saw had a fuse missing. I came across two types of fuses and we saw two types of helicopters, Boeing Chinook and Sikorsky, so one of them should be right."

"There's that *should* again," grumbled the man at the back again.

Rory ignored him, "I was afraid to try either one myself, in case I fried something accidentally."

Myron looked down at the fuses in his hand. His face brightened and he held up one of them, "This one looks exactly like the ones we had for the old Boeing Sea Knight. So I'm positive *this one* is for the Sikorsky."

Harald Schumacher pursed his lips in thought as he glanced at Rory, "But the thing is - you didn't try it - so you're not sure if the helicopter *will* fly. Correct?"

"All I know is the hunter was about to take it out the landing zone and the only thing that looked to be missing to me was the fuse."

Harald Schumacher looked at Myron Connors.

Connors finally shrugged his shoulders, "Like the lady says, what are the alternatives?"

Schumacher nodded his head in return.

"If it does fly," Rory said, "that will mean we have the only helicopter that can fly, since I hid all the other fuses. If we can get airborne, by the time they could get the other helicopters running, we should be home free."

Everyone seemed a little cheered by that news.

"But," Rory added, "I'm going to have to create some type of a diversion to ensure we have enough time. All of the hunters are on their way back up here. We have to make sure the majority of them stay as far away as possible from that hangar back there. We need to gain as much time as possible to get airborne. Anyone have any ideas?"

"Do they have a tank truck for refueling their helicopters?" Myron asked, "maybe we could blow it up."

Rory looked at Missy before answering, "I don't think I ever saw anything like that inside or outside the buildings we looked in."

Missy shook her head, "No. I never saw anything like that." She shrugged, "I mean, we weren't everywhere, but...."

"Do they have an underground bunker for fuel?" Harold asked.

Rory shook his head, "No. We didn't see anything that looked like a fuel bunker above or below ground. If there is, it's well hidden." He looked over at Missy again for confirmation, "I don't think we even saw drums of fuel anywhere, did we?"

Missy shook her head no as she did some thinking.

"Any other ideas?" Rory asked as he looked at the array of hostages in front of him.

"Where did that car hood come from?" Missy asked him.

Rory looked over at her in surprise. He had never even thought about that.

The young platinum-blonds beside Myron Connors asked, "What car hood are you talking about?"

"It's the hood we used to slide down the hill," Missy replied. "We used it like a sled. That's how we got away."

Another red-headed, well-dressed woman looked shocked, "You slid down a hill on a car hood? Isn't that dangerous?"

"That's an understatement. It was like a bullet going downhill," Missy stated. "And I did it in a dress. And not very lady-like, I might add."

"Like the man said, what were the alternatives?" the redhead stated. She and Missy shared smiles.

Missy turned to Rory. He seemed to be lost in thought. "What're you thinking?" she asked him.

Rory chewed his lower lip as he glanced looked at Missy, his mind working in high gear. "When those men took us past the lodge and over to the edge of the hill, do you remember that U-shaped building on our left? It had a number of double doors."

Missy narrowed her eyes, thinking.

"The log one?" he asked, trying to spur her memory.

Missy shook her head reluctantly, "No, I was doing too much praying at the time."

"I don't doubt it," the redhead said.

Rory looked to everyone around him, "It looked to me like it was a large auto garage. Someone up here might be a collector of old cars. It's also possible they have some all-terrain vehicles in there. It would make sense, considering where we are. If they do have vehicles, there should be some drums of gasoline or diesel fuel in there."

"They would have to have some type of aviation fuel in there to run their helicopters as well," Myron Connors added.

"I agree. They have to have some type of fuel stored up here. If I can find it and figure out how to create a spark or set it on fire, maybe we'll have that distraction we need."

A short, beautiful brunette in a long, red ball gown stepped forward, a gold cigarette lighter in her hand, "Will this do? My husband palmed it when they took everything we had, our watches, wallets, rings and cell phones. It was my first gift to him and he wouldn't let them have." She looked back at a thin blond man and glared at him.

The man looked sheepish and shrugged slightly.

The woman beside him said, "I think it's romantic."

"It was stupid. He could have been killed," the brunette said in anger

Rory stepped over to her to cut off the conversation and took the gold lighter from the brunette's hand. He gave her a big hug and a kiss on the cheek, "You're a lifesaver. Thank you." He looked over at her husband and gave a nod of thanks as well.

Missy's eyes flashed a little as she looked over the shapely figure of the short, beautiful brunette Rory had kissed.

Rory turned around and held the gold lighter up to Missy, "I'm going to slip over to that building and see if I can cause some havoc with this. If I can, I want you to get all these people over to that hangar. You get them to the Sikorsky as fast as possible. All right?"

"But what about you?" Missy asked in concern, "we both know how open the ground is to get there. And once you blow something up over there, every hunter is going to be heading in your direction. There's no way you're going to be able to get safely back to the hangar. It's too far and it's too open."

"I'll be okay. You just get everyone over there, all right?"

"No. Someone else can do that. I'm going with you," Missy stated firmly.

"No, you're not!" he said emphatically, "I can move faster–"

"Faster than a golf cart?" Missy interrupted as she looked him in the eye.

Rory stopped short. He hadn't thought of that. He blinked his eyes as he considered her plan.

"We don't need it for the helicopter. So you ride shotgun with that trusty Longbow of yours as I drive us over there. You blow something up and I'll be ready to make a fast getaway," Missy stated. She folded her arms firmly across her chest, "And I'm not taking no for an answer."

Rory looked at her for a moment and then nodded. He turned to the hostages and began to lay out his plan.

With a few suggestions from the hostages and a few modifications to the plan, everyone reached an agreement.

Chapter 53

RORY AND MISSY HEADED OUT through the glass doors at the back of the Lodge. They crossed the veranda and moved down the stairs at a run. Rory headed to the western side of the lodge, Longbow in hand. Missy headed to the eastern corner, where she knelt on one knee and peeked around the corner. A few seconds later, she signaled all clear on her side as she kept watch.

Rory then gave a signal to one of the hostages standing outside the large doors at the back of the lodge.

The hostage stuck his head back inside. Then he ran for the stairs as the entire group of hostages filed out of the back room of the lodge. They ran single-file across the veranda and down the back stairs as quickly and quietly as possible. Turning left, they ran in Rory's direction over to the western corner of the lodge. The hostages settled behind Rory in a long line. The last in line signaled to Missy and she ran back across to lodge to join them.

Moving up the line of hostages, Missy crouched directly behind Rory.

Rory checked his side of the building again to see if everything was clear. When he saw it was, he notched an arrow and gestured for Missy to get moving.

Missy led the way as the men and women, still dressed in their black-tie attire, took off running in their dress shoes and high heels. The long line crossed the open ground to the log crematorium and then hugged the back wall as they headed to the far corner.

Rory followed up behind the line, keeping watch as best he could.

Settling on one knee at the far corner of the crematorium, Missy made sure the hostages lined up behind her.

Rory moved along the line to kneel beside Missy.

"It looks clear."

Rory nodded and set himself, Longbow at the ready.

Missy took off at a run for the hangar holding the Sikorsky. Reaching the nearest window, Missy peered inside. Then she pulled the door open to make sure. Everything looked clear. She ran back to the corner of the hangar and waved her arms.

The hostages took off at a low run across the open ground.

Rory nervously kept an eye peeled for hunters. If they all showed up now, it would be a massacre with everyone in the open. Time passed agonizingly slow until the last of the long line disappeared around the corner of the hangar. It was worse as he waited for the signal from Missy. Finally, it came. Missy signaled to Rory and he took off running for the hangar.

Reaching the corner he saw Missy beside the open door. Together they moved inside the hangar.

One of the hostages had stayed by the door to keep watch. Another one had headed across the hangar to man the control buttons for the hangar door. The rest of the hostages were climbing into the Sikorsky. Missy handed her Longbow and quiver of arrows to the man by the door. Then Rory and Missy headed across the hangar floor at a run to the far door. They stopped and looked back at the Sikorsky helicopter, waiting anxiously.

A few minutes later, Myron slid open the window beside the pilot's seat and give them the thumbs up.

Rory let out his breath. The fuse had worked. No need for any other parts. He turned, opened the door and headed over to the corner of the hangar, Missy right behind him. He peered around the corner. Good fortune was still on their side. Everything was still clear of hunters. They ran across the open space to find the next hangar still empty. Their footsteps echoed loudly in the empty space as they ran hard across the hangar floor to the golf cart.

"Get her started up," Rory said to Missy as he headed over to the hangar door control buttons.

Missy reached up to the visor and caught the keys like she had done before. Jumping into the golf cart, she inserted the key and turned it. The golf cart started with little noise.

"Once I start opening the hangar door," Rory instructed her, "you zip under the door when there's enough room. Once you're out, I can close it back down quickly. If someone looks this way, they won't see a hangar door hanging wide open."

Nodding affirmation, Missy prepared herself over the steering wheel.

Rory pressed the "up" button.

Missy pressed the golf cart accelerator and shot out under the rising hangar door. She stopped abruptly on the other side.

Pressing the "down" button, Rory then ducked under the closing hangar door, heading for the golf cart. Pulling the Longbow from over his shoulder, he jumped in the passenger side of the golf cart and notched an arrow.

"Ready?"Missy asked him.

Rory braced himself and nodded.

Missy pressed the accelerator to the floor.

Rory jerked back as the golf cart shot across the face of the first hangar and headed across the open space at full speed towards the front of the next camouflaged hangar. They shot across the face of the next hangar and then turned sharply left, moving eastward across the open ground behind the redwood log crematorium. They stopped at the eastern corner. Rory got out and checked around the corner. They had decided to take the direct route and chance being spotted crossing the back of the lodge. Rory got back into the golf cart. Dressed like the other hunters, they should only raise minimum suspicion.

At least, that's the theory.

Chapter 54

THEY WERE ABOUT TO CROSS OPEN GROUND and head across the back of the lodge into possible danger. There was no turning back once they started. "Are you ready?" Missy asked.

Rory nodded as he braced himself with his feet to keep from falling out. He had to keep both hands on the bow and arrow, ready to fire.

Missy floored the accelerator and the golf cart shot out from behind the redwood log crematorium and across the open space.

No one spotted them.

Now they were driving across the glass wall at the back of the lodge. They were fully exposed to anyone inside. It was nerve-racking. It seemed to take forever. Finally, the far corner of the lodge was near. Missy slowed the cart to a stop.

Rory got out and peeked around the corner to check between the lodge and the U-shaped building. The way was still clear. He motioned for Missy to pull the golf cart up beside him. "Head to the back of the garage and drive up the far side," Rory said as he climbed back in, "we're less likely to be seen that way."

Missy nodded and bent over the steering wheel of the golf cart as she pressed the accelerator to the floor.

Rory kept an eye peeled for any hunters as they shot across the open space and behind the U-shaped, redwood log building.

Missy slowed the golf cart just a little as they reached the far corner. She did her best to peer around the corner, then accelerated and shot the golf cart around and up along the eastern side of the building.

Rory instructed her to halt again as they reached the front edge of the U-shaped building. Rory got out of the golf cart, prepared to fire an arrow if necessary. Peeking carefully around the corner of the building, he didn't see anyone or anything. Crouching low and with the Longbow up and ready, he moved across the front of the building and peered around the next corner. He could see down into the U-shaped section now and the coast was still clear. *But I have to be sure or we're dead.*

Rory walked in a low crouch against the log was on his right and down inside the U-shape. He examined the first set of double-doors on the right and found it unlocked. He cracked the doors. It was dark inside but quiet. That was good. *But if we're caught down here, with only one way out, we're done for. But then...what choice do we have? Lives depend on us creating a diversion.* It was on. Rory closed the doors, slipped back quickly to Missy, climbed in and instructed her to zip around the corners to the double-doors.

Missy stepped on the accelerator and they shot around the corners. She slid to a stop in front of the double-doors as instructed.

Rory was out and opening the doors in a heartbeat, waving Missy inside. He slipped in behind her, closing the doors.

Once inside, Missy turned the golf cart back around to face the double-doors, prepared for a quick exit if necessary.

The smell of oil and gasoline was definitely present.

Rory slipped the Longbow back into his kit and the arrow into the quiver and started exploring the dark interior.

There was no time to waste and Missy got out of the golf cart and began looking around as well.

Hunting around for a light switch, Rory saw one and switched it on. The interior lit up under a long string of bare light bulbs hanging from the log ceiling.

"What are those?" Missy asked. The light had illuminated several strange looking vehicles painted in camouflage colors.

"Argo all-terrain vehicles," Rory answered. "That one's an eight-wheeled Argo 8 x 8 750. That one with the tracks is an Argo 8 x 8 Titan. They're made up in Canada by a company northwest of Toronto. Amphibious, off-road vehicles like these are great for running around in the wilderness, but they still need fuel," Rory said. He looked at the long workbench behind the all-terrain vehicles. "Here we go." He moved quickly to a 55 gallon, silver colored, galvanized drum to the left of the workbench. The barrel had a heavy-duty lever style barrel pump on top. The galvanized drum had a label spelling 'gasoline' in black lettering across the front. Rory gripped the edge of the barrel with both hands and shook it with a grunt, "It's full," he said with a smile of relief, "I think we found our diversion."

"Look down there, more diversion" Missy said. She was pointing at a line of galvanized drums lining the back the building.

"I'll say. And that piping further down tells me we may have underground fuel bunkers for the helicopters underneath us." He turned and headed over to the workbench where he had spotted a number of Mason jars filled with fasteners. Rory quickly unscrewed the top of one of the Mason jars. He dumped all the wood screws it held onto the workbench. Taking it back to the galvanized drum, he began pumping gasoline into the Mason jar. "Do you see anything we can use as a fuse?" he asked Missy. "We need a piece of cloth or–"

"Will these do?" Missy asked quickly as she reached into the first utility all-terrain vehicle. She picked up a couple of red, work-rags and held them out for Rory to see.

"Perfect. Tie them together on one end to make a longer fuse," Rory instructed.

Missy quickly tied the ends of the two rags together.

Rory carefully placed the Mason jar and its lid on top of the workbench.

Missy walked over to Rory and handed him the long rag fuse she had created.

Rory took it and moved back over to the galvanized barrel. He pumped some gasoline onto the rag, soaking it completely. Rory then took the soaked rags back to the bench. He carefully placed one end of the rag fuse into the Mason jar, leaving most of it hanging outside. He securely held the rag in place by screwing the lid back on tightly - effectively creating a Molotov cocktail. He left it on top of the workbench and moved back to the galvanized barrel. Rory grabbed the hand pump on top of the drum and grunted as he twisted and turned it until he got the spout aiming directly down on top of the silver, galvanized drum. He began to pump gasoline until it formed a half-inch pool nearly 3-feet in circumference on top of the 55-gallon galvanized drum.

"I want you to start the golf cart," Rory said as he moved back to the workbench. "Then stand by the doors. When I give you the okay, I want you to make sure the coast is clear. Once it is, swing the doors open and run for the golf cart."

Missy quickly headed to the doors as Rory gently picked up the Molotov cocktail in his right hand. He moved quickly and smoothly back over to the golf cart and set the Molotov cocktail down on the floor. He took out an arrow set it with the Longbow in between the two seats on the golf cart. Picked up his Molotov cocktail, he climbed back into the passenger side and braced himself again. Pulling the gold lighter from his pocket with his left hand he looked at Missy, "Okay. "

Missy cracked the double-doors and checked outside. The way was clear. Missy quickly swung the double-doors open and then ran for the golf cart.

"As soon as we get outside the building, stop so I can throw this back inside," he said in final instruction.

Missy nodded as she settled in the driver seat and started the golf cart. She jammed the accelerator to the floor, shooting them out of the building where she then swung the golf cart back around to give Rory a clear throw through the open doors.

Rory flicked the gold lighter three times before a flame appeared.

"Hey! Watcha two peeshwanks doin' der?"

Chapter 55

BOTH RORY AND MISSY turned their heads. It sounded like the Cajun hunter they had heard earlier in the hangar. A large hunter stood just outside two open doors, further down in the U-shape. When the Cajun hunter realized it wasn't any of his comrades, he urgently reached back over his shoulder for his Longbow.

"Go, go, go!" Rory yelled as he reacted instantly. He lit the rag and threw the Molotov cocktail through the open doors.

Missy rammed her foot down on the accelerator. The wheels spun as she turned the golf car sharply to the right to escape.

An explosion erupted inside the garage doors behind them, flames darting through the open door.

Missy turned to see the Cajun hunter had notched an arrow and was pulling hard back on his Longbow. She weaved the golf cart back and forth in an evasive maneuver. Suddenly, a loud thunderclap made Missy scream and the golf cart nearly tipped over.

A moment later, a larger fireball burst through the log wall and the Cajun hunter was enveloped in flames. He screamed and released the hunting arrow involuntarily.

It bounced off the top edge of the frame on Rory's side and he heard it whistle past his ear. He ducked involuntarily and realized how close that one had come.

The Cajun hunter was still screaming and flailing around in agony as Missy reached the top of the U-shaped building and headed right.

Rory held on as the golf cart skidded sideways. *Damn! She should have turned left and drove around the back of the building again. We're going to be exposed all the way back to the hangar.* Rory reached for the Longbow but was thrown against the side of the driver's seat as the golf cart slid around the far corner of the building. The screaming stopped on the other side of the U-shaped building.

Missy brought the golf cart out of a skid and aimed it down the alley between the log building and the lodge.

More explosions sounded and fireballs erupted through the roof of the log building on the far side. As more explosions occurred and more fire erupted through the roof and into the sky, Rory suddenly realized the explosions and resulting fireballs were following the U-shape of the building. Sure enough, as the fireballs stepped their way down the far side of the building, the explosions turned and followed the path of the U-shaped building to the west. It was going to come their way! Could they drive past in time?

The far end of the building exploded in a blazing fireball! The explosion shattered the building and spit a fireball fire across their path. They could feel the heat now. They rocketed forward and Rory knew what was going to happen next. Missy and Rory ducked in anticipation. Then their world erupted into a fireball of death.

Chapter 56

RORY AND MISSY CAME OUT of the fireball with their camouflage clothing in flames. They swatted at each other as Missy drove on past the edge of the lodge and headed in a wide skid for the hangar. They could hear the log building continue to explode and erupt in flames behind them.

Missy slapped at a final burning flame off the sleeve of Rory's jacket, "You sure know how to show a girl a hot time, Steele."

Rory slapped the last flame out on Missy, leaving smoking embers in its place, "I can't believe you said that, Amos."

They both laughed in shaky, giddy relief.

The golf cart shot across the back of the lodge. Rory struggled to pick up the Longbow and arrow as they bounced.

Another hunter ran out the back door of the lodge. He skidded to a stop when he saw the golf cart and reached back for his Longbow.

Rory had a hard time getting the arrow notched. This was suddenly like a gunfight with bow and arrow. The fastest man would win. They closed the gap between the hunter and themselves quickly and the hunter was now pulling back on an arrow. He was aiming for Missy. Rory was just a shade quicker. He released the arrow just as the cart bumped again and it flew higher than he intended.

Would it hit?

The hunter screamed as the hunting arrow penetrated his right eye and came out halfway on the other side of his skull.

Missy screamed as the hunter released his arrow in death and this one gouged an angry groove on top of her left shoulder.

"Missy!" Rory yelled in alarm.

"I'm okay, watch for more." Missy grimaced in agony as she steered with her right hand,

Rory reached back and pulled out another arrow. He kept an eye peeled as they started moving swiftly across the open space back to the front side of the hangar.

Missy yelped in pain as she hit a slight bump and jarred her left arm.

Rory glanced at her in concern.

Missy persevered, bringing her left up and gripping the steering hard, keeping her foot on the accelerator to the floor.

Rory looked to the side and behind. *So far, so good.*

Missy finally jammed on the brakes and the golf cart skidded to a stop at the first door of the hangar.

Rory jumped out and started around the front of the ATV.

"I'm fine," Missy said but she was favoring her left arm.

Rory swung the Longbow up, covering her as she ran.

The door swung open and Rory followed Missy into the hangar.

The hostage who had been keeping watch was already heading for the Sikorsky's open passenger door.

Missy ran for the helicopter, her right hand holding onto her left shoulder.

Slamming the door shut, Rory took off at a run.

Reaching the large cargo helicopter, hands helped her up as Missy scrambled inside.

Rory wasn't far behind and the door was slammed shut and locked as soon as he was inside. Most of the hostages were already buckled in, eyes wide as they waited for takeoff. Myron Connors in the pilot seat looked back and gave Rory another thumbs up. Giving a thumbs up back to him, Rory headed for the large side door on the other side of the helicopter.

One of the women jumped to Missy's side, holding a piece of cloth she had torn off the hem of her dress. She told her to remove the jacket so she could bandage the wound. Missy refused, intending to follow Rory. The woman put a firm hand on her arm, insisted she stay put for a moment.

Unlocking the side door, Rory slid it open and secured it in place. Once that was done, he held onto the side post and sat in the large opening, his legs dangling over the edge of the fuselage.

Undoing a button on Missy's jacket, the woman simply stuffed the cloth into the shoulder to stem the flow of blood. Gritting her teeth against the pain, Missy now headed for Rory. She knelt behind him on the floor of the helicopter.

"Are you okay–?"

"Yes," she said firmly. "Don't baby me now." She placed her Longbow and quiver of arrows on the floor.

"Okay. Tie me in." He indicated a strap to the left behind him. "Pass it around my waist and lock it back into the wall here," he instructed her.

Missy picked up the strap with her left and pain registered on her face. She persevered, passing it around Rory as instructed and then back around to lock it firmly in place on the wall of the

Sikorsky. "All set," she said as she tapped Rory on the left shoulder.

Rory gave the hostage at the hangar door control buttons the all-clear sign.

The hostage immediately pressed the up button and set the hangar doors in motion. Then he scrambled for the helicopter.

Rory signaled for him to come straight to the open side door rather than run around to the passenger's door since it was already locked.

The man ran hard and reached the helicopter quickly. Both of them reached down and Rory and Missy pulled him up through the doorway. The man scrambled gratefully for a seat on the far side of the helicopter.

The huge Sikorsky engines started up. The Sikorsky was facing inward, looking towards the back of the hangar. Myron Connors was going to have a delicate maneuver getting the huge beast turned around.

As the huge 72-foot rotor whined and began to spin, a woman came up behind Missy. The woman was in her early 60s and very beautiful. Her white hair was pulled back in a bun, exposing a long, graceful neck that made her look very elegant.

"Are you using that Longbow?" she asked Missy in a genteel, southern voice.

Missy looked at the woman, "No, but...."

"Would you mind?" She held out her right hand.

Missy realized with the injury she would be useless, even if she *could* pull the Longbow back and fire. She reluctantly handed the woman the Longbow and the quiver filled with arrows.

The beautiful, white-haired woman slung the quiver over her shoulder and then fought to keep her glittery, silver dress down with one hand as the wind began to buffet harder through the open door.

As the rotor achieved speed the large cargo helicopter jumped up a few feet off the hangar floor. It also moved backward a couple of feet in the air!

The white-haired lady had to grab the edge of the open doorway with one hand as she held the Longbow in the other, "C'mon Myron, you can do it," she said as she steadied herself.

Rory wondered why she was there and he reached up to help her. The swirling wind pushed her silver dress up over her hips, revealing long, tanned legs and the crotch of white, silk panties. The brief hint of a light floral scent from a delicate perfume brought an image crashing through his mind. He was lying on the floor of the helicopter when they were first taken and - this was the woman who had been there beside him - and now they were side by side again, possibly fighting to the death–

The Sikorsky jerked a quarter-turn turned and Rory's mind went to something else more urgent. He thought the pilot was going to try to fly it out backward! He was about to yell out a warning to not–

Then the massive helicopter stood rock still in the air. It began to slowly rotate inside the hangar.

Rory breathed a sigh of relief.

The helicopter began to turn slowly around towards the open hangar doors. A hand touched Rory on his right shoulder. It was the beautiful, white haired-woman in the silver dress, now crouching right beside him. She gingerly squatted and shuffled her silver high-heeled shoes to the edges of the doorway. Then she sat beside Rory and dangled her feet out the open side door of the huge Sikorsky. The wind from the 72-foot rotor flapped the edges of her glittery, silver dress as she sat there with the Longbow in her left hand.

Missy moved in behind her and picked up the safety strap for that side. She passed it around the white-haired lady's trim waist and locked it into place on the wall of the Sikorsky.

The white-haired lady looked down at the strap going around her waist and then glanced at Missy, "I always wondered how they never fell out in the movies. Now I know, dear."

Rory was puzzled, still not sure why she was there.

The huge Sikorsky slowly continued its turn inside the hangar. Rory and the woman were now facing the fully open hangar doors. Foot by foot, the huge Sikorsky began to move sideways towards the open hangar doors, while it continued to slowly rotate.

Without warning, two hunters appeared outside the hangar doors. Their deadly arrows were notched and ready to fire in their direction. Both were pulling back on their powerful Longbows and taking aim at their prey.

Rory brought his own Longbow up but he knew it was going to be too late. He could already feel the arrow penetrate his heart.

Chapter 57

RORY HEARD A POWERFUL TWANG beside him and a hunting arrow buried itself deeply in the chest of the lead hunter. The hunter screamed and let loose his own arrow. In his death throes, he had raised the Longbow and the arrow shot just over Rory's head into the cabin of the Sikorsky. It struck the roof inside and glanced downward against the back wall where the lethal arrow ricocheted dangerously through the screaming crowd until it buried itself in an empty canvas seat.

The second hunter was aiming his own Longbow towards the open window of the flight cabin. He was aiming right at the pilot of the huge Sikorsky.

Another powerful twang sounded beside Rory.

The second hunter grunted as an arrow buried itself deep in his chest. He released his own arrow as he fell over backward, dead. It ricocheted harmlessly off the Sikorsky's body just above the open window.

Rory looked at the beautiful, elegant woman sitting beside him.

"Two Olympics," the white-haired lady said as she notched another arrow. "Never won a damn thing," she said as she pulled back on the Longbow. "But it all seems so worthwhile, right now," she added grimly. She calmly let loose the arrow. It buried itself deeply in the chest of a third hunter who had appeared just outside the hangar.

The huge cargo helicopter straightened out a little more and began to move low through the open hangar doors. It barely passed over the three dead bodies. The huge Sikorsky was clear of the hangar within moments and began to rise in the air.

We're clear," Missy said with a sigh of relief.

Rory turned to say something–

Bang! The sound of metal banging on metal ripped through the roar of the overhead rotor blades.

The huge Sikorsky jolted to a stop and tilted dangerously to the left.

Screaming ripped through the helicopter as the strapped-in hostages dangled awkwardly sideways their seats. Hostages not strapped in fell from their seats and began sliding across the floor to the open doorway, screaming and clutching for a hand-hold.

Rory grabbed desperately for the door frame but missed. He felt himself sliding out of the doorway and his heart pounded.

The white-haired lady beside him screamed as she slid forward.

Missy screamed as she was thrown against the inner wall of the helicopter.

Several of the screams were cut off abruptly as bodies violently slammed against the wall.

Rory stopped sliding. The safety straps! They kept him from falling out. But the helicopter was tilted at a severe angle and Rory was nearly face down.

The white-haired lady was hanging face down as well. The combination of the sliding and the wind had pushed the edges of her glittery, silver dress back to reveal her long legs. "The bow," she gasped.

Rory looked over.

The white-haired lady was holding it with only her fingers wrapped around the bowstring. The powerful wind from the overhead rotor blades caused the Longbow to twist violently.

Rory reached over and grabbed for the Longbow but his fingers hit the side and it bounced away.

"I'm losing it!" gasped the white-haired lady as the bowstring twisted in her grasp and slipped through her fingers a foot before she stopped it.

"We're caught on something!" Myron Connors yelled from the crew cabin.

How can that be? Rory tried to calm his beating heart as he allowed himself to dangle by the straps as he looked below.

One of the hunters had a grappling hook snagged over one of the helicopter's huge landing skids. The other end was attached to the back hitch on a large, high capacity tracked vehicle. Rory could hear the 225 HP Turbo Diesel growl as the vehicle turned slightly and started to inch the Sikorsky back toward the hangar.

Chapter 58

RORY HAD A HARD TIME believing his own eyes but there it was. The tracked vehicle growled and he could feel the helicopter jerk. He could hear the screams from the others and he felt helpless. He yelled up at them, "They have a hook holding onto the landing skids and attached to a vehicle down there. Someone tell Myron he has to apply more power. He has to counteract it."

The message was relayed by several in shouts of terror, telling Myron to hurry up and do it.

"Everyone hold on," Harald Schumacher yelled from the copilot's seat.

The Sikorsky's engines whined as Myron Connors applied power.

"Look out!" the white-haired lady yelled.

Rory barely pulled his head to the left as an arrow shot by his ear.

Screams sounded behind him as the arrow bounced around inside the helicopter. A sound of pain ripped through the screams. Someone had been hit.

Rory saw the hunter below, reaching back over his shoulder for another arrow.

"The bow!" the white-haired lady yelled again.

Rory threw himself hard to the right and reached for the Longbow. He missed it.

"Hurry!"

Rory swung himself again and snagged the Longbow this time, pulling it up towards the doorway.

The white-haired lady was already pulling an arrow from over her shoulder. Her hand jumped from the bowstring to the grip, she notched the arrow and fired in one move.

His own arrow hitting and glancing over top of the helicopter, the hunter reacted instinctively, ducking for cover under the body of the helicopter,

The huge Sikorsky moved slightly higher - its engines roared as it strained to lift the 22,000-pound load - the back of the tracked vehicle came off the ground.

A second hunter came into view and brought his bow up.

The Sikorsky lifted the high capacity tracked vehicle completely off the ground.

The white-haired lady fired an arrow.

The hunter below ducked without firing.

Connors began to bring the Sikorsky back to level–

With that movement, the high capacity tracked vehicle swung like it was on the end of a pendulum and disappeared out of sight below the helicopter. There was another loud bang and the Sikorsky violently jerked sideways in the air. Screams echoed inside the helicopter as everyone was thrown about again. Connors frantically worked the controls but the Sikorsky remained tilted to the left, unable to budge tracked vehicle again.

"Something happened! We're stuck again," Schumacher yelled.

Rory leaned as far forward as he could. The tracked vehicle had crashed through the side door of the hangar and was stuck there. He yelled, "The vehicle is wedged into the hangar."

The Sikorsky's engines roared but they weren't going anywhere.

"We can't break free. We have to get the hook off," Schumacher yelled back.

Pinging sounds began echoing off the skin of the Sikorsky as hunters fired arrow after arrow.

"Now they're trying to hit something vital," Schumacher yelled.

"Missy," Rory yelled. "You there?" He strained to look over his shoulder.

"Yes," Missy called out. She was against the helicopter wall to Rory's left.

"Undo the straps, and I'll climb down–"

"No! You'll fall out," Missy yelled.

"We're all going to die if we don't do this."

Missy hesitated and then began working on the straps.

Rory held onto the left side of the doorway and looked over at the white-haired lady, "Cover me as best you can, okay?"

The white-haired lady nodded back solemnly. She lifted the Longbow, another arrow notched and ready.

Rory felt the straps loosen and he struggled to keep his body weight from pulling him off his precarious perch in the doorway.

"Be careful," Missy said in a tight, strained voice.

Rory rolled his body to the right, letting himself slide. He caught the bottom edge of the doorway and yelled above the noise, "Tell Myron to drop a little lower to loosen the hold of the hook."

Missy yelled up to the flight deck.

The Sikorsky moved down with a jerk.

Rory yelped as his body was jerked downward with the movement.

Missy yelled his name and grabbed onto his clothing, stopping his fall.

Rory re-gripped the bottom of the doorway, "Thanks. Be right back." He lowered his body and searched for the huge landing skid with his feet.

The powerful twang of Longbows from the ground as well as from the helicopter reached Rory's ears. He ignored them, concentrating on finding the skid. *There it is.* He lowered himself quickly.

Several hunters below the helicopter spotted Rory and realized what he was doing.

Rory saw the hook snagged over the back of the huge skid and he slid that way fast, using the width of the skid as a desperate shield between him and certain death.

Arrows whizzed by him on either side of the skid.

An arrow tore through his upper shirt sleeve, slicing across the flesh of his left arm. He grimaced in pain and fell face down on the skid. He desperately fought to hold on as he felt himself slipping over the edge. His right heel banged against the far side of the skid and he pressed it hard against the metal, using the leverage to stop his momentum.

A hunter below him moved further to the left to get a better shot. He unleashed his arrow.

Rory pulled himself hard to the right and back over the skid. Pain shot through the back of his left thigh as the arrow dug a trench across his pants and skin.

The hunter pulled back on his Longbow again, aiming for Rory's head this time. He never had that chance. His body dropped to the ground as an arrow from above pierced through his Adam's apple.

Rory spun around on the skid and grabbed the grappling hook with both hands. Blood was seeping over the back of his left hand and between his fingers. Lying on his stomach he had no leverage and the steel industrial hook was heavy. He grunted and strained as arrows from below whizzed past the edges of the skid. The hook moved upwards slowly. Then the hook squealed in protest as it scraped sideways on skid until it finally dropped over the side.

"Go, go, go!" Rory yelled as he spun back around on the skid. He heard a cry of pain below but didn't bother looking.

The helicopter moved higher and leveled out.

That movement saved Rory as an arrow cut a gouge through the back of his jacket and his skin. His mouth opened in silent pain as he moved on his stomach along the strut towards the doorway, leaving a trail of blood as he slid.

The Sikorsky moved slowly away from the hangar.

Getting himself back under the open doorway, Rory looked below.

The hunters were aiming for the front of the Sikorsky.

Rory quickly got to his feet in a crouch and jumped up from the skid. He caught the lower edge of the opening. Eager hands pulled him into the helicopter as arrows shot by his leg.

Missy saw the blood on Rory's hand, jacket and pants, "You're hurt!"

"I'm fine," Rory said through clenched teeth.

"Let's go, Myron," the white-haired lady yelled.

The Sikorsky's engines roared...but the huge helicopter only moved sideways towards the hangar.

Chapter 59

THE MASSIVE GENERAL ELECTRIC T64 ENGINES of the Sikorsky CH-53E Super Stallion roared and continued to drive it sideways towards the hangar when they really needed altitude. But it wasn't coming.

"They must have hit the hydraulic servo system to the swashplate," Harald Schumacher yelled from the copilot's seat. "Myron says he can't tilt the blades and we can't go much higher. It's going to take time to switch to manual –"

Arrows began pinging off the skin of the helicopter.

"They're trying to shoot into the flight deck up here!" Schumacher yelled in panic. "If they break through the windows–"

Look out," Myron yelled. There was the sound of breaking glass.

Rory knelt beside Missy and placed his hand against the door frame, leaning out. Dozens of hunters were coming back over the hill now and moving across the open ground towards the buildings. If Myron flew out at this height, there was a good chance an arrow could kill the pilot and or hit something vital and take them down.

The helicopter began moving towards the back of the hangar, seeking shelter, but everyone knew it would be short-lived.

The beautiful, white-haired, still strapped into the doorway turned her head. "Do you still have that gold lighter?" she asked Missy.

Missy quickly tapped Rory on the shoulder and asked for the gold lighter. Rory pulled it from his top pocket and gave it to her.

Missy turned back to the woman and held the lighter out to her.

"No, that's good," the white-haired said, "you hold onto it, for now, dear. I'll tell you when I need it, okay?"

Missy nodded, a puzzled look on her face.

The woman turned her head and shouted loudly back over her shoulder. "There was a large, red Jerry can under the seat just inside the door when we first came in. Is it still there? Can someone check– ?"

"Yes, it's here," yelled a voice. "It's wedged under the seat."

Rory was surprised when he heard that. He couldn't remember ever seeing it when they searched the helicopter before.

The woman looked at Rory, "Can you bring it here?"

Rory nodded and turned quickly, moved over to the seat where a woman in a red gown was crouched down and pointing. He saw the red can and reached for it.

"That wasn't in here before when we looked. Where did it come from?" Missy asked as she joined Rory.

"I was just wondering that myself. I'll bet that dead Cajun Hunter or his dead buddy left it in here," Rory said as he pulled on the can.

"Oh, right. They were going to take this helicopter out."

"Exactly. But it's stuck under there." He pulled hard on the carrying handle. The can had been wedged tightly under the seat in the framework when the helicopter had tilted and he struggled to pull it free.

Missy lay on the floor and worked to push the jerry can from the other side.

Rory finally pulled the jerry can free. It was full and heavy and dropped him on his butt. He struggled to his feet and carried the jerry can back to the doorway.

"Good," the white-haired woman said. "If my hasty plan works, I'll need you to toss it out this doorway."

Rory shook his head, unsure of what *plan* she was talking about. But he had nothing, so he set the can down and sat in the open doorway again, "Okay. Strap me back in Missy."

The white-haired turned her head towards the front crew area and shouted over the noise of the whirling blade, "Harald? Can you have Mr. Connors make a pass over the lodge?"

There was no reply for a moment. Then Harald yelled back, "We can probably get just enough height. But we'll still be in range for their arrows. And being closer to the lodge...."

"I know. But unless you have another choice–?"

Chapter 60

THERE WAS ANOTHER MOMENT OF SILENCE and then the huge Sikorsky began picking up speed, moving across the back of the hangar.

With Missy's help, Rory lifted the red Jerry can to his lap.

The elegant white-haired woman was tying a piece of silver cloth, torn from the hem of her dress, around the tip of an arrow.

The huge Sikorsky reached the back of the hangar and started flying past it, moving above the open ground. It then turned and headed back towards the lodge, gaining a little more altitude.

Black smoke from the roaring flames engulfing the U-shaped garage billowed into the air ahead.

As they approached the Lodge, the combined noise of the huge Sikorsky and the enormous fire were deafening.

"Take off the cap please," the white-haired lady yelled to Rory.

Rory complied as the wind buffeted harder against them.

"Get the lighter out," she yelled to Missy.

Missy nodded and pulled the gold lighter out of her pocket. She moved in between Rory and the lady.

The white-haired lady dipped the arrow into the neck of the Jerry can, soaking the silver cloth. "Hopefully, this diverts their attention long enough for us to get away," she yelled.

Rory still wasn't sure where this was going but it seemed to be their only hope.

The Sikorsky approached the Lodge. Hunters were gathering below, firing more arrows.

"Throw it on the roof as we go over," she yelled to Rory, indicating the red Jerry can in his lap. "And get the lighter ready," she yelled to Missy.

Missy nodded and held the lighter up.

Rory waited until they were directly over the lodge. Then he held the heavy Jerry can out and let it fall. It hit the eastern peak of the roof. Gasoline spilled as it bounced a few times across the cedar shake roof. As it slid down the roof, it left a trail of gasoline.

"Light it up, dear," the woman said as she loaded the arrow and turned sideways toward Missy.

Missy leaned out, flicking the lighter.

Rory grabbed the material of her jacket's arm and held tight, certain she was going over the edge.

Missy flicked the lighter again. A flame sputtered to life and Missy sheltered it with her palm. She held the flame under the rag and it caught fire with a small whoosh!

With the silver rag now on fire, the white-haired lady calmly lifted the Longbow, pulled back and aimed. She led the still sliding red Jerry can perfectly. The arrow sliced through the plastic container and buried itself into the roof. A moment later, the container of gasoline exploded in a huge fireball. Yellow flames eagerly licked back up the roof along the trail of gasoline from the eastern edge up to the peak. A fire quickly began spreading across the red cedar shingles.

The hunters were running for the lodge now, in full panic as the flames began roaring. More black smoke began to fill the sky.

"Just a little farewell present," the white-haired lady yelled in anger.

"Okay, Harald, make a run for it!" Rory yelled.

The Sikorsky's engines roared as Myron applied full power. The helicopter swung around and they fled to the west. Everyone aboard went silent as they held their breath.

Several hunters were running across the open ground towards the lodge from the southwest. They stopped and lifted their longbows towards the helicopter.

The white=haired lady planted an arrow in the chest of the lead hunter and then quickly put another through the neck of another hunter behind him.

The helicopter passed over the hunters and pings ringed off the body.

Then the pings stopped.

Everyone listened through the roar of the engine for more arrow strikes.

But they never came.

Then someone broke the silence, "How do we get over the mountains if we can't go higher?"

No one had an answer.

Rory looked out at the snow-capped mountains in the distance. *Maybe he can fly through between the peak?* He looked across at the white-haired woman who sat stoically, watching for more hunters.

Missy placed her hands on Rory's shoulder–

There was an upward jerk of the huge Sikorsky.

"We're climbing!" someone yelled.

Whoops, and cheers resounded through the huge helicopter.

Rory couldn't help but feel relief and tried to relax as he watched the ground fall away below them.

Missy disappeared up towards the flight deck as Rory and the white-haired lady sat side by side, the wind whipping at them.

Two of the passengers appeared beside Rory with more torn pieces of clothing. They ripped and cut through his own clothing where the arrows had torn at his flesh and worked to stem the bleeding.

As they worked to bandage his wounds, the huge Sikorsky flew past the edge of the western hill and over the dense forest. Moments later, it banked to the southwest towards a high gap in the snow peaked mountains.

Missy appeared beside Rory as the two passengers finished their quick patch job. "Mr. Schumacher says he got the radar working," she announced. "He knows where we are now. He's going to be able to find the way home."

More cheering erupted in the helicopter.

Rory Mack Steele nodded in satisfaction as he looked back towards the lodge.

Thick black smoke rose from the two burning buildings into the blue sky as they headed for home. It wouldn't be long before the structures were nothing but a pile of hot embers.

Missy put her head on Rory's right shoulder and wrapped her arms gently around him.

Rory grimaced from even the light pressure on his wounds.

"Sorry." After a moment she spoke softly, "When we get back I'm going to give my father a call."

"Good for you," Rory replied in a quiet voice.

Missy whispered into his ear, "And then I have to finish what I started at the banquet. You do realize I was going to pick you up that night?"

"You say that now–"

"You have no idea what I had planned for you, Mr. Steele. But you might just find out if you play your cards right. I'll need your phone number."

www.ingramcontent.com/pod-product-compliance
Lightning Source LLC
Chambersburg PA
CBHW020439270626
47155CB00022B/653